"I need you, Holten!" Rebecca pleaded in a hoarse whisper.

"Here? Now?" asked the Scout, casting a wary glance toward the flimsy denim curtain. They were in the back room of one of the busiest general stores in the territory.

The naked blonde grabbed his thigh and said, "Why not? It's more exciting this way, don't you think?"

"What the hell!" Holten cried. He slid his rough hands along the sexy woman's sleek curves, starting at her delicate shoulders, and working down to her firm round buttocks.

Rebecca jumped at his touch and started to moan.

"Shhhh!" warned the Scout. "Not too loud or we might have visitors!"

Then they heard it. The whoosh of the denim curtain.

"Mrs. Ridgeway?" called the sales clerk.

Holten froze. Rebecca's body stiffened. The Scout grabbed her and pulled her as far into the shadows as possible.

"Yes—" replied Rebecca in a cracking voice.

"You sound kind of strange, Mrs. Ridgeway. Are you sure you're all right?"

"I've never been better," she said, smiling at Holten and pulling him down once again . . .

THE GUNN SERIES BY JORY SHERMAN

GUNN #1: DAWN OF REVENGE   (590, $1.95)

Accused of killing his wife, William Gunnison changes his name to Gunn and begins his fight for revenge. He'll kill, maim, turn the west blood red—until he finds the men who murdered his wife.

GUNN #2: MEXICAN SHOWDOWN   (628, $1.95)

When Gunn rode into the town of Cuchillo, he didn't know the rules. But when he walked into Paula's cantina he knew he'd learn them. And he had to learn fast—to catch a ruthless killer who'd murdered a family in cold blood!

GUNN #3: DEATH'S HEAD TRAIL   (648, $1.95)

When Gunn stops off in Bannack City, he finds plenty of gold, girls and a gunslingin' outlaw. With his hands on his holster and his eyes on the sumptuous Angela Larkin, Gunn goes off hot—on his enemy's trail!

GUNN #4: BLOOD JUSTICE   (670, $1.95)

Gunn is enticed into playing a round with a ruthless gambling scoundrel. He also plays a round with the scoundrel's estranged wife—and the stakes are on the rise!

GUNN #5: WINTER HELL   (708, $1.95)

Gunn's journey west arouses more than his suspicion and fear. Especially when he comes across the remains of an Indian massacre—and winds up with a ripe young beauty on his hands . . .

GUNN #6: DUEL IN PERGATORY   (739, $1.95)

Someone in Oxley's gang is out to get Gunn. That's the only explanation for the sniper on his trail. But Oxley's wife is out to get him too—in a very different way.

GUNN #7: LAW OF THE ROPE   (766, $1.95)

The sheriff's posse wants to string Gunn up on the spot—for a murder he didn't commit. And the only person who can save him is the one who pointed the finger at him from the start: the victim's young and luscious daughter!

Available wherever paperbacks are sold, or order direct from the Publisher. Send cover price plus 50¢ per copy for mailing and handling to Zebra Books, 475 Park Avenue South, New York, N.Y. 10016. DO NOT SEND CASH.

THE SCOUT

#2 DAKOTA MASSACRE

BY BUCK GENTRY

ZEBRA BOOKS

KENSINGTON PUBLISHING CORP.

For Ben Ahrendt, a real westerner . . .

ZEBRA BOOKS

are published by

KENSINGTON PUBLISHING CORP.
475 Park Avenue South
New York, N.Y. 10016

Copyright © 1981 by Kensington Publishing Corp.

Printed in the United States of America

Scouting is a congenial profession
leading to a terrible death.
                                   —George Armstrong Custer

I'd rather lose a third of my command
than lose my best scout.
                                   —Gen. George Crook,
                                      famous Indian fighter

CHAPTER ONE

Eli Holten stalked his prey.

The tall, lean chief scout of the army's 12th Cavalry stood as motionless as a poised predator at the edge of the woods. He peered through the inky Dakota prairie night, his nerves as tight as the strings of the fiddle he heard somewhere inside the sprawling ranch in front of him. Holten's senses worked keenly, checking for signs of trouble.

His pulse quickened.

The scout tethered his big sorrel gelding on a nearby tree branch and studied the layout of the famed Rebecca Springs ranch in the clearing just a hundred yards away. He scanned the scene before him, his steely blue eyes quickly studying the massive gray barn off to one side, the long planked bunkhouse, the large circular corral packed with grazing horses, and the big, one-story shingled ranch house that stood proudly in the middle of the quiet compound.

His nerves tingled and his muscles tensed. Twenty years in Indian country had taught Holten to be careful. He had learned that on the plains, survival often meant having total awareness of your immediate surroundings.

The scout knew what he had to do.

Holten quickly pulled off his heavy dust-clogged boots and replaced them with soft leather moccasins from his saddle-bags. He thought about bringing along his 1873 Winchester .44-40, but decided against it. With his fearsome ten-inch Bowie knife strapped to his belt and his

Remington army issue .44 pistol ready at his side, the lean scout slipped into the quiet darkness like a cougar on the prowl.

His prey waited in the shingled house.

The scout glided quietly past the wide rough-fenced corral. A couple of skittish horses whinnied softly at the sudden scent of a man. Within seconds he reached the ranch house.

Then he heard voices.

Holten pressed quickly against the outside shingled wall. Suddenly several chuckling ranch hands appeared out of the darkness. The cowboys passed within five feet of the scout, close enough for him to see the glint from the gold tooth of one of the laughing men.

Holten's heart pounded against his ribs.

Finally the men ambled away and disappeared into the night. Padding as quietly as an Indian stalking an antelope, the scout moved along the outside wall of the large ranch house until he came to a row of curtained windows. Warm lamplight poured out of the house and illuminated the dusty ground in front of him.

The scout stopped to listen.

He heard the strident chords of the fiddle's music drift into the sleepy night from somewhere around the corner of the house, louder now and mixed with the quiet laughter of ranch hands whiling away the lonely evening hours. The snap and crackle of a roaring campfire also pierced the stillness of the cool night air.

Now was his chance.

Slowly, carefully, every muscle tensed for sudden action, Holten eased his long lean frame up to the nearest window and peered through a crack in the lace curtain. The sudden brightness of the lamplight blinded him momentarily. He blinked and then scanned the inside of a large bedroom, his eyes taking in a sturdy mahogany bureau thrust up

6

against the far wall, a big, shiny brass bed, and an ornate porcelain bathtub in the middle of the room.

Then the scout froze.

He spotted his prey—in the bathtub.

Peering intently into the house, being certain not to make a sound, Holten watched as a long lean blonde woman reclined lazily in the heavy tub, her eyes closed and a blissful smile parting her supple lips. Her long silky hair hung loosely over the edge of the shiny porcelain tub. A wide grin spread across the scout's leathery face.

He'd been lucky to find the woman immediately. With a sigh of relief, Holten looked at the flowing golden hair of the widow, Rebecca Ridgeway.

Then he froze again.

Suddenly the door to the bedroom swung open and a squat, pale-faced woman entered carrying a steaming pail of fresh bath water. The stocky middle-aged servant closed the bedroom door and lugged the heavy pail over to the tub.

Holten retreated a few inches into the shadows, but kept his gaze fixed on the room's bright interior. He watched the blonde woman open her eyes slowly, then dismiss the servant with a sudden flick of her delicate hand. The stocky servant blinked once then shrugged her ample shoulders. The scout watched the maid leave the room and close the door behind her.

Suddenly voices sliced through the night.

Holten pulled quickly away from the window and pressed against the darkened wall of the ranch house.

His hand shot to his Bowie knife.

The scout clung to the shadows, his muscles ready to spring into action, and looked at the corner of the house near the campfire. He saw two ranch hands appear suddenly, their voices hushed as they tip-toed toward the row of windows. The scout strained to hear what they were saying.

"You tryin' to get us fired?" asked one in a weak voice. "Or even worse, killed?"

"Aw come on," said the other, "we'll just take a peek and get the hell back to the bunkhouse."

"Well—I dunno," said the first.

The men stopped just before they reached the brightened bedroom window. Holten's palms grew sweaty. Another five feet and the cowboys would have stumbled into him.

"Just a peek," repeated the second.

"You sure she's takin' a bath?"

"I seen lotsa water heatin' in the kitchen," said the second cowboy. "It sure as hell wasn't for coffee!"

The first ranch hand chuckled. "Man, I can just see them big tits!" he shouted, a note of excitement in his voice.

"Shhh!" reminded the second. "Keep your voice down!"

"Okay," said the first cowboy in a hoarse whisper. "Let's do it! But just a peek. I don't reckon to get fired just yet!"

The ranch hands started toward the window. Holten's grip tightened on his knife. His pulse quickened. His mission could be finished before it even started.

Suddenly more voices filled the air. The cowboys panicked.

"Somebody's comin'!" said the first ranch hand.

"Let's get the hell out of here!"

As a small knot of noisy ranch hands passed by the house on their way to the bunkhouse, the two cowboys took off like a couple of scared rabbits. They raced for the bunkhouse and melted into the darkness.

In the shadows near the house, Holten's muscles slackened and his breathing returned to normal. He

8

waited for a few moments until all the men had passed, then inched up to the window and peeked in once again.

His weathered face slackened.

In the middle of the bedroom near the porcelain bath tub, completely naked, passing a thirsty towel over her lean golden body, stood shapely Rebecca Ridgeway. Her long blonde hair glistened in the lamplight.

Holten felt a twinge in his loins.

The scout studied the young widow's gleaming body. He figured her to be about thirty, but she had the firm body of a twenty year old. The scout's blue eyes drank in the woman's sensuous beauty, starting with the silky blonde hair that cascaded over her delicate shoulders and fell to the middle of her gleaming naked back. Holten's eyes roamed over the firm round breasts with their taut, rose-colored buds, the gentle curves of her hips, the flat smooth stomach that led downward to a shiny triangle of kinky pubic hair, the firm round buttocks, and the lovely long legs.

He stood mesmerized at the window and watched the lithe blonde work the fluffy towel over her luscious body with the smooth grace of a cat preening itself.

The scout felt an erection growing in his pants.

He thought about the widow Ridgeway.

The widow's late husband, well known cattleman J. D. Ridgeway, had obviously taken good care of his young bride. Maybe she had proven too much for the old man to handle. A few months ago, two days before his seventieth birthday, old J. D.'s heart gave out while he screwed his wife.

What a way to go, thought the scout.

Holten tore his gaze away from the window and padded to the front of the ranch house. He stopped to listen. Glancing quickly from side to side, his piercing blue eyes scanning the compound and his muscles ready for action, the scout turned the door knob and quickly entered the house.

He squinted at the sudden brightness.

Holten strode purposefully toward the bedroom at the back of the clean, richly decorated ranch house, his senses working keenly and his hardened muscles twitching in readiness.

The scout saw a flash of movement.

He pressed quickly against a corridor wall and watched the pale-faced servant emerge from a room and walk toward the kitchen.

Holten's heart pounded like an Indian war drum.

Without even a glance in the scout's direction, the stocky maid pushed through a swinging door and entered the large kitchen. Holten heard the woman sing an old English folk tune as she went about her work. The scout took a deep breath and continued toward the bedroom, his full-grown erection throbbing in his pants.

Holten reached the bedroom door and stopped in his tracks. He listened for a long moment, his ears straining to pick up any signs of possible trouble. Sensing the way was clear, the scout slowly wrapped his big hand around the glass knob and opened the door a fraction of an inch. He peered through the tiny opening.

Nothing moved in the room.

Suddenly Holten pushed open the heavy oak door and burst into the bedroom, his muscles tensed for action and his eyes quickly scanning the room's interior. Everything was the same—the mahogany bureau, the brass bed, the porcelain tub. And the gorgeous blonde.

Except now she lay waiting in bed.

The widow gasped at the sight of the scout in the doorway, her slender hands going to her mouth. Her sparkling blue eyes grew as big as silver dollars at the sudden intrusion.

10

Holten's piercing blue eyes studied the wide-eyed blonde who lay with her long legs spread under the sheets. His steely eyes quickly visualized the firm round breasts, the flat smooth stomach, and the shiny bush where her long legs came together.

His eyes locked with hers. He closed the door softly.

"Now lady," said Holten, unbuckling his pants as he strode to the bed, "you're goin' to get what you deserve."

A wry grin cracked his leathery face.

Rebecca Ridgeway took her hands from her mouth, smiled seductively, and threw back the bed sheets.

"What took you so long?" she asked, her lean golden frame silhouetted against the white sheet. "I've been waiting for hours."

"Had a little trouble on the trail," said the scout.

Holten was about five hours late for his weekly love-making session with the widow. A sudden problem with a couple of bloodthirsty Cheyennes had delayed him slightly.

"Do you know how lonely it gets around here?" she asked.

"I rode as fast as I could," explained Holten simply. He dropped his pants to the floor.

She glanced at his huge cock and groaned.

"I want it so bad," she said, her big blue eyes fixing on his pulsating penis, "I can almost—"

She caught herself in mid-sentence.

Holten looked up and smiled. "You can almost—taste it?" he said.

Rebecca blushed.

As he tore off his shirt, the scout stared at the naked woman sprawled on the bed. His mind flashed images of the sensuous pleasures he knew lay just ahead. Finally Holten stood buck naked before her, his pulsating cock pointing at the young widow's pretty face. They'd been making love on a regular basis for the past two months. But each time the scout returned from the dusty prairie, he felt a new wave of savage desire course through his veins.

Rebecca's sparkling eyes remained fixed on his cock.

Suddenly, without warning, the lithe young blonde leaped from the bed and glided to where Holten stood gaping, her firm breasts quivering as she walked up to him.

The pain in Holten's iron-hard penis was unbearable.

The scout saw the widow's glistening blue eyes take in his lean naked body, starting at his broad muscled chest, roaming down his rippling stomach muscles, and returning to his incredibly hard and long shaft.

Rebecca reached out with long soft fingers and began to stroke the scout's penis, slowly at first, then faster until her hand was just a blur of motion up and down the ironlike shaft.

Holten moaned in mock protest.

"Serves you right for being late," she chided, her supple lips parted in a sensuous smile.

Holten writhed at her touch. "Remind me to be late all the time," he gasped.

Rebecca slipped her soft fingers from the hard, thick base of his penis to the sensitive, pink tip, lingering a moment there and squeezing gently. The scout thought he'd explode into the air.

"I think we better turn down the lamp," he said in a hoarse whisper.

"The lamp?"

"Peeping Toms," he replied, without further explanation.

With a quick, catlike jab with his right hand, Holten pulled from her grasp and turned off the kerosene lamp near the mahogany bureau. Darkness fell over the bedroom. Only the soft moonlight that filtered through the lace curtains and cast eerie shadows on the smooth wooden floor, provided any illumination.

"That's better," he said.

"But now we can't see each other," protested Rebecca.

The scout smiled to himself. "We'll just have to let our hands be our eyes," he said, reaching through the semidarkness. He began to probe the young widow's soft curvacious body.

"You're right," she said, jerking slightly at his sudden touch. "That's much better."

The scout's rough hands began gently at her delicate shoulders, then slid downward to her plump round breasts and massaged each in gentle circles until Rebecca groaned with ecstasy. His large strong hands stroked each breast with loving care, kneading the soft flesh, lingering for a moment on the now taut nipples, flicking each gently causing the young blonde widow to jump slightly.

"Oooooooo," moaned Rebecca, as she tossed back her head and rolled her eyes with delight.

The scout quickly slid his long fingers down across her smooth, flat stomach until they reached the dense patch of pubic hair at her crotch and lingered at the slick opening of her aroused vagina. Holten shot a finger into the warm and wet channel hidden by the waxy triangle of hair, his strong forefinger pausing for a long moment in the silky folds of flesh at the slick opening, the sudden entrance causing Rebecca to gasp with pleasure.

"Oh Holten!" she said, groaning. "Don't stop!"

He didn't.

With a quick, gentle jab of his finger, the scout probed the innermost regions of the slippery channel, sending his finger deep inside of the writhing widow.

"Ahhhhh!" shrieked the writhing blonde.

The scout plunged his finger into her over and over, the blonde widow writhing with pure animal ecstasy at

13

each savage thrust deep into her fully aroused body, her soft golden flesh pressing against the scout's long lean frame. After a few minutes Holten's hand dripped with her juices.

Suddenly Rebecca reached out for Holten, her long fingers sliding quickly from his back, along his rippling stomach muscles, to the incredibly long and hard penis. She grabbed the ironlike shaft and stroked it quickly, her long fingers racing along the throbbing cock from the thick, hard base to the soft, delicate tip.

The scout felt a sudden savage rage surge through him. Quickly they fell onto the big brass bed, Rebecca's soft hand stroking the scout's rodlike cock and Holten probing deeper and deeper into the widow's innermost regions.

Suddenly Rebecca guided Holten's giant shaft to her warm, wet vagina, moving the iron-hard penis slowly against the silky folds at the channel's opening.

Rebecca closed her eyes and moaned with ecstasy.

Without warning Holten pushed downward and rammed his long, hard cock into the moaning blonde, causing her to gasp slightly as he plunged his penis deep into her slick channel, his savage sexual urge driving him on, causing him to pump into her again and again until she nearly begged for mercy.

"Oh Holten!" she gasped, writhing on top of the big brass bed. "You're the best!"

They thrashed and writhed atop the creaking bed until Holten could feel himself coming inside of her, could feel the savage desire boiling up deep within his body. But he held back, thrusting his rodlike cock against her clitoris over and over, Rebecca responding to every thrust with a trembling fervor of her own.

Finally, in a moment of pure sexual bliss, the scout exploded inside of the writhing blonde, filling her suddenly with a hot flood of milky passion, driving even further inside of her until she gasped and arched her back to meet him again in one final moment of sexual frenzy.

They collapsed on the bed and gasped for air.

Their bodies glistened with sweat.

Holten's muscles felt as limp as cooked rawhide. He lay atop the lithe, shapely widow, his heart pounding against his ribs like a blacksmith's hammer. Then his senses began to work again. His ears strained to hear signs of trouble. Once again he became the frontiersman on guard for danger.

Nothing moved. The ranch was still.

The scout took a deep breath of relief and rolled off Rebecca Ridgeway's soft, limp body. Holten lay back naked on top of the dishevelled bed, his long legs sticking out over the edge, and glanced at the young widow. Even in the sparse silvery moonlight that bathed the dim room, the young blonde woman appeared gorgeous. The scout leaned over and kissed the luscious blonde on the cheek. She smiled.

"You're the best, Holten," she said softly.

He kissed her again. "You're not bad yourself, lady."

Her sparkling blue eyes danced as she turned her head and kissed the scout on the lips, her soft, supple lips lingering as she thanked Holten in her own way.

Then Rebecca sighed and closed her eyes.

Within a few minutes the shapely widow slept like a baby under the covers, her lips parted in a smile as she lay motionless beside the scout. Holten made sure Rebecca was asleep, then swung his long lean frame off the brass bed and padded across the cool wooden floor to the windows. He lit a sweet-smelling cheroot, pulled back the lace curtains, and peered out at the sleeping prairie beyond the gray ranch buildings.

Holten took a long drag on the little cigar, watched the cloud of blue-white smoke drift lazily toward the ceiling, and returned his gaze to the prairie.

His prairie. His home.

Eli Holten, scout and frontiersman, had the look of the plains about him, a tall seasoned man whose long brown hair touched his shoulders and framed a lean leathery face with steely blue eyes that, narrowed from squinting in the sun and wind, could send shivers down the spine of any gunman looking for trouble.

A tall man, wide in the shoulders and narrow at the waist, Holten could ride with the best of them, yet possessed none of the cowboys' awkwardness in walking. When on his own feet, he glided with the grace of a prowling cougar.

Holten knew all about the prairie. He had learned the hard way.

Born in Illinois, orphaned at eight, and a frontier runaway at fifteen, he'd been found by the Indians wandering the plains and spent six years in the camps of the fierce Oglala Sioux. His adopted parents, a brave called Eagle Deer and his squaw called Walking Fawn, had taught him the ways of the plains Indians. Called "Tall Bear" by the Sioux, Holten soon earned the nickname "Hunter-Who-Never-Goes-Out-For-Nothing" because of his great skill with rifle and bow. Holten learned how to hunt, fish, and track like an Indian.

Then one day, yearning for the white man's life, Holten had walked away from a Sioux hunting party and signed on as an army scout. He was one of many frontiersmen given contracts by army quartermasters to perform duties that ranged from guide, hunter, and courier, to interpretor, intelligence officer, and diplomat. For years he chased Indians of many tribes—Sioux, Crow, Arapaho—and renegades from a dozen different bands. A relentless tracker, a deadly shooter, and a ruthless fighter, Holten

16

could trail anybody across the vast Dakota Territory.

And he had. Especially the killers of his Indian family.

The sudden painful memory caused Holten to turn away from the window and crush his cheroot in a nearby ashtray. He took a deep breath and glanced quickly at the sleeping widow in the big brass bed. Then he gazed once again at the shadowy prairie.

Only a few months had passed since the band of brutal murderers had swept into Eagle Deer's peaceful camp of treaty-keeping Sioux and butchered all the men, women, and children as they stood pleading for mercy.

Holten swallowed hard at the thought.

During the massacre he'd lost his only family—his adopted parents, Eagle Deer and Walking Fawn—and White Bird, the only Indian girl who'd captured his fancy in all his years on the plains. The scout had been in shock for a while, then one by one he'd tracked down the killers and gotten his revenge.

But he still felt the loss.

Now he returned from the plains and headed for the army post to get a new assignment. The 12th Cavalry had sent word to Holten; he was always in demand at the fort. On his way he'd stopped at the Rebecca Springs ranch to try and ease his grief in the soft sensuous arms of the blonde widow Rebecca Ridgeway. But even now the massacre played on his mind.

Holten clenched his fists at the painful memories, his muscles tensing at the vivid images of disfigured corpses and mutilated bodies that flashed in his head. He burned with anger at the senseless slaughter of innocent people. He almost exploded with rage when he thought about the blood-drenched soil in Eagle Deer's camp and the butchered children lying in pools of their own blood.

Suddenly Holten felt the fingers on his bare shoulder.

He whirled at the touch, his heart pounding, and almost

knocked Rebecca off her feet. She stood beside him, completely naked, and searched his weathered face with her sparkling blue eyes.

Beads of cold sweat clung to Holten's forehead.

"Thinking about it again?" asked Rebecca, her soft hand touching the scout's leathery face.

He just nodded. He'd told her about the massacre.

"Come," she said softly, grabbing his big hand. "Come to bed and forget about the past."

Rebecca reached with her other hand and started to stroke Holten's flaccid cock. The sleeping shaft began to harden.

The scout smiled. "You've persuaded me," he said.

They walked hand in hand to the big brass bed and lay on the thick mattress. Rebecca rolled over on top of Holten, her flesh soft and warm, and peered into the scout's blue eyes.

"Try and forget about the past," she said. Her hands stroked his penis as she spoke softly.

Holten just nodded. He'd never forget, he knew, but he appreciated her concern. And he appreciated the way she tried to make him forget.

Suddenly his cock throbbed.

With the speed of a stalking sexual animal, Rebecca knelt quickly beside the scout's lean hard frame and began to lick him, her soft sensuous tongue starting at his mouth and lips, working downward across the matted hair of his chest, across the flat, hard stomach muscles, to his incredibly long and pulsating penis.

"So huge!" she said, her sparkling eyes fixed on the throbbing shaft.

"You bring out the best in me," said Holten.

Quickly Rebecca mounted him and with one soft hand grasping the thick, hard base, the luscious blonde widow took his throbbing cock into her mouth, her supple lips sliding rapidly along the iron-hard shaft. The scout

18

moaned with pleasure and watched as her pretty head bobbed up and down, her honey-colored hair splayed across his abdomen.

Holten writhed with pleasure. He felt himself coming.

Suddenly, in a frantic moment of delicious sexual release, the scout exploded, his milky passion bursting from somewhere deep inside of him. The scout grunted deeply, his lean body arching and twisting with the sudden explosion. The sinewy blonde rode his writhing frame like a broncobuster until all the desire had been milked from his long aroused shaft.

Holten lay panting. Rebecca collapsed on top of him.

The blonde widow's firm breasts flattened against the scout's broad chest. Holten's heart pounded almost in unison with hers.

"Feel better?" she asked, her eyes full of mischief.

A wide grin cracked the scout's leathery face. "Thanks," he replied simply.

They lay still for several minutes, Rebecca's soft flesh pressed against the scout's muscled body. Holten listened to the night sounds drift into the bedroom. Noisy crickets played their songs just outside the windows and somewhere out on the lonesome prairie a coyote called.

Then Rebecca's voice sliced through the silence.

"You going to be hunting Injuns again?" she asked in a soft voice.

Holten shrugged. "Maybe," he answered. "I'll find out tomorrow at the fort."

Silence filled the room again. Then the widow spoke.

"Be careful," she said, a note of concern in her voice. The gorgeous blonde turned and studied the scout's weathered face with her sparkling blue eyes. "Be careful," she repeated. "I need you. Except for my folks back East, you're all I got now, Holten."

Holten grasped her hand. "I'm always careful," he said with a smile.

Then as the sumptuous blonde widow snuggled up next to him and started to sleep, satisfied with his answer, Holten wondered why in hell the army had sent all the way to the Black Hills for him. He sighed and tried to sleep. Whatever they wanted, he knew it was dangerous.

They always gave the tough jobs to Holten.

CHAPTER TWO

It looked easy.

The killer called Liver-Eating Jackson peered through the predawn grayness at the sleeping Sioux warriors in the small clearing below. He shifted his wiry frame in his saddle, the leather creaking as he strained to get a better look. A wide smile cracked his thin stubbled face. His yellow snakelike eyes danced with anticipation of the bloody massacre he knew was only minutes away. Jackson turned and faced the giant rider beside him.

"What do ya think, Paco?" he growled.

Paco Riley, hardened frontiersman and longtime scalp hunter, shifted his 300-pound bulk atop his overburdened mount. The ruthless plainsman ran a ham-sized hand over his slick shaven head and flashed a wide, yellow-toothed grin.

"I see lots of scalps down there," he answered in a deep booming voice, his words seeming to reverberate inside his massive body. An experienced Indian killer, the big frontiersman kept his head shaven to, as he put it, "cheat the Injuns out of my scalp."

Jackson and Riley had ridden together for years, killing and raising hell across the entire Dakota Territory. In fact, it was Paco Riley who gave Jackson his nickname. After Jackson had promised to kill and eat the liver of any Indian who tried to kill him—and then did it, his mouth dripping with fresh Sioux blood—Paco began to call him Liver-Eating Jackson. The name stuck; so did the reputation.

"I count a dozen braves," said Jackson, his gaze returning to the slumbering warriors.

Paco nodded his bald head in agreement. "And they're all sleeping like babies."

"We need to get them ponies out of the clearing."

"What about the cannon?"

Jackson brought a thin bony hand across his stubbled face, then turned sharply in his saddle. He glanced behind him at the nine mounted soldiers who waited atop their snorting army mounts in a copse of tall pines.

"Ames!" he shouted.

A few moments later, former Sgt. Luther Ames, a big pot-bellied army deserter, reined in his prancing bay next to Liver-Eating Jackson.

"When we chargin'?" Ames asked quickly. "My men are gettin' anxious. They ain't killed enough Injuns since them goddam treaties were signed!"

Jackson glared at the dim-witted sergeant, a look of disgust on his thin face. In a few days, thought Jackson, I'll be a rich man. Paco, too. In the meantime he'd have to put up with Ames and his ragged band of army dropouts.

"The cannon loaded and ready to fire?" asked Jackson.

"Of course!" snapped Ames. "When we chargin'?"

"See them ponies down there?"

The big sergeant squinted through the fuzzy, predawn light at the small circle of Indian ponies below.

Ames nodded. "What about 'em?"

"How many shells can that big cannon of yours throw right away?" asked Liver-Eating Jackson, his snake eyes narrowing.

"It shoots two twelve-pound balls a minute," answered Ames atop his skittish mount. "Whatcha got in mind?"

"When the sun peeks over that far ridge," said Jackson, "I'll give the order to fire. Put your first shell about ten feet from the ponies. But don't hit 'em. We'll need all the ponies we can get."

"No problem," said Ames.

"Then," continued Jackson, "put your second ball smack in the middle of that campfire."

The big sergeant smiled. "It'll be like shootin' ducks in a pond."

"What about your men?" asked Jackson. "They know what they're supposed to do?"

Ames scowled. "Hell yes!" he said. "They ride into the camp, raise hell, and butcher the goddam savages." The dim-witted sergeant chuckled. "It's great seein' Injun blood again."

"And remember," said Jackson, "grab all the Indian weapons and clothing. Then send some men to get the ponies. We'll need everything later."

Ames nodded. "Right," he said.

"And for those men who want to take scalps," said Jackson with a sideways glance at big Paco Riley, "do it quickly. We ain't got much time to waste. We got us another massacre this afternoon." Liver-Eating Jackson chuckled at his last remark.

Ames nodded again, laughed excitedly, then smacked his mount on the butt and galloped back to the pine trees.

"Damn right I'll be takin' some scalps," boomed Paco, cleaning his big Bowie knife as he spoke. "At fifty bucks apiece in England, I can't afford not to!"

The mammoth killer laughed mightily, his 300-pound bulk quivering like a sack full of jelly, then quickly checked the two .45 pistols at his belt and the big Henry repeater cradled in his massive arms.

"I'm really gonna enjoy this," said Paco finally, a wide smile creasing his large fleshy face.

Liver-Eating Jackson laughed shortly. "We'll give the goddam army so much to worry about they may be busy for the next six months tryin' to figure out what the

23

hell happened."

Jackson drew a fearsome Cheyenne war hatchet from his belt, ran his thumb gingerly along the cutting edge, then squinted up at the rising sun. In a few minutes he'd gallop through the screaming savages, slashing and slicing until the dusty clearing was covered with Injun blood. The sudden thought sent a tingle of excitement through his wiry body. Then after a few more raids, they'd take the gold.

And he'd be rich.

The ruthless plainsman rubbed his tired snake eyes with bony fingers and thought quickly about what he'd do with his share of the money. Maybe he'd just retire in the hills somewhere with a hundred cases of good whiskey and a dozen plump whores. He chuckled for a moment, then forced himself to think about their plans for the day.

He thought about what the boss had told him—raise hell and kill everybody in sight. Both Injuns and whites. And so far, everything was going according to plan.

This morning they'd kill some Injuns.

When Liver-Eating Jackson looked up again at the far ridge, a thin shaft of sunlight smacked him in the eye. A wide grin spread across his thin face.

The time had come to kill.

"Let's get us some Injuns!" he said to Paco Riley.

Jackson whirled the head of his snorting horse around toward the pine trees and faced the small band of anxious deserters. As the early morning sun peeked over the ridge, Jackson raised his right hand. He watched the nervous soldier near the cannon prepare to fire the big deadly gun. When the first streaks of golden sunlight washed over the tops of the tall pines, Jackson slashed downward with his arm.

"Now!" he screamed.

The soldier lit the cannon. The big gun roared.

24

Trying to control his frightened horse, Jackson heard the deadly twelve-pound ball whistle through the early morning air on its way to the clearing below. Thick white smoke and the stench of gun powder permeated the pine covered ridge. Jackson peered through the brightening dawn at the tight circle of Indian ponies.

It was a perfect shot.

The ball exploded in a cloud of alkaline dust about twenty feet from the suddenly horrified horses. Jackson watched with glee as sticks, stones, and clumps of grass rained down upon the now smoky clearing.

Then he heard it.

Strident cries pierced the morning air.

Liver-Eating Jackson glanced quickly at the Sioux campsite. What he saw brought a smile to his thin lips and quickened his pulse.

The stunned Sioux warriors jumped to their feet, their eyes wide with sudden fear, their hands groping for their bows and arrows. A couple of braves pointed to the scampering ponies. Others quickly gathered their thoughts and scanned the hills for signs of trouble.

None of the Indians moved from the campsite.

"Give 'em one right in their laps!" shouted Jackson.

The soldier lit the cannon again. The gun boomed.

Once again Liver-Eating Jackson saw the thick white smoke belch out of the big cannon, smelled the acrid stench of gunpowder, and heard the whistle of the ball as it headed for the unsuspecting warriors below.

The shell hit with deadly accuracy.

Jackson watched the ball explode among the wide-eyed Indians, some of the bodies tossed suddenly in the air like children's rag dolls. Others slammed hard to the ground with the impact.

Now the time had come for the slaughter.

"Let's go get 'em!" yelled Jackson.

With a quick jab of his spurs in his horse's flanks, the wiry plainsman raised his fearsome war hatchet and led the thunderous charge down the slope into the clearing. Behind Jackson, their eyes alive with anticipation and their army .45 revolvers ready in their hands, galloped the wild band of deserters.

It had the makings of a massacre.

The band of killers raced down the hill and into the dusty clearing before the dazed Sioux warriors had a chance to react. Liver-Eating Jackson arrived first, his razor-sharp hatchet slicing downward, his first mighty blow almost decapitating a fleeing brave. The warrior fell heavily in the dust, blood spurting from the gaping wound in his neck.

Behind Jackson, big, potbellied Luther Ames, his dim-witted face aglow with excitement, bounced atop his ragged army mount chasing a fleeing Sioux brave into the woods. As Ames closed in on the stumbling Indian, the warrior looked up at the laughing sergeant, the brave's dark face a contorted mask of pure fear. Taking aim, the big former sergeant pulled the trigger of his .45 at pointblank range and blew a hole in the Indian's head big enough to ram a fist into. The brave lay sprawled on the ground from the impact, his head disintegrating in a bright red spray of blood from the bullet tearing through his skull.

The Indians didn't have a chance.

Throughout the clearing the army deserters killed at will, slashing and shooting until all the Sioux braves lay dead in the alkaline dust. The warriors never had time to even draw an arrow or take a shot.

The dust settled over the bleeding bodies.

"Good job!" shouted Jackson from the back of his prancing horse. "Hell of a good job!"

"Somebody get the ponies!" yelled Luther Ames.

Jackson scanned the clearing, satisfied that all had gone as planned. He turned quickly and caught a glimpse of Paco Riley harvesting his scalps. The mammoth killer knelt in the dust beside the corpses, his big knife flashing in the early morning sunlight as he sliced scalps from the dead Sioux.

The bald giant glanced up at Jackson. "Here's fifty bucks," he roared, holding up a dripping Indian scalp. The big killer tossed the bloody scalp on the ground and continued to work with his knife, slicing the hair neatly from another of the fallen braves.

Jackson looked at the milling deserters. "Start to strip the bodies," he ordered. "We need Indian clothes, lots of bows, and quivers full of arrows."

The excited soldiers ran from corpse to corpse, some of the men hauling off buckskin clothes, others looking for bows and arrows. A few of the deserters joined Paco Riley and deftly scalped the dead Sioux warriors. Two soldiers rode back to the clearing with the Indian ponies in tow.

"See if you can find some war paint among all that Injun gear," added Jackson.

Liver-Eating Jackson smiled broadly at their success, cleaned his bloodied hatchet, and returned the fearsome weapon to his belt. Squinting at the deep blue sky he noticed the whirling buzzards gathering overhead. He felt a twinge of anxiety in his stomach. Jackson knew other warriors lurked in the woods and would soon be attracted by the soaring birds. No sense asking for trouble, he thought.

"Hurry it up!" he shouted. "The buzzards are gettin' hungry!"

Jackson watched the deserters haul armfuls of Indian clothing and quivers of arrows out of the body-strewn clearing. So far, he thought, everything was going according to plan. The first attack of the day had been

27

successful. But the next one, he knew, would be trickier.

And probably more dangerous.

"Let's go!" he yelled. "We still got us some more killin' to do today!"

The laughing band of killers mounted their horses and galloped off into the hills. But before they murdered again, they needed to change their clothes.

They needed to become Indians.

"You look just like a goddam Injun!"

"Look at you!"

"Gimme some of that war paint!"

The gang of deserters acted like kids with new toys on Christmas morning as they pulled on the buckskin clothing they'd taken from the dead warriors in the clearing. Liver-Eating Jackson, dressed now in fringed buckskins, his face slashed with white war paint, a long bow grasped in his hand, a fresh Sioux scalp fastened to his head with an Indian headband, set astride his newly acquired Sioux pony, and surveyed the scene before him.

"Finish dressin'," he ordered. "We ain't got much time."

"These clothes stink!" yelled one of the men.

"Don't them red bastards ever wash?"

Jackson chuckled. "Do the best you can," he said. "All we gotta do is just look like Injuns. We gotta make them white settlers down in that valley think we're a Sioux war party."

"Gimme those arrows," yelled one of the men as the deserters passed around the Sioux weapons.

Jackson turned to Paco Riley. "I want you to stay with the horses," he said with a smile. "If those settlers see your buffalo-sized body and shiny skull, they'll recognize ya sure as hell."

Paco nodded his glistening bald head. "That's okay,"

he boomed in a deep voice. "Ain't no Injun scalps down there anyway."

Liver-Eating Jackson turned back to the now fully dressed deserters, his yellow snake eyes scanning the band of buckskin-clad, feathered "Indians" who stood before him. A big smile cracked his thin face.

"Not bad," he said. "Not bad at all."

Then Jackson glanced at a copse of cottonwoods about a hundred yards away.

"I'll be right back," he told Paco. "Gotta check with the boss."

Liver-Eating Jackson jabbed his spurs into his pony's flanks and galloped off bareback for a rendezvous with the mastermind of their big plan. It wasn't like the boss to meet Jackson out in the open like this. The man must be getting nervous. The ruthless plainsman reined in his pony at the edge of the trees, a shower of dust raining over the horse's legs belonging to the hard-faced rider who held Jackson in an icy stare.

"We're ready," said Jackson tentatively.

The hard-faced figure in the shadow of the trees nodded and stared out at the waiting group of deserters. The brass buttons of his officer's uniform glistened as a few rays of mid-morning sun pierced the shadows. He spoke in a cold clipped voice.

"This is an important part of our plan," said the rider. "The bloodier, the better."

Jackson nodded, his Sioux scalp blowing in the cool breeze that swept in off the plains. "We're ready," he repeated.

"You got to make the settlers believe you're really Indians," said the hard-faced man in the same icy tone. "Leave some arrows stuck in the buildings, scalp most of the men, and rape and butcher some of the women."

Liver-Eating Jackson flashed a yellow-toothed smile.

"I'm sure some of them deserters will be glad to hear that," he said with a chuckle.

"Just do the job," said the cold voice.

"We will," said Jackson. "Don't worry."

"I do worry," snapped the rider. "There's a hell of a lot at stake. For all of us."

Liver-Eating Jackson just nodded.

The rider spoke again from the shadows. "Our plan depends on making every white settler for miles shake with fear at the thought of possible Indian attacks."

"We'll raise hell!"

"I'll check with you at the usual place after all the jobs are done," said the cold-voiced rider. "Then we can talk about gold." The hard-faced man turned his horse's head around and galloped off into the prairie.

Jackson watched the rider for awhile, then whirled and galloped back toward the waiting deserters. He hated hard-assed bosses, especially ones in uniform. As he approached the feathered soldiers, Jackson suddenly felt a warm wave of confidence spread through his chest. The army dropouts, sitting astride their skittish ponies with bows gripped in their hands and war paint glistening on their faces, really did look like a Sioux war party. Jackson smiled and licked his lips.

He looked forward to the day's second massacre.

By mid-afternoon, with the scorching summer sun beating down on them like an invisible hammer, the ragged band of ruthless killers, their regular army mounts trotting alongside them, reined in their Indian ponies on a rocky ridge overlooking a peaceful green valley near the Black Hills. Liver-Eating Jackson peered through the shimmering heat waves at the three sod houses bunched together down below.

"That's them," he said.

30

Paco Riley chuckled. "Looks easy," he said in a deep voice, rivulets of sweat running down his fat face.

"Three families live down there," said Jackson. "According to our count, there's three men, two young boys big enough to shoot straight, and five small children."

The killer paused for effect.

"And," he continued, while eyeing the deserters, "five women over fifteen years old."

An excited murmur spread through the deserters. Several of the men laughed wickedly, their eyes dancing with anticipation of the sensual pleasures that lay below.

"But remember!" snapped Jackson. "Our job is to make it look like an Indian attack. Kill and burn first. Then you can have your fun with the women."

Big Luther Ames laughed. "We know, we know," he said. "Let's get on with it. Can't keep them women folk waitin'!"

"One more thing," reminded Jackson. "Don't speak English. I'm goin' to leave one of them settlers alive. I want him to tell the soldiers what the Injuns did to his family."

"Look!" Paco Riley's voice boomed as he pointed at the valley below.

Liver-Eating Jackson turned sharply in his saddle and glanced down at the sod houses. A thin smile spread across his narrow face as he watched several men emerge from one of the houses, a heavy piano balanced precariously between them.

Jackson cackled. "They're makin' it easy for us," he said. "No guns or nothin' in sight!"

"Let's take 'em!" yelled Luther Ames.

"All right," said Jackson. "Give your army horse to Paco. Then follow me."

One by one the deserters paraded atop their Indian ponies past the enormous bald-headed killer and gave him

31

the reins of their army mounts. Paco Riley grasped the leather strips in his mammoth, ham-sized hands.

"And remember," repeated Jackson. "No English!"

While Paco remained on the rocky ridge with the horses, the feathered and painted soldiers picked their way slowly down the gentle slope until they reached a small stand of thirsty cottonwoods on the floor of the green valley. Jackson halted the group.

"All right," he said. "Let's give 'em hell!"

With a sudden chorus of strident war cries, the deserters burst from the shadows of the trees like screaming phantoms, their bows raised above their heads and their rifles across their laps. The sleek Indian ponies galloped toward the squat sod houses, their shoeless hooves churning up the rich Dakota soil.

The white settlers froze in their tracks.

Liver-Eating Jackson, his fearsome war hatchet drawn and ready for action, watched the three white men suddenly drop the heavy piano like a giant hot potato and rush for the safety of the thick-walled sod houses. Jackson's heart warmed when he caught the look of terror etched in the settlers' faces as they ran.

Suddenly a rifle cracked behind Jackson.

A bullet zipped past his ear, the slug from a Springfield carbine slamming into the chest of one of the settlers. The man jumped off the ground from the impact of the hot lead and lay sprawled in the dust near one of the houses, a splotch of red blossoming on his shirt front.

Then an arrow whistled past Jackson's head.

The ruthless killer watched the deadly shaft strike one of the settlers in the thigh, bright red blood spurting from the wound. Suddenly dozens of arrows zipped through the air, the deserters trying vainly to shoot the sleek shafts with the same accuracy as Sioux warriors. Most of the soldiers, however, relied on their rifles and filled the sweltering

32

prairie air with hot lead aimed at the settlers and the sod houses.

Within minutes the marauding deserters had set fire to the houses and killed all the men in the small settlement, the bloodied bodies bent and broken in the dust, their corpses oozing blood onto the packed ground.

Now came the children.

Without any qualms at all, the whooping painted soldiers hauled the screaming youngsters from the burning houses and at pointblank range blew their brains out with a single shot from their powerful carbines.

Liver-Eating Jackson, surveying the bloody scene, found what he was looking for. Huddled against the wall of a burning sod house, his wide-eyed face etched with fear, sat a young boy of ten or so. Jackson trotted over toward the boy and, stopping beside the cowering youth, raised his fearsome war hatchet as though to strike a blow.

"No!" cried the boy, bolting as he yelled.

Jackson smiled and watched the terrified kid sprint away from the screams and gunshots in the settlement. The boy raced as fast as his little legs would carry him toward the safety of some willow trees at the edge of the clearing.

There's our witness, thought Jackson. Young enough, too, to exaggerate the gory details. The snake-eyed killer turned his pony and joined the others.

Now came the women.

Liver-Eating Jackson trotted up to where Luther Ames held a screaming teenaged settler girl by her flowing red hair. A wide grin cracked the dim-witted deserter's long face.

"Look what I found!" yelled Ames. "Redheads make a hell of a fuck!"

Liver-Eating Jackson froze atop his pony.

The wiry plainsman's thin face darkened with rage. His

33

yellow snake eyes narrowed to tiny slits and the little muscles in his jaw rippled as he grit his teeth. Suddenly, without warning, the ruthless plainsman raised his glistening war hatchet and with a quick, accurate stroke brought the razor-sharp blade down on the trembling settler girl's head. The blow sliced off the top of her skull, leaving wide-eyed Luther Ames holding the girl's hair and the bloodied top of her head. The redheaded teenager slumped dead to the ground.

"Murderers!" came a cry from across the clearing.

Jackson whirled and saw a middle-aged, blonde settler woman sprawled naked in the dust while an aroused deserter, his eyes gleaming with desire, pumped his enlarged cock into her.

"You speak English!" yelled the woman in a frayed voice. "You're white men—"

Jackson exploded. "I told you not to speak English!"

Quickly Liver-Eating Jackson unsheathed his Winchester carbine, aimed down the long barrel, and pumped two shots into the screaming blonde. The settler woman's slender body jerked from the impact of the slugs, then lay still in the dust.

"Hey!" protested the startled deserter atop the woman.

"Fun time is over!" growled Liver-Eating Jackson. "Kill all the women and burn the houses!"

Jackson turned and faced Ames.

"Next time," he snapped, "follow orders."

"But I—"

"Just follow orders!"

Luther Ames swallowed once, glanced up into Liver-Eating Jackson's narrowed yellow eyes, then nodded quickly.

"Sure, sure," he said softly. "Whatever you say."

Jackson smiled. "All right," he shouted. "Let's finish up here. The next move belongs to the army."

Liver-Eating Jackson returned his rifle to its sheath and

quickly scanned the results of the massacre, his narrow snakelike eyes flicking from the burning houses to the butchered bodies on the ground. Then, with a wide grin across his thin leathery face, the ruthless killer turned his pony's head sharply and headed back toward Paco Riley and the horses.

Visions of gold danced in his head.

CHAPTER THREE

"Welcome back to Fort Rawlins, Mr. Holten."

Gen. Frank Corrington rose smoothly from behind his wide shiny mahogany desk, spat tobacco juice into the brass spittoon on the floor, and extended a slender hand toward the scout.

"It's nice to have you back," said the general with a broad smile.

Holten shook Corrington's hand and just nodded.

The scout wasn't looking forward to the meeting. Especially after his stay with the widow. He'd slept late in the big brass bed, eaten a huge breakfast, and escorted Rebecca Ridgeway to the fort, where she planned to pick up some new dresses she'd ordered months ago. Leaving the lovely blonde at the post's general store, Holten had crossed the noisy parade grounds and entered the office of the 12th Cavalry's commanding officer. Now he stood brushing off the prairie dust from his buckskin clothes and waited anxiously for what he knew would be a nasty assignment.

They always gave the tough jobs to Holten.

"I think you know Maj. Nathan Phillips," said the general, indicating the tall hard-faced officer standing next to the big desk.

The scout eyed the major. "We've met," said Holten.

Major Phillips returned the scout's icy stare.

"Fine," said Corrington, sitting heavily in his padded chair. "Now let's get down to business."

The general spat again, making the spittoon ring, then

grabbed a box of cigars and thrust it at the scout.

"Sit down, Mr. Holten," he said, "and have a cigar."

The scout smiled. When they have something dirty for you to do, they always turn on the charm. Holten selected a thin cheroot and sat in a hard-backed chair in front of the desk.

"We have a serious problem Mr. Holten," said Corrington.

"Problem?"

The general nodded. "And we think you're the man who can help us solve it."

Corrington held the cigars in front of Major Phillips, then glanced at Holten again. "Indians," he said simply.

"The killin' kind," added Major Phillips.

The scout stiffened. He didn't like it already.

Holten watched Phillips choose a thick green cigar from the proffered box and saw Corrington replenish the big chaw in his cheek with some fresh chewing tobacco. Then the scout took a match from his buckskin jacket, lit the cheroot, and through a thin veil of blue-white cigar smoke, studied the two stern looking military men who sat in front of him.

Gen. Frank Corrington, a Civil War hero and veteran of the Indian Wars, stood ramrod straight and was almost as thin, his wiry frame hardened from years on campaigns against various ruthless enemies. His narrow hawklike face sported a short iron-gray beard streaked with a thin, amber-colored stain from tobacco spittle that never quite reached its target.

Holten exhaled a cloud of smoke.

The general had taken command of the 12th Cavalry after the previous commander, Maj. George Rowan, died in a Sioux massacre. Corrington had moved the unit's headquarters to Fort Rawlins near the Black Hills, then selected Major Phillips as his right hand man.

Maj. Nathan Phillips, the scout knew, was an ambitious

37

hard-assed soldier with an explosive mean streak. The major's hard chiseled face and cold blue eyes reflected the man's inner toughness. Holten wondered why in hell the generals in Washington had sent such a war-loving officer out to the treaty-bound plains at a time when quiet diplomacy was needed.

"What seems to be the problem?" asked the scout, afraid to hear the general's response. Another renegade uprising wasn't what Holten needed right now.

The general sat back in his chair. "Massacres," he said.

Holten's pulse quickened.

"Whereabouts?" asked the scout.

The general nodded at Phillips. "Tell him, Major."

Major Phillips took a slip of paper from the desk and spoke in a cold, clipped tone. "Jury Wells, Reliance, Cold Springs, Buffalo Canyon—"

Corrington's angry voice cut him off. "Six separate attacks by renegades on white settlements in the past two weeks," snapped the general. He spat tobacco juice for emphasis. "All the settlers—men, women, and children—butchered where they fell!"

A heavy silence fell over the room.

Holten's mind flashed mental images of mutilated corpses, disfigured children, and butchered women.

"Murdering red bastards!" snapped Major Phillips.

"Every one of the attacks was in direct defiance of the terms set down in the treaties signed two months ago," said General Corrington.

The scout saw Phillips squirm in his chair.

"What in hell do these savages want?" shouted the major. "We gave them land to farm. Plenty of tools, too! Now they show their gratitude by killing innocent settlers."

Holten just chewed on his cheroot.

Corrington cleared his throat and looked at Holten. "I know you have some—what shall we call them—

38

'connections'—with the Indians in these parts," said the general.

"I've been around," said the scout.

"He lived with the red bastards!" snapped Phillips.

The scout just eyed the hard-faced major.

"All we'd like you to do," continued the general, "is use these connections of yours to find out who's behind all this killing."

That's all, thought the scout.

Holten exhaled some cigar smoke. "Did anybody see the Indians? Survivors, I mean?" he asked.

Major Phillips shot to his feet, his big green cigar clamped between his teeth, and began to pace across the small office. "What difference does it make, Holten! Indians are Indians!" he snapped, cigar smoke trailing behind him as he paced. "They all have to be taught that a treaty is a treaty!"

General Corrington spat some tobacco juice. "There have been several survivors, Mr. Holten," he said calmly. "From the weapons, language, and ponies used in the attacks, there's no doubt it was the Sioux.

Holten knew what was coming. "And you want me to find out which ones?"

"That's right," said the general. "I don't know of anyone more qualified for the job."

Major Phillips stopped and turned. "Time is running out, Holten," he said in a cold, clipped voice. "The white settlers are beginning to panic all over the Dakota Territory."

The scout had a strange feeling in his gut. Something was wrong and he knew it. But what? Holten had just been in some of the camps of the Oglala and Brule Sioux last week. He's hunted, fished, and smoked with the braves. And he'd heard nothing about any renegades. Yet settlers had been killed, their bodies mutilated and scalped.

But by whom?

General Corrington rose behind his wide desk, his hawklike face creased with concentration, his jaws working frantically on the chewing tobacco in his cheeks. Finally, the general stroked his gray beard and spat a stream of amber-colored juice into the brass spittoon.

"We plan to come down hard on those Indians who are responsible, Mr. Holten," he said. "But first we'd like you to see what you can find out."

The general leaned forward on his desk.

"Find us some Indians, scout," he said through the massive chaw of tobacco in his cheek.

Holten stood suddenly. "I'll do my best," he said. "Far as I know, most of the Sioux are huntin' buffalo up north. Don't know of any who are causin' trouble."

Major Phillips stepped closer to Holten "We've got six hundred crack troops ready to march," snapped Phillips. "The red savages need to be shown that they can't push white men around!"

Holten tossed his cheroot into the brass spittoon where it died a fizzling death, then looked up at General Corrington with his piercing blue eyes.

"Let me check the Sioux camps," said the scout.

"Fine, fine," said a beaming general.

"It may take a week or more," added Holten.

Corrington frowned for a moment and glanced quickly at Phillips before he spoke again. "See if you can't do it a bit faster," he said. "There may be—complications later on."

"Complications?"

Corrington smiled, stroked his beard, and spat again.

"Nothing to concern you right now, Mr. Holten," said the general. "Just find the culprits and report back to us as soon as possible."

Holten nodded, glared for a moment at Maj. Nathan Phillips, and headed for the door. Renegades again on the plains? Why hadn't he heard about it? The scout pulled open the office door and squinted at the sudden bright sunlight on the fort's parade grounds.

Something was wrong. He'd find out what it was.

Holten was standing at the back of the fort's general store, near the fitting rooms, when a slender golden hand reached from behind some curtains and grabbed his crotch.

The scout jumped. Then he heard the giggling.

Glancing first at the dozen or so customers in the store, Holten pulled back the denim curtain and saw Rebecca Ridgeway, in all her glorious beauty—a radiant new yellow and cream chiffon dress draped sensuously over her sumptuous body.

"I had you by the balls," she said, a glint of mischief in her big blue eyes.

Holten smiled. "Lucky nobody saw us."

"Who's going to see us?" asked the sexy widow.

"Only the whole 12th Cavalry."

"It's more exciting that way," purred Rebecca, "don't you think?"

"More exciting—?"

Before Holten could say another word, the sinewy golden-haired yong widow slipped the chiffon dress over her head with a quick rustle of material and stood like a naked goddess before the scout.

Holten felt a twinge of desire in his groin.

Quickly his steely blue eyes roamed her golden body, lingering for a moment at the firm round breasts, dropping over the smooth flat stomach, and settling at the shiny, triangular patch of pubic hair at her crotch.

Then reality hit him like an Indian war club.

"Get away from the curtain," he whispered quickly, and grabbed the soft sensuous blonde by the arm. Looking nervously over his shoulder, the scout herded her to a corner of the large storeroom that doubled as a fitting room.

The closeness of her almost overwhelmed him.

"Are you ashamed of my body?" she asked playfully.

"Ashamed?"

"It's yours, Holten," she said.

Suddenly the gorgeous widow grasped the scout's hand and gently rubbed it against one of her firm round breasts.

"It's all yours," she breathed, closing her big eyes.

Holten's cock throbbed.

Rebecca Ridgeway pressed the scout's rough hand harder against the soft, billowy flesh of her sumptuous breasts, running his fingers gently over her fully aroused nipples. She moaned softly with pleasure.

"I need you, Holten!" she pleaded in a hoarse whisper, her sparkling eyes open now and searching the scout's weathered face.

"Here?" asked the scout, casting a wary glance toward the flimsy denim curtain.

Rebecca was almost panting. "Why not? It's more exciting this way, don't you think?" she groaned softly.

The naked blonde shot a hand to the scout's crotch and rubbed his penis through his buckskin pants, reaching down after a moment and grabbing his balls.

Holten couldn't stand it any longer. "What the hell!"

Quickly the scout tore off his buckskin clothes and his boots and stood buck naked in front of an appreciative Rebecca Ridgeway, his long shaft pointing up at her and his lean muscled body tingling with excitement.

His cock pounded like a hammer.

"So huge!" she said, her glistening blue eyes fixed on his incredibly long erection.

"Like I told you before," said Holten, his pulse beating like an Indian drum, "you bring out the best in me."

"Let's do it!" she said hoarsely, her delicate fingers

42

reaching out to gently grasp the scout's iron-hard shaft, her firm, golden thighs brushing up against his lean frame.

Holten smiled broadly.

Why not, he thought. Already he'd been told about a new extraordinary situation on the plains—a renegade uprising by Sioux warriors he didn't even know. Now, one of the most gorgeous women he'd ever met wanted to make love in the back room of one of the busiest general stores in the territory. Might as well keep the afternoon extraordinary!

Holten's hands began to go to work.

Quickly the scout slid his big rough hands along the sexy blonde widow's sleek curves, starting at her delicate shoulders, working down her flat smooth stomach, and reaching her firm round buttocks.

Rebecca jumped at his touch. Her hands grabbed his arms.

"Oh, Holten!"

"Shhhh!" warned the scout in a hoarse whisper. "Not too loud or we might get some visitors."

"I don't care!" said the fully aroused blonde. "Do it to me!"

He did.

Gently the scout slid his strong hands along the soft warm flesh of Rebecca's golden thighs until he reached the waxy patch of pubic hair at her crotch, pausing for a long moment as his long fingers began to massage the silky folds of flesh at the warm, wet opening. Rebecca jerked in a sudden reflex action, her whole body trembling as Holten's fingers probed deeper and deeper into her slippery channel, his long fingers reaching her innermost region.

Rebecca Ridgeway gasped.

"Ooooooo," she moaned.

As they stood panting in the corner of the shadowy

storeroom, Holten pumped his fingers into the writhing blonde, each thrust of his hand sending Rebecca Ridgeway into spasms of pure sexual delight.

"Let's do it!" she gasped. "Now—!"

Holten bent down and took one of the luscious widow's breasts in his mouth, gently massaging the billowy flesh with his lips, flicking the taut rose-colored nipple with his tongue, sending a new tremor of desire shooting through Rebecca's lean and willowy frame.

"Aiiiii," shrieked Rebecca. "Oh Holten. . . ."

Quickly the blonde widow reached out with her long tapered fingers and grasped the scout's pulsating penis, her hand a blur of motion as she slid her fingers up and down Holten's long hard shaft from its thick, hard base to the now dripping pink tip.

"Jesus!" breathed the scout.

"Enter me," pleaded Rebecca. "Please—!"

Slowly they sank to the floor and collapsed on top of a pile of burlap sacks, Holten mounting the writhing widow, her firm breasts flattening against his broad hairy chest as the scout's long lean frame pressed down on her.

"Now!" pleaded Rebecca Ridgeway, her big blue eyes rolling with delight.

The sensuous blonde quickly guided the scout's long rod-like cock to her glistening bush, pausing for a moment at the silky opening and rubbing Holten's penis slowly in gentle circles, Rebecca gasping with delight at the feel of the scout's throbbing cock as it massaged the soft delicate folds of flesh hidden in the mat of pubic hair.

Suddenly Holten pushed downward, his huge penis ramming into the writhing blonde, her body jerking slightly as his fully aroused penis slid through her slippery channel and struck the hard slick wall deep inside of her.

Rebecca Ridgeway shrieked with delight.

As uniformed soldiers and chattering visitors milled

about in the general store on the other side of the flimsy denim curtain, Holten and Rebecca Ridgeway thrashed and rolled in pure sexual bliss atop the small pile of burlap potato sacks, their glistening bodies glued together as each brought the other closer to a glorious sexual climax.

Holten pumped and pumped into her.

Rebecca's head rolled from side to side.

"Oh!" she said suddenly.

In a frantic instant of complete sexual release, their bodies seemingly glued together, they came at the same moment, Holten pushing into the writhing sinewy body one final time, Rebecca arching her back to meet him. The scout exploded into her, his hot passion filling Rebecca, their bodies frozen for a long moment until each was completely satisfied.

Then they collapsed onto the burlap.

Rebecca gasped for air. Holten's heart pounded.

They lay still for several long moments, their bodies completely spent, their emotions drained. Holten lay atop the soft sensuous widow, his ears starting to pick up the sounds from the busy general store, his sharpened senses working again as though he was out on the treacherous prairie.

Rebecca looked into his eyes. "Thank you," she said softly.

"Why not?" said Holten playfully.

Then they heard it.

The clump of army boots. The whoosh of the denim curtain.

"Mrs. Ridgeway?" called the army sales clerk.

Holten froze. Rebecca's body stiffened.

"Mrs. Ridgeway," repeated the young clerk, "is everything all right?"

Holten grabbed the lean widow and pulled her as far into the shadows as possible. The scout heard the clerk plod further into the back room.

Holten whispered. "Better answer him."

"Are you all right, Mrs. Ridgeway?"

"Yes—" replied Rebecca in a cracking voice. "Yes, I'm fine. I'll be finished in a minute."

The clerk paused. "You sound kind of strange, Mrs. Ridgeway. Are you sure you're all right?"

Rebecca smiled, her sparkling blue eyes locking with the scout's. Her long fingers grasped Holten's face gently and pulled him down to her. She kissed him on the mouth, her supple lips lingering for a moment.

"I've never been better," said the blonde widow.

"Well," replied the puzzled clerk. "I'll be in the store if you need any help."

"Thank you corporal," said Rebecca.

The lean sexy widow glanced again at Holten.

"And thank *you* again," she said with a smile.

The scout grinned. "Anytime."

Hell of a woman, thought Holten.

They dressed quickly, Holten hauling on his buckskin clothes and fastening his weapons to his belt. As he watched the sinewy blonde pull a new dress over her luscious body, the scout's mind began to drift toward his new assignment.

Renegades on the plains?

By the time Rebecca Ridgeway had finished and stood in front of him, her sparkling blue eyes studying his leathery face, Holten's mind was already out on the prairie.

Something was wrong. He had to find out what it was.

CHAPTER FOUR

Shrill war cries pierced the air.

Holten froze.

The scout pulled up short in the middle of the dusty trail, his big horse snorting in protest. With the merciless sun beating down on him like an Indian war club, Holten stopped in his tracks and listened.

Gunshots echoed. Indians screamed.

The familiar sounds of an Indian attack reached him on the gentle summer breeze that wafted over the Dakota prairie. He'd heard them many times before.

And he'd seen the bloody results.

Holten had been tracking for several hours through the burning alkaline dust, his tired eyes glued to the sun-baked trail looking for signs of the Sioux. Ever since he left Fort Rawlins at midday he'd been searching for some kind of sign that Sioux renegades were near.

Then he'd heard the war cries.

Holten's senses worked keenly, his muscles tensed for action. Finally, the scout clucked to his big horse and quickly headed toward the source of the whooping and hollering. As he urged his mount through the sweltering heat, the gelding's long powerful legs churning up the dusty trail, Holten's mind played with the puzzle General Corrington had given him.

Renegades on the prairie. But who?

Maybe the ruckus in the clearing over the next rise would give him some answers. The scout spurred the gelding and raced through the tall buffalo grass and scraggly sage brush toward the rocky knoll off to his left.

Holten reined in his big snorting mount, a shower of dust falling over the knoll as he braked the gelding, and peered through the shimmering summer heat to the frantic scene in the small dusty clearing below.

What he saw quickened his pulse.

At the bottom of a slight hill the scout spotted two beleaguered frontiersmen, their fallen horses and pack mules lay sprawled dead in the dust in front of them. The wide-eyed plainsmen shouldered glistening Henry repeaters and shot steadily from behind their dead horses at a band of about a dozen screaming Sioux braves. The whooping Indians circled the desperate white men, their swift ponies racing around the clearing kicking up a thin veil of fine dust. As they rode, hanging from their mounts for protection, the painted warriors ducked under their mounts' necks and bellies and let loose with a barrage of whistling arrows. The deadly shafts had already wounded one of the frontiersmen as Holten noticed several arrows stuck in the man's side and back.

The scout knew the men couldn't last much longer.

He went into action.

Holten tethered the gelding on a nearby tree branch, then hauled his Winchester .44-40 repeater from its saddle sheath. Checking the .44 Remington revolver at his belt, the scout slipped quietly down the grassy slope toward the fighting below.

Gliding through the undulating buffalo grass like a big cougar stalking its prey, his footfalls barely audible, the gunshots and war cries ringing in his ears, Holten studied the broad dark faces of the circling Sioux warriors.

Who were they? Did he know them?

The scout slid down the grassy embankment, his Winchester grasped firmly in his big hands, his steely blue eyes fixed on the whooping braves.

Holten had met most of the Sioux braves in the vast

Dakota Territory. He knew their way of life and the location of their summer and winter camps. He knew how they thought and acted under various conditions. And he knew that, for the most part, they wanted peace.

So why did these warriors break the treaties?

Holten reached the edge of the dusty clearing and quickly shouldered his rifle. The scout aimed down the long barrel, caught a screaming warrior in his sights, and gently squeezed the trigger.

The Winchester spat fire.

Across the clearing the warrior's arms flew over his head and his body jerked suddenly at the impact of the hot lead. The startled Sioux brave slammed to the hard ground near a copse of cottonwoods, blood spurting from the gaping wound in his chest.

Quickly Holten levered another shell into the Winchester. He fired again. And again. The acrid stench of gunpowder assailed his nostrils. In front of him Sioux warriors literally bit the dust, their wide glistening faces twisted into masks of agony as the hot slugs tore into their flesh and sent them spinning from their ponies.

As he fired over and over, the scout recognized some of the circling braves. His pulse quickened as he studied the painted faces. The warriors came from the camp of Red Hawk, a war-loving subchief with a deep hatred for white men. Once, a long time ago, the scout had been close friends with some of the braves who now rode in front of him.

Were these Corrington's renegades?

Holten levered and fired, his Winchester spitting hot lead at the warriors he'd known in a different time as blood brothers and hunting partners.

Crazy Dog. The scout shot him in the chest.

Four Horns. Holten's bullet caught him in the head.

Left Hand Bull. Dead before he hit the ground.

Suddenly the Indians retreated, their bows held high

49

above their heads as they raced from the clearing and disappeared into the prairie like yelping dogs with their tails stuck between their legs.

Silence filled the dusty clearing.

But just for a moment.

"Damn good shootin', mister!" called a gruff voice.

Holten turned sharply and glanced at the smiling frontiersmen, their haggard faces flush with relief, their smoking Henry rifles clutched in their shaking hands.

"Them Injuns dropped like flies!"

The scout rose from his spot in the buffalo grass and strode carefully to where the plainsmen lay behind their bleeding animals. Holten cradled his Winchester, his piercing eyes quickly scanning the two men and their immediate surroundings. A major rule of survival on the prairie, Holten knew, was to be ready for anything.

And to trust nobody.

The scout studied the gruff-voiced man, a wiry plainsman with long unkempt hair that fell to the fringed shoulders of his dusty buckskin jacket. His wounded partner lay moaning in the alkaline dust, a heavy-set frontiersman with a wide fleshy face, three Sioux arrows embedded in his back and side.

"Jesus!" breathed the wounded heavyset man, his fat face creased with pain. "Thought for sure we was goners!"

The wiry man stood. Holten tensed his muscles.

"Lucky thing you came along when you did, stranger," said the wiry plainsman in his gruff voice. "Another few minutes and we woulda been out of ammunition."

The scout studied the two frontiersmen carefully, his mind working frantically to place the faces. Were they friends or foes? Had he ever seen them before? Holten quickly drained his memory and gave the two plainsmen a clean bill of health.

He'd never seen them before. But he'd be careful just the same.

It takes only one mistake to be dead.

"Name's Burke," said the wiry man extending a bony hand at the scout. "Tom Burke."

"Holten," said the scout simply, shifting the Winchester in his arms and shaking the man's skeletal hand.

"This here is Luke LaPointe," said Burke. "Or what's left of him." The wiry plainsman chuckled.

"Damn arrows hurt like hell!" said LaPointe.

Holten watched the men for a long moment then relaxed his muscles a little. They needed help. He'd give them a hand then continue his trek to the Sioux camps.

"Let me get those arrows out," said the scout, moving forward. He placed the Winchester next to him on the ground and knelt beside the bleeding Luke LaPointe.

A wounded mule bleated several feet away.

"Looks like one of your animals survived," said Holten as he examined the arrow shafts in LaPointe's stocky body.

"I'll have a look," said Burke.

Holten returned his gaze to the wounded man.

"This is goin' to hurt," warned the scout as he grasped the first arrow.

Luke LaPointe nodded glumly. "Let's get it over with."

Holten squeezed the Sioux arrow's long wooden shaft, twisted it slightly, then, with a quick deliberate motion pulled it free from the fallen frontiersman's upper back.

"Aiiii!" shouted LaPointe, his face paling suddenly.

"Two more to go," cautioned the scout. LaPointe nodded. The deadly arrowheads hadn't pierced any vital organs or broken any bones. Holten quickly hauled out the remaining two arrow shafts in quick succession, then tore LaPointe's cotton shirt into strips and made crude compresses to stop the flow of blood. Once the bleeding had stopped, the scout washed the wounds with water from his canteen and placed several poultices made from nearby yarrow plants onto the nasty gashes.

"Almost as good as new," said the scout.

LaPointe smiled weakly. "Appreciate it, Holten."

Burke returned after having hauled an arrow out of the lone surviving mule. The wounded pack animal stood unsteadily at the far side of the clearing.

Burke shook his head, his scraggly hair shaking from side to side as he did so. "Shoulda known this was goin' to happen. After all, we was warned."

"Warned?" asked the puzzled scout.

"Back in Deadwood," explained Burke. "Couple of trailsmen told us to expect Injun trouble in these parts."

Holten blinked and tried to understand. First General Corrington mentioned something about Sioux war parties and now a couple of frontiersmen were told about the Indians by some drifters in Deadwood. What in hell was going on?

LaPointe stood shakily. "Hell," he said grimacing with pain as he steadied his stocky frame. "Never thought anything Liver-Eating Jackson said would ever come true."

Holten froze. The name struck him like an arrow.

"Who?" asked the scout wanting to be sure.

"Liver-Eating Jackson," repeated LaPointe, shaking his big head slowly. "How can ya believe anything from a crazy bastard who ate the goddam liver from some dead Injun!"

Liver-Eating Jackson, thought the scout.

"Know him?" asked Burke.

Holten nodded. "I know the son of a bitch," he said.

Holten had met Jackson once in a hail of bullets, their argument settled with a blast from the scout's .44 pistol. It happened several years ago at Fort Sampson. Holten's army patrol had just brought in the bloodied corpses of several Sioux warriors, former friends of Holten who had died gloriously in battle against the soldiers. The stiffening corpses lay draped over the backs of some ragged army mounts. Liver-Eating Jackson had met them at the main gates, a glistening butcher's knife in his hand, waiting eagerly to scalp the dead Sioux braves.

Holten had stepped in quickly to claim the bodies, hauling them off to give them a proper burial. Jackson followed, enraged at the prospect of losing a few fifty dollar scalps, and tried to ambush the scout just outside the fort. Holten had been quicker, though, and to this day Liver-Eating Jackson still wore the scout's lead embedded in his shoulder.

Liver-Eating Jackson. Holten knew him all right.

"Paco Riley," said LaPointe.

The voice brought Holten out of his thoughts.

"What?" he asked.

"The other man was Paco Riley," said the wounded frontiersman, saying the name like it was some kind of deadly critter to be avoided. "A big fat killer. He warned us about the Injuns, too."

"Said they got the information from a special source," added Burke. "Whatever the hell that means."

Holten just nodded his head. Paco Riley? It figures. The scout knew that where you find Jackson, Paco Riley is sure to be close at hand. But what did they know about Indians? A couple of two-bit drifters; they'd know as much about a new renegade uprising as the painted whores who hovered around the green gambling tables in Deadwood. It didn't make sense.

"One more thing," said Burke, a bony hand stroking his lean face. "Both Jackson and Riley got to drinkin' quite heavy. Then they started boastin' how they's gonna be rich real soon."

"Rich?" asked Holten.

Burke shrugged his narrow shoulders. "That's all they said. Soon after that they shot the saloon all to hell and killed some poor drifter standing at the bar."

"Sounds just like Jackson," said the scout.

The new information rankled Holten ever more. Maybe

53

it was nothing to be concerned about. But suddenly everyone seemed to be talking about Indian uprisings. And what did Liver-Eating Jackson have to do with anything?

The mule bleated from across the clearing.

"We best be movin' on, Holten," said Burke in his gruff voice. "Thanks for your help."

"Much obliged," said LaPointe, shaking the scout's hand.

"Can you make it all right?" asked Holten.

Burke nodded. "Got us a cabin just over that ridge over there," he said. "We'll be fine."

"Be back on the trail huntin' buffalo before you know it," said LaPointe, smiling through his pain.

The two frontiersmen gathered what belongings they could carry, strapped some packs onto the wounded mule, then turned and waved to the scout. Holten watched the men trudge into the prairie until they disappeared over the next slope.

Liver-Eating Jackson and Paco Riley?

And why did Red Hawk's warriors go on the war path?

Holten collected his Winchester and headed back up the gentle slope toward the tethered gelding. The more he looked for General Corrington's Sioux renegades the more questions he stumbled across. He walked faster up the grassy hill. He wanted to be in Sioux country by morning.

Then he'd get some answers.

Holten headed for buffalo country.

He pointed the gelding toward the dark brooding hills to the north and trotted along the tree-lined trail. The scout edged the big horse through narrow rock-strewn ravines and past plush stands of tall, stately pine trees, his eyes always alert and his senses tingling.

Indian country was no place to be careless.

As he rode, Holten reviewed the situation so far. At least

54

the situation as far as he knew it. Some band of Sioux warriors had run wild across the territory burning, looting, and killing. Trouble was, as the scout searched his memory for the names of tribal troublemakers, the ones eager for any kind of treaty, he came up blank.

Who in hell was responsible for the raids?

The scout clucked to the gelding and urged the big horse into a gallop. The sooner Holten reached the camp of Chief Black Spotted Horse the sooner he'd get some facts. Red Hawk's braves had been responsible for the attack on the two frontiersmen back in the clearing, but that could have been just an isolated incident. Red Hawk always enjoyed raising hell. Somebody was bent on starting a full scale uprising across the plains, and the sooner the scout talked with his former Sioux brothers the less chance there was for more mayhem.

Holten galloped into the late afternoon sunshine, and by the time the early evening shadows began to stretch across the darkening prairie, the scout had reached a small wooded clearing with a sad-looking sod house stuck in the middle. Holten reined in the gelding and scanned the scene before him.

Nothing moved. Not a sound cracked the silence.

Then he froze.

He saw arrows in the house. Dozens of them.

Holten spurred the gelding and trotted into the clearing, his steely blue eyes flicking from side to side looking for signs of a possible ambush, his muscles tensing and ready for action, his fingers twitching and ready to go for his weapons.

The scout slowed the gelding to a walk and scanned the immediate surroundings, his gaze passing quickly over the lonely house with arrows bristling from its exterior, the small wooden corn crib off to one side of the building, and the pitiful garden baking in the last rays of the unrelenting midsummer sun.

Holten glanced at the fresh grave to his left.

Then it happened.

The flimsy slab door of the sod house flew open, a slim figure appeared suddenly in the doorway, and the double barrel shotgun in his hands roared to life as its deadly load of buckshot burst into the clearing.

It was aimed at Holten's head.

The scout dove to the ground, the gelding reared on its hind legs, and the slim figure in the door slammed backwards from the impact of the big gun. The gunman, dazed from the gunshot, lay sprawled just inside the house.

Holten quickly regained his footing. The slim figure, just a young boy, reached for the gun. The scout had no real choice.

As quick as a wildcat's paw, Holten's hand shot to his belt and unsheathed his fearsome Bowie knife. The scout raised the glistening blade and started to throw it toward the scrambling youth in the doorway.

"No!" came a plaintive cry from the corn crib. "Don't kill my boy!"

Holten paused suddenly as a slim dark-haired woman burst from the battered corn crib and raced to the house. The haggard woman thrust her body onto the slim youth, shielding him from any attack by the scout.

Holten lowered the knife and looked suddenly at the activity near the corn crib. Four more youngsters, aged from above five to nine, scampered out of the dusty shelter and ran wide-eyed toward their mother at the house.

"Don't kill my boy!" sobbed the semihysterical woman. "Don't, don't, don't!"

Holten stared for a long moment at the pitiful scene in front of him, then started forward. He stopped when he saw the woman reach for the shotgun, her eyes wide with sudden fear. Something terrible must have happened here, thought the scout, to turn a strong settler woman into a frightened hysterical animal.

The woman grabbed the shotgun, levelled it at the scout, and with trembling hands aimed it at his head.

"Stay away!" she snapped, her haggard, blanched face a contorted mask of fear and hatred.

Holten froze in his tracks. "I'm a friend," he said gently. "I want to help you."

"Stay away!"

Holten looked at the pack of youngsters huddled around their fallen big brother and trembling mother. The scout also noticed the obvious lack of a man on the premises. Then he thought quickly about the fresh grave he'd passed on his way to the house.

Holten tried again. "I'm here to help you," he repeated. "You need help against the Indians. I can help you."

The woman fell silent. Her hands continued to tremble.

"Let me help your children. It'll be all right."

Then Holten watched the woman's face soften and her grip on the shotgun loosen. Suddenly the beaten settler woman lowered the big gun and began to cry, the dam of tears inside of her bursting and letting loose a torrent of pent-up feelings. She knelt on the ground in front of the darkened house and sobbed uncontrollably, her narrow shoulders heaving as she cried.

"It's okay Ma," said a small boy.

"Don't cry Momma," added a little girl.

Finally, the dark-haired woman jumped to her feet and sprinted past the startled scout to the freshly dug grave. She threw herself over the mound of soil and cried even harder.

The scout moved forward and took the gun.

As the big orange sun dipped in the western sky, Holten slipped into the neighboring fields and quickly shot four big jack rabbits. Returning to the sod house, the scout lit several kerosene lamps and cooked the freshly killed animals on the family's blackened stove. Mixing the sweet rabbit meat with some potatoes and onions he found next to the stove, Holten prepared a small feast for the half-starved children who watched him with big sparkling eyes. They all ate ravenously and in complete silence at the rough-planked table in the middle of the house. All except the woman, who remained sobbing at the grave.

After the meal, the younger children fell fast asleep on beds at the back of the small house. The oldest boy, the one who'd tried to shoot the scout, apologized and then explained what had happened earlier that day.

"The Injuns came at us whoopin' and hollerin'," he said dully. "They galloped a long way across the prairie, so it gave my pa a chance to send us off into the woods to hide."

Holten watched the boy, who he figured to be about ten or eleven, tell the gruesome story.

"We all hid down in the bushes," he continued. "My ma was scared as all get out, and told us to keep our heads down. But I had to look. I had to see what was happenin' to my pa."

The scout saw the boy lower his head.

"The Injuns sliced him to pieces," he said in a soft voice, "then scalped him. I saw 'em do it."

Holten reached out and touched the boy's shoulder.

"And there's somethin' else," said the boy looking up into the scout's blue eyes.

"Something else?"

"While we was waitin' in the bushes, I heard some horses snorting just a little ways off. So I sneaked away from my ma and peeked at a small stand of trees."

"And?" asked the scout.

"I seen this giant bald-headed man waitin' with about a dozen horses," said the boy. "I ain't never seen such a big man before in my life."

Holten froze. Paco Riley.

The scout's mind raced dizzily. Twice on the same day the mammoth frontiersman's name had cropped up. And now the big killer was reported out on the Dakota plains with a band of raiding Indians.

But why?

Holten turned to the boy. "Then what happened?" asked the scout shakily.

The boy shrugged. "When the Injuns finished killin' all our animals, they raced onto the prairie. The big fat man raced after 'em with the horses."

Holten studied the boy for a moment in the sparse light of the flickering lamp, then rose and strode out the door into the inky prairie night. As crickets sang and a cool breeze rustled his long brown hair, the scout pulled one of the arrows from the sod house and studied it.

It was Sioux all right. But whose?

As the grieving woman's constant sobbing rose into the cool night air, Holten snapped the arrow in two and tossed it to the dusty ground. Could Paco Riley be behind the Indian attacks? And where in hell was Liver-Eating Jackson?

Holten would find out in the morning.

Chief Black Spotted Horse would know.

CHAPTER FIVE

A sea of buffalo.

Holten reined in the snorting gelding on the crest of a rocky ridge that overlooked a vast grassy plain. With a sense of awe he glanced down at the grazing mass of big furry buffalo that spread out for miles before him. The sight always took his breath away. The scout knew that midsummer to early fall was the time the great herds of bison thundered down from the north country and fattened themselves on the succulent Dakota grass for the icy winter. The herd in the plain below was one of the biggest he'd ever seen.

At least ten thousand animals.

Holten clucked to the gelding and continued along the jagged ridge toward the plains below. While watching the great mass of buffalo, his thoughts returned to the problems at hand. He'd left the sobbing settler woman and her young brood at a nearby trading post, figuring at least they'd be safe there from any further Indian attacks.

Or attacks by Paco Riley and Liver-Eating Jackson.

Holten pulled his mind away for a moment and checked his immediate surroundings. After a few minutes the scout urged the big gelding down the grassy slope leading to the flat plain below, his eyes alert and his senses working overtime. He'd entered the Sioux hunting grounds several hours ago and now his nerves tingled with anticipation. The scout imagined warriors lurking behind every tree and rock.

Then his thoughts returned to the problem of a possible

Indian uprising. He began to think about Paco Riley, Liver-Eating Jackson, the young boy's story, and General Corrington's assignment. The scout tried to put all the different parts together and come up with some kind of logical answer to his puzzle. As he rode his mind played with names and faces.

Then it happened.

The scout froze in his tracks.

A flash of activity down on the grassy plain caught Holten's eye. He turned sharply and glanced at the massive buffalo herd. Peering through the shimmering early morning heat, Holten watched two columns of whooping, fast-riding Sioux warriors attack the suddenly panic-stricken buffalo herd.

It was called a surround. A dangerous hunting technique.

Holten sat atop his big mount and smiled with admiration as the galloping Sioux warriors attacked a portion of the large herd from two sides, the braves shouting at the top of their lungs while their well-trained buffalo hunting horses headed off any bison that tried to escape. The scout remembered similar surrounds during his days with the Sioux and the excitement that built up inside him on the day of the great hunt. Now he watched with interest as the Indians burst onto the prairie. Within minutes the braves had about a hundred galloping buffalo trapped in a tight circle of screaming Indians and prancing horses.

Now came the tough part.

With seeming disregard for their personal safety, a few of the bravest warriors plunged their wild-eyed ponies deep into the thrashing swarm of frightened buffalo, their short razor-sharp lances piercing the big furry prey just behind the last ribs in order to collapse the big animals' lungs. Holten watched the crazed buffalo turn and slash a couple of Indian ponies, the startled braves hanging on to their wounded mounts for dear life rather than risk being trampled to death under the heavy hooves of dozens of frantic, two-thousand-pound buffaloes. Other warriors sat atop their sturdy horses and shot arrow after arrow into the massed herd.

The surround was a complete success.

The scout watched the Sioux braves finish off the last of the remaining buffaloes, the animals' death screams rising into the sweltering morning air. Then after all the buffalo had been neatly slaughtered, Holten looked at the edge of the wide plain for the squaws he knew would come running. Within minutes he saw about fifty or sixty brown-skinned women burst from the woods and race onto the plain, their little legs pumping to reach the fallen buffalo, their hands full of knives and other carcass cleaning tools.

Holten knew what came next. He'd done it himself.

For the next five or six hours, the women would slice and slash the buffalo carcasses to pieces. Not one bit of the giant furry animal would be wasted. Huge strips of meat would be lugged back to camp and dried for winter. Every part of the buffalo not used for food was put to some other good use. Horns, bones, hooves, and innards became household items. The hides had many uses, both with and without the thick, downy fur. Even the stomach lining of an unborn calf had its use—as a bag for harvesting cherries.

Only the bloodied hearts of the giant beasts would be left on the grassy plain, the Sioux believing the hearts would help bring more healthy buffalo next year.

The Sioux lived on the buffalo. It was life itself.

Holten became involved with the scene below, his blue eyes fixed on the milling warriors, the fallen buffalo carcasses, and the chattering women. The scout became involved with a part of plains Indian life that had remained unchanged for thousands of years and that had been a part of his own life not too many years ago.

In fact, Holten became too involved.

A twig snapped. A horse whinnied. The scout froze.

The scout whirled sharply in the saddle, realizing too late that he'd let his guard down for just an instant. His hands began to go for his weapons, but stopped halfway. Holten's steely blue eyes quickly scanned the small circle of scowling mounted warriors that held him in their icy glares. The scout's heart skipped a beat when he saw the drawn bows aimed right at his head.

It looked bad.

"Tall Bear," said a deep voice suddenly in Lakota, the Sioux language. "You lose your touch. We kill you easy."

Holten turned. His weathered face cracked into a smile.

"Black Spotted Horse," said Holten in Lakota. "It has been many moons since I last saw my Sioux brother."

The scout breathed a little easier when he saw the tall mounted warrior rein in his snorting pony next to the gelding.

"How goes the buffalo hunt?" asked Holten in Lakota.

The Sioux chief gestured toward the plain. "You see for yourself," he said. "Many buffalo this year. It will be a comfortable winter for my people."

"May their lodges be full of buffalo robes."

Black Spotted Horse signalled for the warriors to lower their drawn bows, then returned his attention to the scout. Holten quickly studied the great Sioux chief, one of the greatest of all buffalo hunters who ever rode the plains, a tall handsome warrior with a big hawklike nose and flashing brown eyes. The chief and Holten went back years together, back to the time when the scout first joined the camps of Sitting Bull and Crazy Horse. The scout considered the lean bronzed chief one of his best friends among the plains Indians.

He hoped Black Spotted Horse thought the same.

"What brings Tall Bear to the hunting grounds of the

Oglala Sioux?" asked the chief.

Holten scanned the dark stoic faces of the braves behind Black Spotted Horse, his piercing eyes trying to recognize any of the warriors. He wondered how many of them, if any, rode against the two frontiersmen in the clearing back on the trail.

"I seek Black Spotted Horse's wise counsel," said the scout diplomatically.

"My counsel?"

"Many whites have died during the past two weeks," said Holten. "Their scalped and mutilated bodies were found near their burned houses on the prairie."

"And Tall Bear thinks Sioux warriors are responsible?" asked the Oglala chief.

Be careful, thought the scout.

"Perhaps Black Spotted Horse knows who was to blame," said Holten. "And from which tribe they came."

Black Spotted Horse sighed deeply and looked out at the activity on the hunting grounds below. Then he turned and his flashing brown eyes locked with the scout's.

"It is not safe to be a white man in Sioux land these days, Tall Bear," said the chief coldly. "Many Indians, too, have died during the past few weeks."

Holten's eyebrows shot up. "White men killed them?"

The scout watched Black Spotted Horse signal to his braves and saw several ponies being brought forward, dead Sioux warriors draped over their backs. The bodies had been stripped, scalped, and mutilated.

It wasn't a pretty sight.

"More than twenty Oglala braves have died," said Black Spotted Horse.

Holten stroked his leathery face. "But the white men have signed treaties. The soldiers remain in the fort."

Black Spotted Horse stared at the scout for a long moment, his flashing brown eyes fixed on Holten's lean puzzled face. Then the tall chief turned and dismissed the warriors behind him. As the braves galloped away in a cloud of dust, the Sioux chief turned and looked at the scout again. Black Spotted Horse spoke in an even voice.

"I can not hold back my young warriors much longer, Tall Bear," said the chief. "They did not like the white man's treaty in the first place. Now, they are ready to kill all the whites on the plains."

"Who did this to your braves?" asked the scout.

"Several warriors have survived the attacks," said the chief. "They say many whites—maybe ten or more— riding army horses attacked without warning."

"The white men were soldiers?"

Black Spotted Horse shook his head. "They are run-away soldiers—how do you say it—?"

"Deserters?"

The chief nodded. "All of them are deserters except two," said Black Spotted Horse. "One of the others, say my braves, is as big as a pregnant bear. An evil man. He takes Indian scalps."

Holten's pulse quickened. He knew who it was.

"We call him 'Bear-Who-Likes-Indian-Scalps'" said the Sioux chief. "And he has no scalp himself. His head is clean and shiny like a baby's."

Paco Riley.

"And the other one?" asked Holten, although he already knew who it was.

"Thin and bony," said Black Spotted Horse, "with long brown hair. Some braves say this white man once ate an Indian's liver, but I do not believe it."

I do, thought the scout.

Liver-Eating Jackson.

"The white men killed our braves," continued the chief, "and then stripped them clean—ponies, weapons, and clothes. And they took scalps, too."

Holten sat atop the prancing gelding, his mind working rapidly, and started to put the pieces together. Liver-

Eating Jackson and big Paco Riley rode at the head of a band of marauding army deserters. The scout had seen other groups of army runaways on the plains; the soldiers had tired of the discipline and boredom of military life and decided to fight their own Indian war. The end result of most deserter-type adventures was a renewed series of attacks by the Indians.

But why hadn't Corrington mentioned the deserters?

And what was Paco Riley doing with a raiding war party?

"Have your warriors struck back?" asked Holten.

The chief shrugged. "Maybe some, like Red Hawk, have lost their tempers," he said. "But if these attacks by the whites continue, then I cannot guarantee that others—maybe all—will not follow them to the war path."

Holten winced. Another uprising was in the wind.

For some reason, Liver-Eating Jackson and the deserters had deliberately provoked the treaty-keeping Indians. They'd brutally murdered many braves and picked them clean. And some of the warriors had gone to the war path already. But had Red Hawk's braves killed all of the whites? The scout knew that the only way he'd get answers to his many questions was to find Jackson and Riley. And the sooner the better.

The chief's voice sliced through his thoughts.

"Come to our camp, Tall Bear," said Black Spotted Horse. "Eat and smoke in my teepee. We can talk more there. You are always welcome in our lodges."

Holten glanced at the squaws down on the plains. The Indian women's glistening knives butchered the freshly killed buffaloes where they had fallen. Hunting season was always a good time to visit Indian camps; the scout could almost taste the broiled buffalo steaks he knew hung dripping over cooking fires in the Oglala camp. He turned and nodded at Black Spotted Horse.

"I am honored to go with the wise chief of the Oglala to

his camp," said Holten.

Black Spotted Horse smiled and turned the head of his pony sharply. The scout clucked to the gelding and followed the chief at a gallop. As he rode, sudden images of mutilated and scalped white men flashed through Holten's mind. Black Spotted Horse had said that the scout was always welcome in the Sioux camp.

Holten hoped to hell he was right.

"I offer this pipe in honor of Tall Bear."

The scout watched Black Spotted Horse sing an incantation to the Sioux gods, a long stone pipe held over his head and pointed toward the heavens.

"I am honored," said Holten simply.

Then the tall hawk-nosed Sioux chief lowered the smoldering ceremonial pipe, took a long deep drag, and passed the pipe to the scout at his right. Holten accepted the highly polished stone pipe, noticing its smooth coating of buffalo grease, the long shaft decorated with yellow beads, and the half a dozen eagle feathers dangling from the narrow bowl. The scout inhaled deeply and filled his lungs with rich, thick tobacco smoke. Then following the Sioux custom of passing a pipe from left to right, never from right to left, Holten handed the long pipe to the elderly brave seated cross-legged next to him.

Holten had entered the Oglala camp trotting alongside Black Spotted Horse, his steely blue eyes scanning the bustling hunting village while curious Sioux braves glared back at him. The scout had noticed mourning squaws, crying beside the corpses Holten had seen earlier draped across the ponies, quickly take knives and lop off one or two fingers in the accepted public display of grief. As he pulled up in front of the chief's tall clean teepee, the scout had smelled the rich aroma of cooking buffalo meat that permeated the campsite.

The scout had entered Black Spotted Horse's teepee and,

following Sioux custom, had gone to the right and seated himself on a downy buffalo robe spread on the ground. Now, in a teepee filled with the tribe's subchiefs and honored warriors, he accepted Black Spotted Horse's ceremonial pipe and the honor that went with it.

But it was difficult for the scout to relax. He kept his muscles tensed and his eyes glued on the hard-faced brave who sat directly across from him.

Red Hawk.

After the pipe had circled the entire group a couple of times, the conversation turned to the inevitable, with Holten on hand—the army and the killing of Indians.

The scout's heart began to pound.

Perhaps he'd find some more answers to his questions, but the icy glares he received from the assembled warriors reminded him where he was and kept his nerves on edge.

"What does Tall Bear say about the white men who kill our braves?" asked Red Hawk, his broad dark face twisted into an ugly scowl.

Holten knew about Red Hawk, the tribe's most warlike subchief. The scout had heard many stories of the fearsome warrior's battle exploits, his prowess with gun and bow, and his seemingly never-ending hatred of all whites. It was only natural, thought Holten, that Red Hawk would be the first to speak about the current killings.

"They are bad whites," said Holten simply. "They will be punished for their mistakes."

Red Hawk's eyes flashed. "They will be punished all right!" snapped the powerfully built subchief. "I will punish them!"

The assembled warriors murmured. Then the chief spoke.

"We must follow the treaties," said Black Spotted Horse suddenly. "Let the white men punish their own people."

Red Hawk's eyes widened. "Treaties?" he said. "How

can the chief of the Oglala tribe talk of treaties when the whites continue to slaughter his people?"

Once again the assembled braves murmured.

"Tall Bear will bring back news of the white men's attacks to the soldiers at the fort," said Black Spotted Horse. "Then the whites will punish the whites."

Suddenly Red Hawk shot to his feet. "Tall Bear?" he said, his flashing brown eyes fixed on the scout. "He is white, too!"

"He is our honored guest!"

"He killed some of my braves yesterday!"

The assembled braves talked loudly among themselves and turned suddenly to face the scout. Holten felt a wave of anxiety spread quickly through his stomach. Holten looked at Black Spotted Horse.

"Red Hawk broke the treaty," said the scout, aware of the cold stares of the warriors. "I helped the innocent whites his warriors tried to kill."

"Innocent whites?" said Red Hawk. "All whites must die! Either the whites die, or the Indian is no more!"

The muscular subchief took a menacing step closer to where Holten sat next to Black Spotted Horse. The scout tensed his muscles, his hand ready to go for his Bowie knife. Black Spotted Horse rose quickly.

"Stop!" he shouted. "I have spoken! Tall Bear will go back to the soldiers and tell them that it is bad whites who start the trouble and not Sioux warriors. We have signed treaties with the whites and we will honor them!"

Holten watched Red Hawk seethe at the other side of the big teepee, the muscles of his jaw working as he grit his teeth. The scout was ready for anything.

"Be careful, Tall Bear!" warned the subchief.

Finally Red Hawk turned sharply and strode from the lodge. Holten thought it significant that several of the other warriors got up and followed the warlike subchief out of Black Spotted Horse's teepee.

69

Tension crackled in the air.

The Sioux chief sat and looked at Holten with the forlorn expression of a lost puppy. "You see," he said in a sad voice trying to convince the scout. "It is just as I told you Tall Bear. My people are divided. I am counting on you to talk to the soldiers. Make them understand that the Oglala Sioux people want peace."

The scout nodded. "I'll do my best," he said.

Black Spotted Horse smiled, patted Holten's shoulder, and turned toward the teepee flap. He clapped his hands sharply and yelled at the women who hovered nearby.

"Bring some meat!" snapped the chief. "Now we feast!"

Holten felt his pulse race. Now, after the unexpected showdown in Black Spotted Horse's teepee, he had Red Hawk's renegades to worry about as well as the army deserters.

'Be careful!' Red Hawk had told the scout.

Holten would talk with General Corrington all right, but he couldn't guarantee any results. First, however, he'd have to find Liver-Eating Jackson and Paco Riley and find out what in hell they were up to.

The scout would make them talk. Or else.

The sumptuous feast brought back memories.

Holten gorged himself on lean buffalo steaks still crackling from the sizzling cooking pits, boiled buffalo tongue as sweet as he remembered, long sausages made from buffalo intestines stuffed with bone marrow, fat, and scraps of meat, boiled roots, yams, and potatoes, succulent fruits such as plump, juicy persimmons and deep red chokecherries, and rich sweets made from the leaves of delicate prairie plants.

All during the feast Holten heard the beat of drums as the Oglala Sioux danced in celebration of the successful hunt.

TUM, tum, tum, tum. TUM, tum, tum, tum.

The scout watched the proud warriors dance in a wide outer circle and the laughing women in a tight inner circle, the two concentric circles merging at times with a rush of feet and a chorus of high pitched yells.

TUM, tum, tum, tum. TUM, tum, tum, tum.

The entire morning brought back sweet memories of Holten's early days with the Sioux and the happy times he spent with his adopted parents, Eagle Deer and Walking Fawn. It was almost enough to make the scout forget Liver-Eating Jackson and Paco Riley.

Soon Black Spotted Horse finished eating, belched mightily, and rose from his place at the campfire. The hawk-nosed chief glanced down at the scout.

"Now, Tall Bear," he said, "we sweat for a while. Then we hunt buffalo."

Holten's jaw dropped. Hunt with Black Spotted Horse?

The scout rose quickly beside the chief and followed the Oglala leader across the bustling Sioux camp. To refuse the chief's invitation to go hunting, Holten knew, was tantamount to challenging Black Spotted Horse to a knife fight. It just wasn't done. The scout sighed, resigned himself to a quick hunting trip with the chief, and knew he'd be on the trail after Jackson and Riley by early evening.

Black Spotted Horse and Holten reached the edge of the hunting camp. They quickly stripped naked, wrapped their loins in breechcloths, and entered the steamy circular buffalo-robe-covered hut known as the sweat lodge. While other braves poured gourds full of water over sizzling round stones, the scout and the Oglala chief sat in quiet meditation for about twenty minutes and let the hot moist air gently massage their bodies and their souls. With his muscles as limp as cooked cereal and his brain cleansed of all pressing thoughts, the scout nearly forgot all about the deserters.

Finally Black Spotted Horse stood, pulled back the

71

soggy buffalo robes that covered the hut, and leaped out of the sweat lodge. Holten followed the tall chief and raced Black Spotted Horse to the cool swift flowing stream at the Sioux camp's perimeter. With a flying leap the two racers dove headlong into the icy mountain-fed waters, the sudden contrast of temperature smacking the scout in the face like an Indian coup stick.

Black Spotted Horse beamed. "You are almost Sioux!" he shouted as he splashed in the cold water.

"Just like the old days!" replied Holten, his body and soul completely refreshed.

"Now," yelled the chief, "we hunt buffalo!"

Holten galloped after the big bull buffalo.

Dressed only in a skimpy breechcloth and moccasins, and armed with just a short iron-tipped lance, the scout closed in for the kill atop one of Black Spotted Horse's prize buffalo horses. Holten's gelding, although a superb trail horse, was no match for the highly trained buffalo ponies the Sioux held in such high regard. The scout was glad the Oglala chief had offered his fleet courageous horse.

Holten charged with his lance raised.

The scout had spotted the big bull almost as soon as he'd trotted onto the prairie along with the Sioux braves. After the glorious sweat bath and the romp in the icy stream, the scout, Black Spotted Horse, and five other braves had galloped toward the plains in search of the biggest bull buffaloes they could find. They had arrived on the vast grassy prairie and almost immediately spotted a huge hairy bull grazing nearby.

"Take him, Tall Bear!" Black Spotted Horse had shouted. "He is worthy of you!"

The scout had jabbed the buffalo pony in the flanks with his bare heels and raced after the bull. Now he closed in for the kill.

72

The fleet buffalo pony's hooves churned up the rich Dakota soil beneath the long undulating grass as Holten's snorting mount closed the distance between the scout and his pounding quarry.

The scout gripped the lance and readied.

As the brave buffalo pony galloped to within five feet of the enormous two-thousand-pound bull, Holten saw the buffalo's beady eyes flashing with hatred at the sudden intrusion by the mounted hunter, saw the rippling shoulder muscles beneath the thick shaggy coat, and saw the long curved horns that could disembowel a pony with one swift swipe.

Holten aimed his lance.

In the middle of the plain, frightened buffalo scattering in all directions around him, the scout pulled his fearless pony to within a few feet of the fleeing bull buffalo. Grasping the horse's reins with his left hand and the short deadly lance with his right, Holten reached to his right and jabbed the sharp iron tip into the buffalo's thick hide. The bull screamed as the lance's tip tore through its side and punctured its lungs, the pained cry a deep, horrible bleating sound that carried through the shimmering noon air.

But the buffalo raced on as though unaffected.

Again the scout jabbed with the short lance, and again the bull buffalo screamed with pain as the lance struck bone and ripped through into its lungs. Finally, after several more quick thrusts with the now bloodied lance, the buffalo slowed to a trot, then fell to its knees in the grass.

Holten reined in the snorting hunting pony and circled the fallen buffalo. The scout knew a wounded bull buffalo was one of the most ferocious animals on the prairie.

Holten kept his distance.

Finally, in the shade of a small stand of trees at the edge of the plain where they had stopped, the big bull gasped one final time and pitched over onto its side, blood oozing onto the grass from the many wounds in its side.

The scout sat smiling atop the pony.

Holten started forward to inspect his prize, his heart pounding with excitement and the exhilaration of the chase. The bull must have weighed at least a ton. Holten began to dismount and check his fallen quarry.

Then he saw it.

The toe of a booted foot near the trees.

The scout stiffened as he gazed through the midday heat toward the copse of cottonwoods. Finally, with his senses working keenly and his muscles twitching, the scout eased the hunting pony into a trot and headed for the trees.

And the boot.

Holten reined in the snorting horse and stared down at the bloodied ground at the base of a scraggly cottonwood. During the heat of the buffalo hunt he'd forgotten completely about the trouble with Red Hawk and the deserters. Now, as he glanced down at the scalped and mutilated bodies of the two frontiersmen named Burke and LaPointe, the scout's mind returned suddenly to the brutal killings plaguing the Dakota Territory.

As Black Spotted Horse and his warriors trotted over to where Holten sat atop the prancing buffalo pony looking down at the bent and broken bodies, the scout knew what he had to do.

Stop Liver-Eating Jackson, Paco Riley, and the deserters.

Before it was too late.

CHAPTER SIX

Holten headed for Fort Rawlins.

As the scout galloped along the grassy trail away from Black Spotted Horse's hunting camp, the merciless early afternoon sun beat down on him like a hammer. With tiny rivulets of sweat running down his long leathery face, Holten pointed the big gelding toward the fort and a meeting with Gen. Frank Corrington. He had to let the army know about the explosive situation that had developed out on the prairie.

Before it was too late.

Holten urged his big powerful mount up a steep incline and stopped the snorting horse on a narrow rocky ridge that overlooked a small grassy valley. A tiny settler town sat quietly in the middle of the valley. Peering through the shimmering afternoon heat, the scout noticed four or five medium-sized wooden buildings nestled among some towering pines in the valley. As the impatient gelding pawed the ground, Holten scanned the dusty street—the dilapidated gray shacks, the one big building that housed the saloon, and the half dozen drowsy horses tethered at the only visible hitching post in the town.

The scout searched the map in his mind and quickly identified the sleepy settler town that lay in the valley before him. Buffalo Creek stood between the white man's world at the fort and the Sioux hunting grounds near the Black Hills and was a logical stopping place for weary hunters.

And for marauding deserters, thought Holten.

Studying the sleepy town one more time, the scout decided everything was in order. He turned the head of the gelding and trotted down a narrow rock-strewn trail toward Fort Rawlins. Holten ran his tongue over his parched lips and thought how nice a tall glass of ice cold beer would feel going down his scorched throat. He quickly cleared his mind and stared straight ahead at the dusty prairie.

Holten couldn't waste much time at desolate prairie outposts, especially with Jackson and Riley on the loose. Not to mention Red Hawk. He'd come back to Buffalo Creek after talking with the army. Then he'd warn the settlers before they ended up butchered and scalped like the two frontiersmen, Burke and LaPointe.

Then he heard it. The crack of a gunshot.

Then another shot and another.

The scout pulled back on the reins and stopped the gelding in its tracks. Holten turned sharply in his saddle and peered back at Buffalo Creek. The scout's practiced ears identified the gun as an army .45 pistol.

Then he saw him.

Holten's piercing blue eyes squinted through the dusty heat and quickly focused on the front of the saloon. Suddenly the swinging wooden doors burst open and a big soldier, his long arms flailing wildly in the air, flew out of the saloon and sprawled in the alkaline dust near the hitching post.

The scout stiffened.

Holten watched the half-drunk man stagger to his feet, grab onto the hitching post for support, and charge back into the Buffalo Creek saloon. The scout noticed the man's piece-meal uniform and three day beard. He saw a glistening gold pocket watch, probably stolen, dangling from the soldier's pants pocket. And Holten saw something else, too.

An Indian knife sheath strapped to his side.

Holten knew the man was a deserter and he'd done some raiding recently.

Quickly the scout wheeled the gelding around and headed for the town at a gallop. This could be the chance he'd been hoping for—a chance to grab one of the deserters and ask him some questions. Or beat the shit out of him. Holten spurred his big horse and raced back to Buffalo Creek.

As he neared the dusty street and the front of the saloon, Holten slowed the gelding to a trot. Then stopping his horse across from the saloon, the scout dismounted slowly, tethered the gelding, and listened carefully.

He heard the voices clearly.

"I saw her first you wiry son of a bitch!"

"Come any closer and I'll kill ya!"

"You're drunk!"

"Damn right!"

The gruff voices drifted out of the saloon and across the street to where the scout stood listening. His mind worked dizzily. Holten figured there must be at least two deserters, and from the sound of things at least one woman. The scout checked his .44 Remington revolver and the ten-inch Bowie knife strapped to his side. Then, with his muscles tensed and his senses fully alert, Holten padded quietly across the street like an Indian stalking an antelope.

Surprise was on his side.

As the scout approached the entrance to the saloon, he scanned the rest of Buffalo Creek. His steely eyes searched the four other buildings, the stables, and the parched street. Not a soul moved. Holten figured the deserters must have herded the town's half dozen residents into the saloon and robbed them there.

Or worse.

The scout gripped the butt of his .44, drew the deadly pistol, and listened again. The voices poured out of the saloon once again, only louder.

"Have another drink, Rogers."

"I don't want another drink. I want that woman!"

"Get your hands off my wife!" cried a frightened voice.

"Get away you good-for-nothin' farmer!"

A shot. A scream.

"Pa!" came the high pitched voice of a young boy.

Holten flew into action. The scout burst from his hiding place in the shadows of the saloon and sprinted up to the front entrance of the building. Holten pressed his long lean frame against the outer wall of the saloon and peered carefully over the flimsy swinging doors into the long dark barroom.

The scout's pulse quickened.

Holten quickly scanned the interior of the saloon and saw one small wiry deserter, his left arm around the waist of a wide-eyed, middle-aged settler woman, a smoking .45 army pistol in his right hand. Against the long polished bar stood the staggering half-drunk deserter, his holster empty and his face twisted into a fierce scowl. Sprawled on the floor, blood gushing from a hole in his chest, was a tall thin settler. The scout spotted a crying boy of twelve or thirteen bent over the fallen man. Three other settlers, two men and another middle-aged woman, cowered at the back of the dimly lit saloon. Everyone stared at the dying settler on the floor.

Now was Holten's chance.

Like a coyote bursting into a den of unsuspecting jack rabbits, the scout smashed through the swinging doors, his .44 Remington pistol leading the way, and took aim at the wiry deserter with the woman.

The scout's surprise was complete.

Before the two ex-soldiers could react through their alcoholic haze, the scout fired a neat shot that missed the woman but struck the wiry deserter's gun hand and sent his .45 flying into the air. Holten crouched and aimed a second shot at the deserter at the bar. The half-drunk soldier had just gone for the knife at his side when the scout squeezed the trigger. The hot slug tore into the deserter's stomach, the .44-caliber bullet ripping through the man's gut and exiting through his back in a bloody spray. The big man jumped backward from the impact and lay sprawled on the bar.

A flash of movement caught Holten's eye.

Suddenly the wiry deserter shoved the startled, wide-eyed settler woman toward the scout, the stumbling woman falling into Holten's arms and blocking his view.

The wiry deserter bolted.

As Holten pushed the woman aside, the wounded soldier burst out of a small back door and raced toward the prairie. The scout took aim with his .44 but stopped quickly as the three cowering settlers at the back of the saloon began to scream and run into his line of fire.

Holten swore under his breath. He ran out the front.

Quickly the scout sprinted across the dusty street to where the gelding stood pawing the ground. Holten pulled his Winchester .44-40 from its saddle sheath and ran back toward the saloon.

A stocky settler blocked his path.

"Oh thank you!" sobbed the man.

"Get out of the way!" snapped the scout.

The man grabbed Holten. "You saved our lives!"

"Look out!" said the scout, pulling free of the man.

Holten peered through the shimmering waves of heat and tried to locate the fleeing deserter. Suddenly the scout heard the pounding of hooves from behind the saloon. He raised the Winchester and aimed down the long barrel at a point just past the corner of the building. He waited for the rider to show himself.

"You saved our lives!" repeated the stocky settler.

"Quiet!"

Then the scout saw him.

The wiry deserter jabbed his spurs into the gleaming

79

flanks of a ragged army horse, the frightened mount galloping like hell toward the grassy plains beyond. The soldier crouched in the saddle and smacked the horse on the butt. The range was about two hundred yards.

Holten sighted down the barrel. He squeezed the trigger.

The Winchester barked once, a shaft of fire spitting from its barrel. In the distance the wiry deserter jerked in the saddle and flew from the back of his horse. The soldier hit the ground in a cloud of alkaline dust.

"What a shot!" shouted the stocky settler.

Holten shook his head. "It was a terrible shot."

"A terrible—?" said the puzzled settler. "Why hitting a man like that at this distance is a hell of a shot!"

"I was aiming for the horse," snapped the disgusted scout.

"The horse?"

"I wanted the bastard alive."

The stocky settler stroked his fleshy face and glanced out at the fallen body of the wiry deserter.

"Uncle Jed!" screamed the young boy from the saloon. "Come quick! This one's still alive!"

Holten's pulse quickened. He raced for the saloon.

The scout pushed back the swinging doors and burst into the darkened saloon. Sprawled on top of the bar in a pool of blood, his jaws working slightly, lay the big half-drunk deserter. The scout strode quickly to the man. Holten knew the badly wounded ex-soldier didn't have much time to live. The scout looked down into the man's glazed eyes.

"Where's Jackson?" asked Holten.

The man moved his head slightly to glance at the scout. He tried to move his jaws. Holten grabbed the soldier's shirt front and lifted him slightly off the bar.

"What were you doin' here?" asked the scout.

The man's lips moved. He spoke in a hoarse whisper. "We—are—just the advance—scouts," he said weakly.

"And Jackson?"

The soldier licked his lips. He was going fast.

"What about Jackson and Riley?" snapped Holten.

The dying deserter moved his lips, then opened his glazed eyes as wide as silver dollars. His face blanched suddenly and beads of sweat appeared on his broad forehead. Then the man slumped on the bar. He died in Holten's hands. The scout lowered the soldier's body.

So close to the truth, yet still no information.

Holten helped them bury the bodies.

Working under the blistering sun, the scout and the other settlers dug simple graves for the dead settler and the two army deserters. Then with the orange sun dipping behind the rolling hills on the prairie, the scout explained the new danger to the surviving settlers. He suggested they head for Fort Rawlins.

"But this is our home," said the stocky man.

Holten nodded. "I know," he said, "but the renegades and the other deserters are burnin' and killin' all around these parts."

"Why would they want to bother us?"

Holten looked into the broad fleshy face of the stocky settler and wondered if the man really understood the danger he faced.

"The Indians because they hate your guts," explained the scout, "and the deserters because they ain't got nothin' better to do."

The scout swung his tall frame into his creaking saddle and grabbed the reins. He glanced around quickly at the simple town. He'd almost obtained some information about Liver-Eating Jackson. Now he'd just have to go back to the fort and give Corrington a general summary of

81

the killers' activities. Holten looked down at the small knot of settlers in Buffalo Creek's only street.

"If you left now and traveled all night," said the scout, "you'd be at the fort by noon tomorrow."

The stocky man shook his head. "Thanks all the same," he said, glancing around at the simple buildings. "This is all we got. We'll stick it out here and hope for the best."

Holten shrugged. "Suit yourself," he said. "Best of luck to you and yours." The scout tipped his dusty hat.

"Much obliged," said the stocky man.

The scout clucked to the gelding and headed out of Buffalo Creek. Behind him he left a couple of dead deserters and a handful of frightened but determined settlers. He spurred the gelding and galloped out onto the prairie toward the fort.

As he rode, Holten formulated his plans. He'd spend the night under the stars and reach Fort Rawlins in the morning. Maybe, just maybe, Jackson and the others were close at hand.

As the sun's last rays cast eerie shadows across the landscape, the scout pointed the gelding toward the darkening prairie. Maybe he would hear from Jackson tonight.

The thought quickened his pulse.

It was a great place to camp.

The scout selected a small clearing surrounded by tall stately pine trees and bordered by a swift-flowing mountain stream. Holten stripped his horse, set up his bedroll, and built a small campfire.

Then he slipped into the prairie and shot two quail. Placing his Winchester within easy reach, his .44 under his bedroll, and the Bowie knife next to the tiny campfire, the scout roasted the plump birds and whiled away the minutes with sexy thoughts about Rebecca Ridgeway.

He started to get horny.

Turning the quail on the simple roasting spit he'd made from some nearby sticks, Holten let his mind drift back to the glorious times he'd spent with the luscious widow. The scout had never really given much thought to settling down—he was too much a part of the wide prairie to ever stay put in one place for very long. But if he ever decided to stop running around and find himself a good woman, the soft and sensuous widow, Rebecca, would be as good a choice as any.

He felt a twinge in his loins.

Holten tore off a little sliver of quail and chewed the juicy meat while he thought. Rebecca was another reason he had to get back to the fort. Her ranch would be a prime target for marauding bands of Indians and deserters. After talking to the general, he'd ride out to the Rebecca Springs ranch and persuade her to stay at Fort Rawlins for a while until the prairie returned to normal.

If it ever did return to normal.

The scout ate hungrily, finishing the quail and washing down the sweet-tasting meat with strong black coffee. Then after one final check of his surroundings, Holten tossed some more wood on his small campfire and tried to get some rest. He closed his eyes, but his sharpened senses kept working. He'd developed the ability to sleep while still keeping a lookout with his animallike senses. Holten closed his eyes and rested while visions of bull buffalo, half-drunk deserters, and sumptuous blonde widows danced in his head.

At daybreak he heard the gelding whinny softly.

The scout opened an eye. His instincts spoke to him.

As the sun peeked over the eastern horizon, he heard unmistakable sounds in the woods around him. Holten's senses began to work at full speed—his nerves tingled and his muscles tightened. A wave of anxiety passed quickly through his now empty stomach. The trees around him came alive with the sounds of birds chirping, insects playing, and small animals squeaking.

Indians. And they were close.

Slowly, cautiously, without any quick movements, the scout reached for the Bowie knife near the fire. Wrapping his big hand around the handle, Holten then slowly moved his eyes and glanced at the Winchester next to his saddle. He felt the hard bulk of the .44 under his bedroll.

He was ready for the attack he knew would come.

As sweat poured down his weathered face, the scout listened carefully to the sounds around him. His palm grew sweaty around the Bowie knife's big handle and his heart pounded like an Indian war drum. From the sounds he heard, Holten figured at least five warriors lurked in the early morning shadows near his campsite, all of them watching him intently and waiting to pounce like a pack of wolves on a sleeping mule deer. He tensed his muscles for what he knew would have to be a superior effort on his part.

Holten's mind worked feverishly, trying to reconstruct the camp's layout. The warriors could have him surrounded on only three sides; the cold stream flowed off to his left. Holten pictured the campsite in his mind and knew how he would move. With his pulse pounding in his ears, he lay coiled and ready like a snake.

Then they struck.

The first warrior burst from the bushes behind the scout, a fearsome knife leading him into the clearing, his broad dark face slashed with yellow war paint, his rippling muscles gleaming in the sparse early morning light.

With the blinding reflexes of a rattlesnake, Holten whirled suddenly and threw his Bowie knife at the charging brave, the long glistening blade burying itself to the hilt in the Sioux warrior's chest. The Indian cried out sharply and lay sprawled on the dusty ground near the campfire.

Holten sprang into action.

The scout reached quickly for the Winchester, grabbed the big repeater, and whirled to face the other side of the clearing.

He'd guessed right.

Just as he squared around, the scout caught three more warriors leaping out of the underbrush. The Winchester spat fire three times, the slugs finding their mark in the chest of one charging brave, the stomach of another, and the head of the third. The three painted warriors fell dead on the ground, their bows and arrows flying into the air from the impact of the .44-40 slugs.

Holten heard the twang of a bow. He turned suddenly.

Even before the arrow struck him he knew he was too late. The long iron-tipped shaft whistled through the air and tore into Holten's left thigh, blood spurting from the flesh wound as the arrow embedded itself deeply. He yelped as a hot streak of pain lanced through his leg. The sudden wound caused the Winchester to fly from the scout's hands and land several feet away. Holten stood hurt and helpless.

Then he heard the war cries.

From the bushes near the gelding, Holten saw two big warriors burst into the clearing, one of them notching another arrow as he ran while the other arced a .45 army revolver upward and aimed it at the scout's head.

Holten had to think quickly.

In a flash of motion the scout dove to the ground, reached under his bedroll, and pulled out the .44 Remington revolver. At the same time, the brave with the pistol fired. His .45 roared.

The scout rolled quickly to his left. The hot slug from

85

the Indian's pistol thudded into the hard-packed dirt beside Holten's head. The scout came quickly to his knees and fired the .44. A bullet slammed into the chest of the brave with the gun, sending the startled warrior spinning to the ground, a blossoming splotch of crimson across his bare chest.

A flash of movement. The scout looked up.

Holten arced the .44 upward and fired into the broad glistening face of the final warrior. The Sioux brave unloosed his arrow just as the scout squeezed the trigger, the long shaft whistling past the scout's ear and thudding harmlessly in the dirt. The warrior's head exploded across the clearing, bone fragments, brain matter, and a shower of blood flew over the dusty ground.

It was over in seconds.

A heavy silence filled the tiny clearing.

Holten's heart beat against his ribs. His breath came in uneven gasps. Slowly the scout stood and surveyed the sudden slaughter all around him.

He studied the faces of the braves. He quickly recognized one warrior from the feast at Black Spotted Horse's teepee. They must have trailed him all the way from the hunting camp. Holten walked to his bedroll and dropped the .44 on his blanket. Red Hawk wasted little time in making good on his threat.

Holten winced at the pain in his leg.

The scout reached down, grabbed the arrow in his thigh, and with a quick thrust pushed it through his leg to the other side. Another surge of pain sliced through his entire lower body as the iron-tipped arrowhead burst through his skin. Then the scout snapped the arrow in two and removed the pieces from his bloodied leg.

Holten steadied himself as a sudden wave of dizziness swept over him. Beads of sweat appeared on his forehead. Taking a deep breath, the scout walked shakily to the gelding and grabbed his canteen.

He began to cleanse his wound.

Holten looked around at the dead warriors and knew one thing for sure. He hadn't seen the last of Red Hawk's warriors. They'd be after him until they succeeded in killing him.

Or until the scout killed Red Hawk.

CHAPTER SEVEN

Holten saw the buzzards before he saw the body.

The scout squinted up into the brassy Dakota sky at the wheeling scavengers above him and wondered who lay dying over the next ridge. Even on his way back to the fort he encountered death. Holten smacked the gelding on the butt and galloped up the boulder-strewn slope toward the jagged ridge ahead of him.

He stopped in his tracks on the ridge.

Holten peered through the shimmering midsummer heat at the two butchered pack mules and the bloodied gold digger who lay sprawled in the wide grassy clearing below. As the scent of death carried up to the ridge on the gentle prairie breeze, the gelding's nostrils flared and the big horse whinnied softly. The scout patted his mount gently on the neck and started the descent to investigate the mayhem below.

As the gelding picked its way down the hill, Holten's sharpened senses worked hard. His piercing blue eyes scanned the clearing for signs of a possible ambush. The scout was close to Fort Rawlins now, but he had known Sioux warriors to attack a white man as close as the main gate of an army post. He wasn't taking any chances today.

Then he saw the gold digger move. Holten stopped.

With his fingers twitching in readiness and his weapons hanging loosely at his side, Holten quickly studied the scene in front of him. The two mules had been shot many times at close range, a dozen fist-sized holes in their torsos oozing blood onto the sun-baked soil. The gold digger, it appeared, had been bushwacked while he sat eating his dinner. Glancing at the parched ground, the scout noticed many hoofprints in the dust. He could tell right away they weren't Indian ponies.

The gold digger moved again. Then he groaned.

The scout clucked to the gelding and trotted over to where the wizened old man lay dying in the dust. Despite the throbbing arrow wound in his thigh, Holten dismounted smoothly, grabbed his canteen, and knelt in the dust next to the white-haired old prospector. The scout lifted the gold digger's head and looked into his weathered face, its skin as dry and wrinkled as aged rawhide. The old man moved his parched lips.

"Water," he rasped.

"Easy now old-timer," said the scout.

Holten poured a little cool water on the gold digger's cracked lips. The old man winced with pain. The scout waited a moment then repeated the action. This time the old man's lips accepted the water and he drank freely. The scout let the dying old-timer drink for a long moment before he removed the canteen.

"What happened?" asked the scout.

The gold digger licked his lips. "Ambushed," he said in a rasping voice.

"Who?"

The old man began to speak, winced slightly, then motioned for more water. Holten put the canteen to the gold digger's cracked lips and once again the old man drank deeply. The wizened prospector finished drinking and lay back on the dusty ground. He looked at the scout through glazed eyes.

"Who ambushed you?" repeated the scout.

"They came from nowhere," rasped the old-timer.

"Indians?"

The old man shook his head. Then he winced as a sudden jab of pain lanced through his bony frame. Holten noticed three gaping bullet holes in the old-timer's side and back. The scout wondered how in hell he'd survived this long. Holten raised the gold digger's head again.

"If it wasn't the Indians," said the scout, "then who was it?"

The old timer moved his lips. "Soldiers," he breathed weakly. "And a couple of drifters."

Holten's pulse quickened suddenly.

"Did you recognize them?"

A thin smile cracked the old man's leathery face. "Hell yes," he rasped. "Two of the meanest sons of bitches this side of hell!"

"Who?" prodded the scout gently.

Suddenly the old man began to cough harshly. Holten watched a trickle of blood seep from the corners of the prospector's mouth. The old-timer was fading fast.

"Who were the drifters?"

The gold digger tried to speak but could only gasp softly. The old man moved his lips and tried to form the words. The scout moved closer to the dying prospector's mouth.

"Liv—Liver," gasped the old-timer.

Holten stiffened.

"Liver-Eating Jackson?" asked the scout.

The gold digger nodded slowly.

"And big Paco Riley?" continued Holten.

Again the old man nodded slowly, but painfully.

The scout looked up for a moment, his mind working quickly. Jackson, Riley, and the deserters seemed to be working the entire Dakota Territory. They'd taken time out from their attacks on Indians to shoot an innocent prospector.

Suddenly the gold digger cried out in a frayed voice.

Then he died.

Holten lay down the wizened old body and strode toward the gold digger's pack mules. The scout took a short-handled shovel from the gear strapped to the back of one of the dead animals and began to dig a grave for the old man.

Liver-Eating Jackson had struck again.

He planned to make the fort by dusk.

Holten clucked to the gelding and galloped along the dusty trail leading toward Fort Rawlins. The discovery of the ambushed prospector just confirmed what he already knew—Liver-Eating Jackson and Paco Riley rode at the head of a band of marauding army deserters. And for some reason they wanted to provoke trouble all around the Territory.

So far, they'd done a good job.

The scout urged the big horse across the grassy prairie, through small stands of scraggly cottonwoods, and over rolling sand hills dotted with green and white Spanish dagger plants, delicate blue turnip blossoms, and bright red prairie roses. Holten rode hard for several hours, his mind playing with the problems at hand—deserters and renegades.

By mid-afternoon both the scout and his tired horse needed a rest. Holten reined in the gelding under a majestic willow at the edge of the trail, dismounted slowly due to the stiffness in his thigh wound, and tethered his panting mount.

Then the voices came to him—in Lakota.

Holten froze.

The scout stopped and listened. Somewhere off the trail, back behind the stand of willows, at least two Sioux warriors chattered excitedly. Holten unsheathed his Winchester and slipped into the brush that rimmed the dusty trail.

The scout's pulse quickened.

Pushing quietly through clawing berry bushes and scraggly plum branches, Holten eased his lean frame past several sturdy box elder trees and pressed up against a wide rutted cottonwood trunk. Gripping the Winchester, he peered carefully into a small shaded clearing near a slow moving stream. His nerves tingled and his heart pounded as he looked.

Holten saw them haggling over their loot.

Two lean Sioux warriors stood beside several large trunks full of clothes, household goods, and books. A battered wagon stood sadly in the background. As the scout watched, the painted braves argued animately about the ownership of a large mirror clutched in one of the Indian's hands. Then Holten saw the settlers.

Dead and scalped.

A middle-aged man and his portly wife lay sprawled in the grass beside their worldly possessions. The two braves must have surprised them as they watered their horses. The scout glanced beyond the Indians and saw two haggard work horses grazing in the lush midsummer grass.

A sudden crash pierced the air.

Holten returned his gaze to the warriors. In disgust, one of the braves had tossed the ornate mirror to the ground, breaking it into a hundred tinkling fragments. The argument ended as Holten knew it would. Neither of the warriors had the mirror.

Suddenly one of the warriors unsheathed a long hunting knife. The two warriors faced each other. Holten stiffened. The scout watched as the chattering brave with the knife turned sharply and strode over to the bodies of the settler couple.

Holten knew what was coming. He'd seen it before.

Raising his glistening blade high in the air, the lean muscular warrior slashed downward and ripped a foot-long gash in the white settler's rotund belly. Holten heard the ripping of flesh, like the gutting of a dead antelope, and saw the man's guts spill onto the green grass. The warrior continued to slash and slice, mutilating the dead man in the accepted Sioux fashion.

Holten had seen enough.

Knowing there was nothing he could do for the settler couple, and not wanting any extra problems, the scout turned slowly away from the butchery in the clearing and padded back to where the tethered gelding stood grazing.

He mounted his horse and headed down the trail. The scout knew the prairie was a beautiful place, full of natural beauty and wide open spaces. It was also a deadly place full of treachery, brutality, and danger. The scout wondered if the little scene he'd just witnessed was part of the growing renegade uprising or just a typical example of overmatched settlers running into a couple of feisty buck Indians.

Holten galloped toward Fort Rawlins.

Holten peered through the gathering dusk.

He couldn't believe his eyes. Renegades attacking wagons.

Holten had almost reached the fort. Now the scout dismounted quickly and glanced at the embattled settlers beside the river below. Gunshots and screams rose into the early evening air. Tongues of yellow flames licked the sky from several burning wagons. A small party of white settlers was on the verge of losing a hard fought battle against a screaming horde of renegade braves.

Or were they braves? Something was wrong.

Holten reached into his saddlebags and extracted his army field glasses. He hunkered in the tall buffalo grass on

93

the knoll above the river and looked through the glasses at the faces of the attackers.

As the last of the dozen or so white settlers bit the dust, his bullet riddled body slumping to the ground, Holten focused on the mounted warriors who milled around the burning wagon train.

Some of the warriors dismounted quickly and ran toward one of the wagons. Holten followed them with the glasses. After a moment the braves jumped from the smoking wagons with a couple of settlers in tow.

The scout's grip on the glasses tightened.

The screaming warriors hauled two sobbing young white women from the sanctuary of the wagons and threw them onto the ground. A couple of the braves rushed up to the teenagers and with a violent jerk of material, ripped the fronts of the young settler girls' dresses. The crying girls stood in the middle of the smoky clearing, their small young breasts exposed, while the warriors roared with laughter. Quickly the young women covered themselves with their arms.

Something was wrong. Something was out of place.

The scout watched the renegades through the field glasses. Holten studied the way the warriors walked, the types of weapons they carried, the ponies they rode, and the clothing they wore. The scout passed the glasses over each brave from head to foot.

Then he stiffened. He knew what it was.

Holten fixed the glasses on the hair of one of the warriors resting beside a smoking wagon. The scout's heart leaped to his throat with excitement at his discovery. The hair was not hair at all but some kind of wig. The man he watched wore the wig at a slight angle, his real hair peeking out from beneath. Then, to the scout's complete surprise, the man removed his hair, wiped his sweaty brow with his forearm, and replaced the long black wig.

Holten lowered the field glasses.

It suddenly struck him with the force of a war club.

Black Spotted Horse's words came back to the scout. He remembered what the Oglala chief had said about the massacres of his braves. The whites had taken clothes, ponies, weapons—and scalps.

Now they used the scalps as wigs.

Holten raised the glasses again and peered out at the milling band of killers. His heart jumped a beat. If the scout had any doubts about the identities of the men masquerading as Indians down near the river in front of him, they disappeared when Liver-Eating Jackson and Paco Riley galloped out of the shadows and onto the prairie.

The scout's heart pounded. He'd found the deserters.

Holten watched the wiry killer stop his army mount beside the sobbing young settler girls and talk animately with the aroused deserters who had hauled them from the wagons. Suddenly, without warning, Liver-Eating Jackson pulled a big .45 from its holster and shot the two settler girls in the head, the teenagers' brains flying over the clearing. The young women jumped from the impact of the bullets and fell to the dusty prairie, dead before they knew what had happened.

Jackson pointed the gun at the deserters. Holten watched the soldiers shrug their shoulders and mount their Indian ponies. The evil killer had made whatever point he had tried to get across. Then the band of costumed raiders spurred their ponies and raced away from the smoldering settler wagons toward the purple hills in the distance.

The scout had the urge to follow, but thought better of it. Besides, General Corrington waited for his report. Holten watched them splash through the shallow summer-parched river and gallop off in the gathering darkness.

95

All except one.

The scout focused the field glasses on the lone soldier who had remained near the wagons. The young deserter, his long black Indian hair now stuck in his saddlebags, dismounted and walked quickly to where several settler men lay sprawled in the grass. The soldier unsheathed a long glistening knife and started to scalp the settlers.

Holten lowered the glasses. He went into action.

The scout hauled off his heavy boots and slipped into a pair of soft leather moccasins. Then Holten unsheathed the Winchester .44-40 and padded after the lone deserter in the clearing below. He wanted the bastard alive if possible.

He'd make a nice gift for General Corrington.

Holten slipped through the tall buffalo grass like a sleek predator stalking its prey, his eyes fixed on the busy deserter and his muscles tensed for action. With the powerful Winchester gripped in one hand, the scout reached a position just fifty yards away from the kneeling soldier. He peered through the undulating blades of green grass and decided what he would do.

Quickly the scout slid through the grass on his stomach like a rattlesnake sneaking up on an unsuspecting jack rabbit. Within minutes he lay just twenty feet from the deserter. Holten studied the young soldier, watching the deserter grasp the hair of the fallen settlers and slice through the skin until the bloodied scalp pulled free. The soldier finished his grisly chore and lay his gleaming blade on the grass.

Now was Holten's chance.

"Put your hands up!" snapped Holten.

The deserter froze.

"Get 'em up!"

"Who are you?"

Holten fired the Winchester, the bullet kicking up the dust beside the young soldier's feet. The deserter's hands shot into the air.

"All right, all right," said the deserter in a thin, frightened voice.

The scout watched the soldier's eyes flick from side to side trying to locate his ambusher. Suddenly Holten stood in the grass, the Winchester levelled at the deserter's mid-section.

The deserter swallowed hard. "Who are you?"

"A friend of General Corrington," said Holten with a smile.

The scout kept the big rifle pointed at the deserter's stomach and eased forward.

"The army boys will be glad to see you," said Holten.

Suddenly the scout heard the drumbeat of hooves out on the prairie. He turned sharply and saw several deserters racing toward the scene of the settler massacre. The young soldier saw them, too.

He bolted. The scout swore under his breath.

Quickly Holten arced the Winchester upward and fired two shots, the big rifle spitting fire into the early evening air. The fleeing deserter jumped a foot in the air as the hot lead slammed into his back, the .44-40 slugs tearing through the young soldier's lungs and heart killing him instantly.

Holten didn't waste any time. He turned and strode rapidly from the clearing, the sound of the hooves pounding in his ears as he sprinted toward the ridge and his horse. The scout reached the grassy knoll and looked down at the river bank. He watched three deserters rein in their horses, glance down at the dead deserter, and quickly scan the surrounding hills. Then with swift kicks to the flanks of their mounts, the soldiers broke into a gallop and disappeared into the gathering dusk.

Holten returned the Winchester to its sheath and hauled his long frame onto the gelding's wide, strong back. He clucked to his horse and headed for the clearing below. At least now the scout had a body to show the general. Even so, Holten still had to face Corrington and tell him some of his boys were responsible for the killings on the prairie.

He didn't look forward to the meeting.

CHAPTER EIGHT

"Deserters are becoming a big problem, Mr. Holten."

"So are renegades."

"We'll take care of them both."

"You better hurry."

After Holten gave his report, Gen. Frank Corrington paced his office with his hands behind his back. Hard-faced Maj. Nathan Phillips stood near a wall map of the Dakota Territory, his cold blue eyes fixed on the scout. Finally the general stopped and spat a stream of amber-colored tobacco juice into the brass spittoon on the floor. He turned toward Holten.

"I mentioned complications during our last meeting, Mr. Holten," said Corrington.

Holten nodded. "Yes general, you did."

"Now you know what I meant."

"You could have told me about the deserters."

"We weren't sure."

"But you had some idea," insisted the scout.

The general shrugged. "Would it have done any good if we had mentioned it?"

"I wouldn't have felt like such a fool when Chief Black Spotted Horse told me white men had killed his braves."

Corrington spat again. "Well," he said returning to his shiny mahogany desk, "now you know. And now we have a double problem on our hands."

Major Phillips' voice cut through the air. "We have a band of bloodthirsty savages running loose," he said in a cold clipped voice.

"The deserters provoked them," said Holten.

"The Indians are to blame!" snapped the major, his face darkening with rage.

Corrington cut into the conversation. "It makes no difference who started what, gentlemen," he said. "What remains is an explosive situation out on the plains. It's a situation that needs to be dealt with."

The general stroked his iron-gray beard and eyed Phillips.

"Especially," he said in a low conspiratorial voice, "since the largest gold shipment ever sent this way is due to arrive in the Dakota Territory in about a week."

Holten's eyebrows shot up. "Gold?"

"Another 'complication' Mr. Holten," said the general.

Major Phillips lit a cigar. "Over one hundred thousand dollars in gold coins," he said exhaling a cloud of blue-white smoke. "All of it headed for the three new Indian reservations set up by the last treaties."

Phillips turned and glared at Holten.

"The treaties broken by the renegades," continued the major in an icy tone.

Holten ignored the major's remark. Instead, the scout's mind drifted back to the statement made by the two frontiersmen, Burke and LaPointe. They mentioned Jackson and Riley strutting through Deadwood boasting about how they would soon be rich.

Holten's pulse quickened.

Suddenly it all came together. Jackson and Riley had used the deserters to deliberately provoke the Sioux warriors and to raise hell out on the plains. Then, under the cover of all the confusion they knew their attacks would provide, they planned to swoop down and attack the gold shipment.

But were Jackson and Riley that smart?

Corrington's voice sliced through the scout's thoughts.

"Regarding the deserters," said the general rising from

his desk, "the army will punish them. After treaties are signed, we always have a few good-for-nothings who insist on causing problems with the Indians."

"And Liver-Eating Jackson?" asked the scout.

Major Phillips cut in. "The army will deal with both Jackson and Riley," he snapped. "But our main job right now, Holten, is to keep the peace on the prairie."

"And the gold?"

"The army will take care of it," said Phillips coldly.

Corrington moved away from his desk, spat some tobacco juice into the brass spittoon, and turned to face the scout.

"Not only are these deserters a disgrace to the U.S. Army," said the general, "but they are a threat to the peace of the entire Territory. And, they pose a threat to the gold shipment. Without that gold, Mr. Holten, the army will lose the plum it promised to deliver to the Indians. And I'm sure your Sioux friends wouldn't take that sitting down."

"When is the gold due to arrive?" asked Holten.

"In one week," said Corrington. "We have seven days to pacify the prairie and stop the deserters."

"Can't you postpone the shipment?"

The general spat again. "Wish we could," he said. "But the treaties call for prompt delivery of the gold to the reservations. Any delay and I'm sure the Sioux would think it's just another white man's trick."

Knowing the Oglala, Holten figured the general was right.

"We have lots to do," added Phillips in a clipped tone.

Corrington grabbed his officer's hat. "You're right, major," he said as he headed for the door. "I'm leaving you two alone for a while to plan the details of this campaign. I trust you'll both work together and bring this potentially explosive situation under control."

Phillips saluted. "We will, sir."

Holten nodded toward the general.

Gen. Frank Corrington smiled, spat tobacco juice into the brass spittoon one last time, and strode briskly from his office.

A heavy silence descended upon the room.

Major Phillips broke the spell. "So, Holten," he began, "you now understand the problem."

The scout nodded. "I hope you do, too, major."

Phillips glared at the scout for a long moment, then turned and began to pace the office. He stopped near the large wall map of the Territory and turned toward Holten.

"Your job is simple," he said to the scout. "Ride out into the prairie and warn all the settlers you can find about the renegade uprising."

The scout stiffened. "What about the deserters?"

"The army will take care of them," said the major. "And we'll handle the renegades, too."

Phillips walked away from the map and stared at Holten.

"You know this prairie better than anyone, Holten," said the hard-faced major. "Your job is to scour the countryside and warn people. That's all."

Holten rose from his chair and looked into the cold blue eyes of Maj. Nathan Phillips. What a waste of his prairie savvy. But, if that's the way the army wanted it, thought the scout, then that's the way it would have to be.

"Good luck, major," said Holten.

Phillips nodded. "Good luck to you, scout."

Holten turned and strode to the door. Major Phillips' voice stopped him just as the scout grabbed the polished brass knob.

"And Holten," said Phillips coldly. "Don't interfere."

The scout stared at the hard chiseled facial features of Maj. Nathan Phillips for a moment. Then Holten nodded curtly, pulled open the door, and stepped onto the sun-baked parade grounds where soldiers drilled atop weary horses.

Hell of a meeting, thought the scout.

As the sure-handed army barber sliced off Holten's three day stubble with swift sure strokes of his long razor, the scout sat back in the chair and reviewed the strange meeting with the army brass.

Just round up the settlers, he'd been told.

Why would the army want to keep him out of the picture, wondered Holten. And why hadn't he been told about the deserters earlier? And about the gold shipment? The scout just sighed and pushed the thoughts from his tired mind. At least his assignment would let him visit Rebecca at her ranch on his way across the plains.

With that last thought warming his insides, the scout paid the barber and headed for the mess hall for a big meal. He'd be eating beef jerky and hardtack for the next week or ten days, so a big hot meal sounded mighty good.

"Don't interfere" were Phillips' last words.

As Holten stuffed himself with roast chicken and hot biscuits, the major's cold words echoed inside his head. Something didn't feel right about the whole affair. The scout felt uncomfortable with his new assignment, especially since the prairie was poised to explode in a full scale uprising. Why was he taken out of the action? Why didn't Major Phillips want him to interfere?

The scout washed down his dinner with a couple of bottles of ice cold beer, headed for the stables, and retrieved the well-rested gelding. Hauling his long lean frame into the saddle, the scout felt glad about one thing. At least the army planned to make good on its promise of spending some cold hard cash on the Indians and the reservations. At least Holten's Indian friends wouldn't freeze or starve this winter. The gold would come in handy.

103

If Jackson and Riley didn't get it first.

Holten smacked the gelding on the butt and trotted out of Fort Rawlins' bustling enclosed compound. Pulling down his dusty wide-brimmed hat, the scout headed for the plains to warn the settlers about marauding deserters and Red Hawk's renegades. He'd even stop at the Rebecca Springs ranch and send Rebecca Ridgeway to the fort for safety. The scout spurred the gelding into a gallop and left the fort in a cloud of dust. He had a job to do.

Holten hoped Phillips would do his job, too.

He spotted the pony tracks a mile from the fort.

Holten kept his steely blue eyes glued to the dusty trail and studied the three sets of Indian pony tracks that led from Fort Rawlins up toward the hills that loomed dark and mysterious above the prairie. The scout galloped along the tree-lined trail until he stopped and froze in his tracks. With the snorting gelding prancing impatiently in the trail, Holten stared down at the alkaline dust beneath him.

Another set of tracks merged with the ponies.

The tracks of a heavily shod horse.

Holten nudged the gelding and continued along the trail, his tired eyes fixed on the tracks in the dust below. As he rode, the scout kept his senses working and his nerves ready for instant action. In times of renegade uprisings, you could expect almost anything out on the prairie. While his eyes followed the trail, the scout's ears listened for signs of possible trouble. He'd survived this long on the plains by always being prepared.

Suddenly the pounding of hooves struck his ears.

Holten reined in the gelding and stopped to listen. A galloping horse headed his way from over a slight rise just ahead. Quickly the scout pulled his big horse's head and raced off the main trail to a spot in the shadows of several towering pine trees.

In just seconds Holten saw a big army horse pound into view, its tall rider jabbing his spurs into the horse's gleaming flanks. The scout clung to the shadows and studied the face of the big figure atop the mount as it galloped past.

Holten froze. He recognized Major Phillips' chiseled features.

The scout remained in the shadows and watched the snorting army horse race down the trail and gallop out of sight. Holten stared after the dusty figure until the sudden sharp whinny of a horse near the slight rise caught his attention.

Had Phillips met with someone?

Holten spurred the gelding and trotted toward the rise. He eased the big horse over the dusty main trail until he approached the small hill. Then the scout reined in his horse and dismounted.

He heard muffled voices speaking English.

Holten tethered the gelding and slipped into the thick underbrush that lined the rocky trail. Sneaking through the bushes like a silent Indian hunter, the scout reached a small tree-lined clearing. He pressed against the thick trunk of a tall willow and peered at the three figures who stood talking in the shade.

Holten's pulse quickened.

He spotted Jackson, Riley, and a big deserter.

The scout watched the laughing killers talk among themselves for a moment, their evil faces twisted into wide devilish smiles, then mount their skittish Sioux ponies. Holten moved to get a better view.

Then it happened. Five quail shot into the air.

Holten froze.

"What's that?" said a voice.

"What?"

"Over there!"

A cackling laugh rose in the air. "You're gettin' jumpy,

Ames," said a harsh voice. "It's just some prairie chickens."

"Let's get the hell outta here."

The laughing killers slapped their ponies and galloped off toward the hills. Holten breathed deeply and watched them ride away.

As the scout returned to his horse, his mind raced dizzily. Had Major Phillips met with Jackson and the others? Or was it just a coincidence? Holten pulled himself into the saddle and headed toward the plains to warn settlers.

He didn't believe in coincidences.

CHAPTER NINE

The old woman looked up. "Eli Holten!"

"Hello, Ma," said the scout.

"Well bless my soul!"

Plump silver-haired Ma Beaudeen, house madame of the Dakota plains' smallest but choicest whorehouse, waddled over to where the scout stood in the doorway and wrapped her fleshy arms around him. The jolly old dame stepped back from Holten, her blue eyes twinkling, and studied him with grandmotherly concern.

"Why you're as skinny as a scarecrow!" she said.

The scout smiled. "Just lotsa hard livin', Ma."

"And you're as dusty as a scarecrow, too!"

"I like him anyway," purred a sexy voice from across the large parlor.

Holten turned sharply. A wide smile cracked his leathery trail weary face.

"Bridget!" snapped Ma Beaudeen, "get some clothes on!"

The scout watched a sinewy whore named Bridget stand provocatively in the doorway leading from the parlor, her shapely naked body gleaming in the sparse lamplight of the curtained whorehouse. Holten's blue eyes roamed the lovely girl's sexy frame, from the big plump breasts, down her lean flat stomach, to the firm round buttocks.

"Remember me, Holten?" asked Bridget.

The scout looked at the pretty oval face framed by long, silky black hair that touched her delicate shoulders. Vivid memories of sweat-soaked orgies with the slender sexpot flooded Holten's brain. His cock began to harden.

"How could I ever forget?" he replied simply.

Ma Beaudeen chased the whore. "Scat!" she said. "You know better than to come out front like that!"

Holten chuckled. "Same old Bridget," he said.

"Hummph!" snorted the old house madame. "I love all my girls, but that Bridget is goin' to be the death of me yet."

"That's what I came to see ya'bout, Ma."

"Bridget?"

The scout sat on a long padded sofa. "Death," he said.

Ma Beaudeen's fat face paled. She waddled over to the scout, lit a tiny cigar, and sat next to him. Her twinkling blue eyes searched the scout's weathered face.

She spoke in a somber voice. "What's wrong, Holten?"

"Renegades," he said simply.

Her eyebrows arched. "Again?"

"A Sioux brave called Red Hawk," said the scout. "Been killin' and scalpin' all around the territory."

Ma Beaudeen took a long drag on her little cigar, smoothed her cotton print dress over her plump little legs, and stared at the scout with a strange gleam in her eye.

"What about them runaway soldiers?" she asked.

Holten's face slackened. "You know about 'em?"

"Hell," she said exhaling a cloud of smoke, "in a place like this, ain't much we don't know!"

Holten chuckled. "I shoulda guessed."

"In fact," said the house madame, "a couple of them deserters came by the other night."

"And?"

"Sons of bitches!" snapped Ma. "Screwed the hell out of all my girls, drank a gallon of whiskey, and then run off without payin' a plug nickel!"

"What about a drifter named Liver-Eating Jackson?"

The old gal's face darkened. "I heard about that one!" she said in a harsh voice. "Hope we never see the pig!"

108

The scout watched Ma Beaudeen crush her cigar in a nearby ashtray. Holten knew the old madame had been on the plains for nearly twenty years, her clean houses gaining the reputation they richly deserved. She'd seen good times and bad. And she'd survived. That's more than a lot of them, thought the scout.

"I come to ask you to head for the fort for a couple of days, Ma," said Holten. "At least until things are under control."

"The fort!" she said, her voice edged with excitement.

"For protection only," added Holten quickly. "I'm sure General Corrington wouldn't want the girls plyin' their trade in the soldiers' barracks."

The scout saw the disappointment spread over Ma Beaudeen's fleshy face. "All right," she said slowly. "But it's a long hard trip to the fort. Who'll protect us along the way?"

"I will," said the scout. "We'll pick up any nearby settler families and then head back to Fort Rawlins."

"The widow Rebecca Ridgeway for example?" asked Ma with a gleam in her eye.

Holten smiled. "Her, too."

Ma's face brightened. "Well," she said, "since you're behind all this, I don't see no harm." She stood quickly, much faster than Holten would have thought for a plump old gal.

"But," she added, "only for a few days. We got our regular customers to think about, ya know."

Holten smiled. "Just for a few days," he promised.

Ma Beaudeen's round fleshy face spread into a big smile. She turned and headed for the back of the whorehouse.

"Just let me pack a few things, Holten," she said at the doorway, "and we'll be right with ya."

Ma glanced covertly at the sleeping quarters, then returned her gaze to the scout. She laughed deeply, her whole fleshy frame quivering as she did so.

"I think the girls have somethin' planned for ya," she said laughing, and then disappeared into another room.

Holten blinked. What in hell did that mean?

Quickly the scout rose to his feet and walked to the darkened window. Pulling back the rough denim curtain, Holten squinted into the blinding midday sunshine and wondered how many settlers would be willing to come along with them. Maybe if they saw the mutilated corpses of Burke, LaPointe, and the plump settler with the trunks of clothes, they'd be more receptive to the scout's offer.

Then he felt the fingers at his belt.

The scout whirled—and almost knocked over three of the prettiest, sexiest, and shapeliest whores he'd ever laid his blue eyes upon. Bridget, and her two companions, Katie and Lil, stood stark naked in front of the scout, their round plump breasts just inches from his rough hands, their lean sinewy bodies just waiting to be grabbed and caressed.

"What in hell—?"

"Hi Holten!" said Katie, the half-breed.

Holten noticed the Indian blood in her high cheekbones, long black hair, and copper-colored skin. She smiled up at him and searched his face with glistening brown eyes.

"Remember the girls?" asked Bridget.

"But—?" stammered Holten.

"Of course he remembers," said Lil, the stacked little redhead. "I remember everything he did to me—"

Lil sidled up to the scout, reached out with long slender fingers, and began to massage his cock through his buckskin pants.

Holten's penis throbbed.

"We ain't got much time," protested Holten. "Those renegades might show at any moment."

"Then we better hurry," purred Bridget.

Before the scout had time to think about what was

110

happening, the three worked-up whores converged on him and pulled off every stitch of clothing from his long lean and fully aroused body. Holten stood naked before them, his long hard penis pounding with desire.

"Wow!" gasped Lil. "Look at that!"

"I'll do more 'an look at it," said Bridget.

Before the scout could react, Bridget grasped his long ironlike shaft and twisted it gently against her soft lean body, a slight gasp of pleasure escaping from her supple lips.

Quickly the three naked girls led the scout to the long padded sofa and pushed him back gently against the pillows. Then like a pack of sexual animals they began to work on his lean muscled body, Bridget stroking his incredibly long cock, Lil massaging his broad hairy chest, and Katie, the half-breed, gently stroking the inside of the scout's thighs.

Holten writhed with pleasure. "Damn!" he breathed.

Suddenly Bridget took his aroused penis into her small mouth, her supple lips sliding up and down the pulsating shaft with blinding speed, her long delicate fingers grasping his balls at the same time.

The scout almost exploded right then.

At the same time, redheaded Lil smothered Holten with long wet kisses all over his leathery face, her lips and tongue massaging him in her own special way.

Then, without warning, Bridget sucked one last time on the scout's shaft, stood quickly, and let the half-breed Katie sit astride Holten's groin, her long fingers gently grasping his fully aroused penis and rubbing it slowly against her wet and ready vagina.

Holten groaned with ecstasy. Katie writhed with desire.

Suddenly Katie shoved Holten's cock into her slick wet channel, his rodlike shaft burying itself inside of her twisting, writhing body, the iron-hard penis driving deep inside of the gasping whore as she sat atop the thrashing scout. Before he exploded into the sinewy half-breed, the gasping whore slipped away and let the redhead mount him.

For what seemed like hours but was only minutes, the worked-up whores took turns with Holten, first one mounting his long frame and then another. Each of the soft sexy girls brought him closer to climax, their twisting gyrating bodies drawing the passion out of the scout's throbbing penis with each wild turn of their buttocks atop his groin.

Finally, as he approached the verge of a glorious sexual release, the girls slipped off of him. Bridget quickly knelt beside the panting scout and took his long overworked shaft into her mouth, her supple lips sliding up and down the throbbing cock, drawing out the scout's juices, until Holten burst into her, his pent-up passion exploding with a fervor he'd rarely known before, his hot milky fluid pouring into Bridget as she drained him completely, her mouth clinging to him until he'd been fully satisfied.

Holten felt as limp as cooked rawhide.

He lay gasping on the sofa with his eyes closed.

After a minute or so he opened his eyes and looked around the dimly lit parlor. The whores had disappeared, slipping away like naked phantoms to the back of the whorehouse. The scout sat slowly, his limp frame as loose and pain-free as never before. Even the arrow wound in his leg stopped throbbing as much.

Holten found his clothes and started to dress. In a few minutes he stood in the middle of the darkened parlor strapping on his weapons and thinking about the luscious girls who'd worked him over. He glanced up suddenly as Ma Beaudeen waddled into the room lugging a big straw suitcase.

"Sorry I took so long," she said, her blue eyes twinkling. "You weren't bored were you?"

Holten smiled. "I found something to do," he said.

*   *   *

The merciless sun beat down on them.

Holten turned in his saddle, his clothes drenched with sweat, and checked the buckboard full of whores behind him. Ma Beaudeen sat up front next to Bridget, who drove, and talked up a storm. Katie and Lil sat nestled among the baggage in the back, their long hair blowing in the breeze as they bounced over the countryside.

The scout smiled and turned back to the trail. He urged the gelding toward the three ranches that lay sprawled in the wide green valley just ahead, including Rebecca Springs. He chuckled to himself when he thought of Rebecca's probable reaction to a wagon full of whores.

Holten removed his wide-brimmed hat and wiped the sweat from his brow with his forearm. The thought of Rebecca Ridgeway struck a chord inside of him. She was a hell of a woman, the kind a man wouldn't mind settling down with.

If, of course, a man wanted to settle down.

They rode steadily along the dusty trail, Holten trotting atop the big gelding and the whores bouncing in the creaking buckboard. It was a beautiful day for a trip, clear and sunny. Then they spotted the smoke rising in the brassy afternoon sky.

Holten froze. The buckboard stopped.

"What's the matter?" asked Ma Beaudeen.

The scout felt a lump in the pit of his stomach.

"I don't know," he said, peering at the billowing white smoke that rose above the tops of the next few ridges. "Maybe renegades."

"What are we going to do?" asked Bridget.

"Take a look," said Holten. He clucked to the gelding.

With his heart beginning to beat against his ribs, and the fear starting to rise in him, the scout galloped over the next couple of rocky ridges and headed for the green valley he knew lay just ahead. Several ranches stood at the edge of

113

the grassy plains, but he knew which came first.

Rebecca Ridgeway's place.

Pulling far ahead of the slower buckboard, the scout raced along the trail, the gelding's big legs churning up the dirt with long powerful strides. Holten reached the crest of a boulder-strewn ridge that overlooked the valley and reined in the gelding, a cloud of alkaline dust rising into the sweltering air as he stopped the big snorting horse. Holten peered through the waves of shimmering afternoon heat at the scene in the green valley below.

He felt a sudden jab of fear in his chest.

The scout glanced down at what used to be the famous Rebecca Springs cattle ranch, but what was now just a pile of smoldering ruins.

Holten swallowed hard and spurred the gelding.

Galloping as fast as his big mount could take him, the scout raced down the grassy slope toward the sprawling ranch compound where the lovely blonde widow, Rebecca Ridgeway, lived.

Or used to live.

Holten reached the smoking ruins and leaped from the gelding. Hitting the ground at a full run, the scout sprinted toward the charred remains of the shingled ranch house, his hopes of finding the widow alive fading as fast as the great fire that had ravaged the ranch.

The scout burst into the smoking frame of the house, his eyes checking the blackened timbers for signs of life and his heart pounding like an Indian tom-tom. He stopped in his tracks at what used to be the bedroom, his steely blue eyes scanning the room. Holten spotted the once glistening mahogany bureau now charred and scarred by the roaring fire. He glanced quickly at the long porcelain bathtub, now just a big black container. And the scout's smoke-burned eyes fell on the big brass bed where he'd spent so many delicious hours, the once gleaming bed now just a charred skeleton.

114

The scout heard sounds from the ranch compound.

Holten whirled and saw the wagon full of whores skid to a stop in the dust, the wide-eyed girls scanning the blackened destruction in front of them.

"Holy shit!" exclaimed Ma Beaudeen.

"Look at that!" yelled Bridget.

Katie shook her head. "Wow!"

Then Holten heard it. A low moan rose in the air.

The scout turned and strode briskly from the smoldering ranch house, his sensitive ears following the sounds to the smoking remains of the bunkhouse on the other side of the ranch compound.

"What's that?" asked redheaded Lil.

Holten walked quickly past the girls toward the ranch hands' quarters, his eyes taking in the complete destruction around him. When the scout spotted the slaughtered horses in the wide log corral to his left, their bloodied corpses piled atop one another like firewood, he knew at once it hadn't been renegades who'd attacked Rebecca Ridgeway's place. The Sioux worshipped horses and prized them even more than a good woman. They'd never butcher prize mounts like that.

It had to be Jackson and his boys.

The moaning grew louder now, the obvious death groans of a badly wounded cowboy. Holten stopped at the smoking timbers of the bunkhouse and peered through the thin veil of white smoke. Then he saw the bloodied body sticking out from beneath a jumbled pile of smoldering timbers.

The scout bent down and uncovered the broken body of a dying cowboy, the man's blood oozing from several gunshot wounds in his chest and stomach. It was a miracle he was still alive, thought Holten. The scout noticed five or six other bodies sprawled beneath the ruins.

"Help me," gasped the cowboy.

Holten raised the man's head. "What happened?"

The cowboy swallowed hard. "They—surprised—us," rasped the dying man, his breath coming in uneven gasps.

Bridget raced up to Holten.

"Bring some water," said the scout. Bridget turned and ran back toward the gelding as fast as her shapely legs would take her.

"Who surprised you?"

"Injuns—" gasped the man. "But—"

The cowboy winced with sudden pain, his soot covered face contorted into a mask of agony. Bridget returned with Holten's canteen and thrust it at the scout. Holten let the cowboy drink a little water, the cool soothing liquid seeming to pump new life into the dying man.

"But what?" asked Holten.

The man swallowed. "They—weren't—Injuns."

Holten stiffened. He'd guessed as much.

"Who were they?"

"White men," gasped the cowboy. "Soldiers."

Liver-Eating Jackson and Paco Riley, thought the scout.

"Why—?" asked the dying ranch hand in a frayed voice. "Why—would soldiers—attack us—?"

Suddenly the coyboy coughed, blood oozing from his mouth as he tried to catch his breath. Holten knew the man didn't have long to live.

The scout had to know. "And the widow Ridgeway?"

"Gone," said the man in a hoarse whisper.

"Gone where? Did they take her with them?"

The man winced with pain, then nodded slowly.

Then he died.

Bridget the whore gasped and brought a hand to her mouth.

Holten laid the man's head on the ground and rose slowly. As the scout scanned the ruins all around him, it became suddenly apparent that Liver-Eating Jackson and the deserters not only wanted to provoke trouble in the

116

Dakota Territory, but they intended to raid and loot as many homesteads as possible before the army took action.

And now they'd kidnapped Rebecca Ridgeway.

"What now?" asked Bridget.

The scout started forward, his long legs taking him across the smoking ranch compound toward his gelding. He felt the anger boil up inside of him. Raiding and looting were one thing, but kidnapping was something all together different.

Liver-Eating Jackson had gone too far.

"Got some trackin' to do," said Holten.

A thin cloud of smoke hung over the plains.

Tracking the deserters' pony prints in the dusty trail, Holten and the wagon full of whores passed the other two ranches in the wide green Dakota valley—or what was left of them. Their proud buildings were just smoldering ruins, plumes of thick white smoke rising above the tall green pines like Indian signal fires.

Once the scout stopped and examined the butchered bodies of several ranchers that lay sprawled in the dust, their shiny scalped heads glistening in the sunlight.

"Damn!" said Ma Beaudeen. "The butcherin' bastards!"

"What kind of person could do somethin' like that?" asked Bridget, her pretty face paling as she looked at the bodies.

Holten saw vivid mental images of Liver-Eating Jackson, his evil yellow eyes narrowed, and giant Paco Riley, his 300-pound frame bent over a fallen rancher slicing off the man's scalp.

Holten's voice hardened. "Crazy men," he replied.

The scout clucked to the gelding and continued on his mission of mercy. While he followed the pony tracks in the trail, Holten wondered what kind of hell Rebecca Ridgeway was going through at that very moment. The

117

thought sent a new wave of anger through his chest.

He kept on tracking.

Moving slowly because of the wagon full of girls behind him, Holten eventually guided his small party out of the smoking valley and up a slight incline toward the purple hills that lay ahead.

Then he saw them. It was another disaster.

Pulling back quickly on the gelding's reins, Holten peered through the afternoon heat at a struggling slow-moving train of crippled wagons, arrows bristling from the wooden frames and wounded settlers limping alongside the creaking vehicles.

Liver-Eating Jackson again?

The scout smacked the gelding on the butt and galloped down the grassy slope to meet the battered settlers. As Holten approached the half-burned wagons he saw the survivors glance up at him quickly, wide-eyed expressions of fear on their haggard faces. They'd had a horrifying glimpse of death back on the trail, thought the scout, and didn't like what they had seen.

Holten slowed his big horse and trotted up to the lead wagon. As the scout approached, a short stocky settler removed his floppy hat, wiped the trail dust from his fleshy face, and stared up at him. Holten stopped his snorting gelding beside the man.

"Run into some trouble?" asked the scout.

The stocky settler looked at Holten. "That's right," he said in a tight voice. "And we're not lookin' for any more."

"Indians?"

The man nodded somberly. "About ten of 'em jumped us back around the bend," he answered.

Holten had to know. "Did they have a white woman ridin' with 'em?"

The stocky man's eyebrows shot up. "Why yes," he said. "They did. Looked pretty scared, too."

The deserters. And they were nearby.

"Which way did they go?"

"Headed for the hills. Could have finished us off, but just stopped real sudden like and whooped off into the hills."

"You're luckier than most," said Holten.

"That woman family of yours?" asked the man.

Holten just stared for a moment, his mind flashing sudden images of silky blonde hair, plump round breasts, and a smile that could melt a man's insides.

"Yep," Holten said finally.

"Too bad," said the settler shaking his head. "Them Injuns had her half-naked already. Hate to think what they're doin' to her now."

Holten grit his teeth.

Suddenly the wagon full of Ma Beaudeen and her girls rattled over the rise in a cloud of dust. The stocky settler glanced up quickly.

"Who's that?" asked the man.

"Some more victims," said the scout. "I'm helpin' anyone who needs to get to Fort Rawlins until this renegade problem is finished."

"Much obliged," said the stocky settler. "We're just kinda stunned. Don't rightly know where we're headin'."

"Follow me," said the scout. "I'll take you as far as the trail that leads to Fort Rawlins. Then I've got me some business in the hills."

Ma Beaudeen's buckboard approached the lead wagon in a cloud of alkaline dust, the girls' hair dishevelled and their skimpy clothing ruffled by the wind. While he waited for the whores to pull alongside, Holten scanned the crippled settler wagon train and quickly studied the surviving homesteaders. He counted about five men, four women, and six or seven children staring out at him. He noticed the disgusted looks on the women's faces when they spotted Ma and her whores.

"Jesus H. Christ, Holten!" shouted Ma. "You coulda

waited for us!"

Holten nodded at the wagons. "More victims," he said.

"Oh," said Ma Beaudeen, glancing at the settlers. "Is everyone all right?"

The stocky man removed his floppy hat. "The name's Mason, ma'am," he said. "We lost some of our people back on the trail, but the rest of us are determined to get to the fort."

"They're comin' with us," said Holten. "I'll take you all as far as the trail that leads to the fort. Then I got me some trackin' to do."

"The deserters again?" asked Bridget, her big glistening eyes scanning the arrow-studded wagons.

Holten nodded. "They ain't too far away," he said, looking into the shadowy hills in the distance. The scout also knew they were in Sioux hunting ground. "Maybe Red Hawk's warriors are nearby, too."

Mason put on his hat and sighed. "This territory's sure full of treacherous characters," he said.

The scout's mind flashed sudden images of Liver-Eating Jackson, Paco Riley, and Red Hawk. He couldn't agree more with the man.

"Follow me," said Holten.

The scout clucked to the gelding, headed off down the trail, and hoped to hell he could get his growing party of survivors safely over the hills to the trail that led to the army post.

Then he'd go after Jackson and Riley. And Rebecca.

The rotting bodies lay covered with buffalo robes atop tall burial platforms, Indian weapons propped against the corpses. An eerie late afternoon breeze whistled through the shadowy clearing. A strange silence hung over the cemetery like a heavy burial shroud.

Mason stroked his face. "Why can't we cross?"

"It's a sacred Sioux burial ground," said Holten.

"We'd be across in less than ten minutes."

The scout shook his head. "Can't do it."

"Why not?"

"The Sioux don't take kindly to white folks stompin' across sacred ground," said Holten. "Big medicine."

"Not just this once?"

"No," repeated the scout.

Holten had stopped abruptly at the beginning of a narrow trail that led through the hills. On the other side of the brooding mountains he could see part of the wide, grassy, and relatively safe trail to Fort Rawlins. The trip would take only a few hours, but Holten's little wagon train had run into a complication.

An Oglala Sioux burial ground.

"I don't see no Injuns," said Mason looking around.

"They're out there," said the scout.

"If Holten says we can't cross," interjected Ma Beaudeen, shifting her fleshy body atop the buckboard, "then we can't."

"Well," said Mason. "Where's the next crossin'?"

"In the neighboring hill," replied Holten. "It's a little dangerous, but with some care we should make it with no problems."

"Dangerous?"

"Steep canyons," said the scout. "Tell your people to stay in a tight line. And control their teams."

Mason sighed and nodded. "Let's go," he said finally.

Holten turned the head of his gelding around and led the small train of fleeing settlers toward the next hill. The trip would take a couple of hours longer, the scout knew, but he'd seen what could happen to whites who violated the sacred ground of an Oglala Sioux burial ground.

It wasn't pretty.

Holten led the struggling settler wagons over a rocky trail bordered on one side by a steep, wooded cliff and on the other by a deep ravine with a drop of about two hundred feet to the bottom. The dangerous trek began well enough, the wagons keeping in a neat straight line. Then the tired settlers, eager to reach the warm safety of Fort Rawlins, ignored the scout's advice and started to push ahead en masse.

Disaster struck almost immediately.

Trotting ahead of the narrow line of wagons, his senses working and his eyes searching the sides of the trail, Holten heard the sudden screams of the settlers first, followed right away by the sharp whinnying of the startled horses. The scout whirled around in his saddle and watched two wagons slip and slide off the trail toward the ravine and the steep drop-off. The wide-eyed drivers of the wagons tried desperately to pull the horses away from the ravine, but fought a losing battle.

Holten went into action.

The scout turned the gelding sharply and galloped back to where the two wagons slid inexorably toward the drop-off. In just seconds Holten reached a couple of the hysterical women, the screaming small children, and one of the stunned settler men. He hauled them off the sliding wagons and dropped them on the rocky trail. Then, urging his big horse once again, the scout raced back to the wagons and tried to haul them back onto the trail.

He was too late.

Two settler men still on the wagons screamed with horror.

With a sickening crash of broken wagon wheels and splintered axles, the two wagons skidded off the edge of the narrow trail and fell silently for a few seconds toward the boulder-covered ravine bottom two hundred feet below. They landed in a cloud of dust with a loud crash, wagon parts and settler household goods scattering in all directions as though a cannon shell had struck the wagons.

The settlers stared dumbfounded for a few minutes.

Then Mason turned to face Holten, the stocky settler's

blanched face lined with horror, his eyes filled with fear. Holten noticed the man's trembling hands. The scout just nodded.

"All right," said Holten with a sigh. "We'll take the other trail."

With the orange sun sinking in the western sky, the scout led the remaining settlers back toward the Indian burial ground. Maybe they would be lucky and sneak past the Indians.

Holten had his doubts.

CHAPTER TEN

They headed up the narrow trail, passed quickly through the Sioux burial ground, and stopped on the other side. Holten held up his hand.

"Quiet!"

"What is it?" asked Mason.

"I don't know. Let me listen."

"I don't hear a thing."

"Shhhh!"

The scout strained his ears and tried to pick up the forest sounds that came to him on the warm prairie wind. A casual cricket call, the press of feet on tall buffalo grass, a prairie chicken calling to its mate, all were normal sounds on the Dakota plains.

And normal sounds of the Oglala Sioux, too.

"I still don't hear anything," said Mason, his stocky body frozen atop his wagon as he listened intently.

"I do," said Holten simply.

The scout's heart beat against his ribs.

Holten had hoped it was Jackson and his boys. It would have made his tracking job easier. Instead, it seemed Red Hawk was hot on his tail; the tall subchief wouldn't be satisfied until Holten's scalp hung from his lodge pole. Holten's instincts spoke to him and told him the Indians were close at hand.

Maybe too close.

The scout dismounted and tethered the gelding to Ma Beaudeen's buckboard. Then he hauled off his boots and replaced them with soft deerskin moccasins from his saddlebags. Ready at last, the scout took his Winchester .44-40 from its sheath and padded off toward the burial ground they'd just crossed.

"Where you goin', Holten?" asked Ma Beaudeen.

"Don't leave us," pleaded Mason in a thin frightened voice.

Holten glided toward the trees. "I'll be right back," he said over his shoulder.

"What if the Injuns attack?" shouted Mason.

Holten ignored the question, sprinted up a slight hill, and crouched in the tall grass. Then sneaking like a cougar through the shadowy wooded area that bordered the Sioux burial ground, his Winchester gripped firmly in one hand, the scout finally reached the wide clearing and its grisly platforms. He peered through the shadows and froze.

Holten's heart jumped to his throat.

On the far side of the Indian cemetery he spotted two wiry braves with about twenty ponies, their dark painted faces staring glumly into the surrounding trees. The warriors were sentries assigned to guard the ponies. Holten knew a large war party lurked somewhere in the surrounding trees ready to pounce on his small wagon train.

Suddenly gunshots pierced the air.

Then screams of horror from the assembled settlers behind the scout reached his ears. The war party had attacked the wagons.

As Indian war cries rose from the clearing where he'd left the settlers, the scout quickly shouldered his big rifle and fired twice at the Indians guarding the ponies. The hot slugs from the Winchester ripped through the braves' chests. The young warriors jerked off their horses as though yanked off by a giant lasso and landed heavily in the grass. At the same time the Indian ponies panicked and raced off toward the hills beyond.

Holten didn't have any time to lose. He ran.

The scout sprinted toward the embattled settlers in the clearing below, his heart beating wildly as he raced through the tall buffalo grass. Holten reached the rise that overlooked the wagons and froze in his tracks.

All hell had broken loose.

The scout watched about two dozen Sioux warriors rise from behind rocks that surrounded the small wagon train and fire at will. Bows twanged and arrows whistled through the air. Holten saw two settlers dead on the ground already, arrows deeply embedded in their chests. The scout heard the screams of the settlers, the whinnying of the frightened horses, and the cracks of rifles fill the clearing below.

It had all the makings of another massacre.

Holten started down. Then the braves hit him.

The two lean Sioux warriors burst from the bushes on the scout's right and struck him with the force of a charging bull buffalo. The sudden contact sent the Winchester flying from the scout's hands. Holten and the two braves sprawled in the grass, quickly regained their footing, and faced each other with glistening knives clutched in their hands.

Suddenly, Holten was locked in a fight for his life.

As the three combatants circled warily like wolves sizing up their prey, the scout watched the flashing brown eyes of the sinewy warriors. The Indians held their long knives flat and ready to strike. Holten's steely blue eyes darted from the glistening blades in the braves' hands to their broad dark faces slashed with white war paint. With his muscles tensed like coiled springs, the scout waited for any sudden movement.

It came almost immediately.

The hard-eyed warrior to the scout's right struck with blinding speed, his glistening blade leading the way. Holten swerved quickly to the side, parried the warrior's vicious thrust with a smash to the brave's head, and turned to face the other Indian.

He did it just in time.

The other lean warrior had already launched himself toward the scout, his flashing eyes set with determination as he slashed his long blade at Holten's mid-section. Quickly the scout tucked in his belly and just avoided the deadly thrust. The Indian's knife ripped through Holten's buckskin jacket, while at the same time the scout jabbed with his Bowie knife at the startled brave.

His fearsome blade struck flesh.

The lean warrior's eyes widened with shock as the scout's wide blade pierced his chest, ripped through layers of muscle, and tore into his heart. The Indian shrieked once, then fell dead to the ground, blood spurting from the ugly gash in his chest.

Holten saw a sudden flash of movement.

The remaining warrior lunged at the scout, his glistening knife whooshing through the air toward Holten's back. The scout whirled quickly, caught the brave's wrist, and fell heavily to the ground. The two knife fighters grappled on the buffalo grass, Holten grasping the Sioux warrior's wrist to keep the deadly blade from striking, the lean brown-skinned brave fending off the scout's slashing thrusts with the Bowie knife. The scout knew he had to act fast.

Holten brought his knee into the Indian's groin.

The warrior's eyes widened with shock, his broad gleaming face slackening as the sudden sharp pain in his crotch broke his concentration.

The scout lashed out with his knife.

As the stunned brave began to scream with pain from the knee in his groin, Holten tore his Bowie knife clear of the Indian's clutches and jabbed the long fearsome blade into the warrior's stomach. The scout drove the blade to the hilt in the Indian's writhing body, the sharp deadly point reaching upwards toward the brave's heart.

The warrior froze. Blood splashed onto the ground.

Holten laid the dead warrior on the grass and stood quickly. The scout's heart pounded against his ribs like a blacksmith's hammer. He quickly regained his bearings and glanced down at the fighting in the clearing below.

It looked bad.

The scout watched several Sioux warriors leap from their hiding places and charge the overmatched settlers. One of the settlers pulled both barrels of a shotgun and nearly blew the head off one of the lunging Indians, a spray of blood and bone fragments exploding in the air. But then Holten saw two of Red Hawk's warriors leap onto the settler with the shotgun and with quick slashes of their glistening war hatchets almost decapitate the man.

Holten scanned the chaos below him and spotted the wagon full of whores, their wide-eyed expressions reflecting the sudden horror they faced. Ma Beaudeen stood in the buckboard and pointed at several Indians who charged from the woods. The frightened gelding, tied to the wagon, reared onto its hind legs and whinnied sharply. Sioux warriors began to charge from every direction.

The scout grabbed his Winchester and went to work.

Holten hunkered in the tall grass and began to pick his targets. He aimed down the long barrel of his repeating rifle and caught a charging warrior in his sights. The scout squeezed the trigger.

The Winchester spat fire and threw hot lead toward the startled brave. The Indian never knew what hit him. The charging warrior's arms flew over his head as the slug tore through his body and slammed him to the ground, a widening circle of crimson running over his muscled chest.

Holten levered the Winchester and fired again. Another Sioux warrior bit the dust. The scout fired again and again. Each time charging warriors slammed to the grassy floor of the clearing, dead before they hit the ground.

Suddenly, a blood-curdling scream rent the air.

Holten turned and looked at the buckboard. What he saw quickened his pulse. Two Sioux warriors grabbed Bridget and Katie and started to haul the screaming whores from the wagon. Lil fell heavily to the ground, where a brave grabbed her flailing arms. A fourth brave wrestled with fat old Ma Beaudeen.

What happened next sickened the scout.

As Holten watched helplessly, the scowling Sioux brave grappling with Ma Beaudeen pulled a long glistening knife from his belt and jabbed it into the old whorehouse madame's fleshy body. Ma Beaudeen flinched slightly, but kept on fighting, her fat little fingers clawing at the warrior's scowling face. The brave slashed again and again until Ma's dark red blood spilled down the warrior's muscled forearm and dripped onto the buckboard.

Holten bolted down the hill.

The scout grasped his Winchester and sprinted toward the wagons. Suddenly a warrior leaped into Holten's path, a fearsome war club in his hand and an evil smile across his dark painted face. Without breaking stride, the scout reversed his grip on the rifle and used it like a war club. He brought the heavy rifle butt down on the stunned warrior's head, the brave's skull cracking from the impact.

Holten glanced at the buckboard. He raced ahead.

Suddenly two more braves leaped in the scout's path, one of them with a knife and the other grasping a Spencer repeating rifle.

Holten didn't stop.

The scout lowered his broad shoulder and smashed into the warrior with the rifle. The brave grunted with the sudden impact, his Spencer flying into the air. A quick jab with his elbow to the other warrior's jaw cleared the way.

The buckboard glistened with Ma Beaudeen's blood.

Holten reached the embattled wagon train and leaped at

the buckboard. The scout struck the brave with the knife just as the Indian withdrew the knife from Ma Beaudeen's fat stomach for the twentieth time or so. With a swift kick to the brave's ribs, the scout sent the Indian to the ground gasping for breath. Holten then levered a cartridge into the Winchester, aimed the long barrel at the fallen warrior, and squeezed the trigger.

The repeater barked. And barked again. And again.

Taking his anger out on the fallen warrior with the bloodied knife, Holten shot six times, the rifle's slugs ripping into the Indian's body just seconds apart. The body danced on the ground like a puppet at a traveling carnival, the warrior's blood spurting from his many wounds as he writhed in the dust.

Holten whirled and stared at Ma Beaudeen.

The fat old dame stood wavering on the buckboard, her pudgy fingers dripping with her own blood as they tried to keep her guts inside of her slashed stomach, her once sparkling blue eyes now dulled with shock.

The scout watched Ma's eyes roll toward the heavens as she pitched forward off the buckboard, her stomach and intestines splashing onto the ground before she landed in the dust with a heavy thump. The scout stood staring for a second, his mind racing with hatred at his attackers.

Gunshots brought him back to reality.

Holten quickly scanned the two remaining settler wagons, his piercing eyes surveying the carnage before him. Mason, the stocky settler leader, lay dead in a pool of blood next to his wagon. Beside him lay the butchered corpses of several small children, wide-eyed expressions of terror etched on their innocent young faces. Behind the bodies several other overmatched settlers grappled with whooping Sioux warriors in the clearing, their bodies dripping with blood from the arrows stuck in their sides.

It was a massacre.

"Holten!" came a plaintive cry. "Help us, Holten!"

The scout whirled and saw Bridget, Katie, and Lil being dragged away from the clearing by half a dozen yelping Sioux warriors.

Holten flew into action.

The scout quickly shouldered his Winchester and aimed at the braves next to the whores. He'd have to make a hell of a clean shot, but it could be done. He sighted the rifle and started to squeeze the trigger.

Then an arrow whistled and thudded into the scout's right arm. Another arrow whistled past his head, while a third struck him in the right leg just above the knee.

Pain knifed through his body. He dropped the rifle.

The scout fell to the ground.

Holten turned and started to pull the arrows from his body. Then he spotted three screaming warriors bearing down on him, heavy-headed war clubs grasped in their hands. The scout braced himself for the attack, lunged at the first brave, and sent the warrior spinning to the ground. A second Sioux brave lashed out with his war club, the stone head whooshing just inches from Holten's skull. The scout jabbed his balled fist into the Indian's stomach, the brave gasping suddenly and dropping heavily to the dusty clearing.

Then it happened.

Holten whirled to face another charging warrior. He turned too late. His head snapped forward. The scout felt a dull thud on the back of his head, saw a sudden starburst in front of his eyes, and felt himself falling and falling until his face smacked against the packed dirt of the clearing. A black blanket of unconsciousness covered his face.

He rolled once, then lay still in the dust.

Holten woke with the sudden pain.

The scout sat bolt upright as two hard-faced Sioux warriors yanked the arrows from his body. The scowling braves pulled viciously at the shafts, sudden pain slicing through the scout's lean frame. Blood spurted from the wound in Holten's arm. The scout quickly shook his head to clear his brain and tried to stop the flow of blood with his dusty kerchief.

"How is the pain, Tall Bear?"

Holten glanced up quickly, the sudden effort making his aching head throb. The scout felt more awake now and started to remember what had happened before he got clouted. He looked up at the tall muscled warrior hovering nearby.

Red Hawk.

"Surely the great white man's scout can stand the pain of two little arrows," chided the Sioux subchief.

Holten glanced at the body-cluttered clearing. "Red Hawk takes pleasure these days in butchering women and children," said the scout in Lakota.

"All whites must die!"

"Even harmless children?" asked Holten. "Red Hawk has won great honor today. He has killed five small children."

The scout watched the anger rise in Red Hawk's lean hard face. Holten thought the Oglala subchief would explode. Instead, Red Hawk's flashing eyes narrowed as he glared down at the scout.

"Enjoy your brief rest from the pain, Tall Bear," snapped the renegade warrior chief. "Soon you will feel pain like never before in your life!"

With that last ominous statement, Red Hawk turned on his heel and strode briskly toward some braves across the small clearing. Other braves returned with the ponies that had scattered earlier. Holten took advantage of the sudden respite from the hostilities to check the results of the massacre.

What he saw turned his stomach.

The scout scanned the small clearing and surveyed the carnage. Holten knew the Sioux disfigured their dead enemies to render the enemies' spirits helpless in the afterlife. This time, he noted, they'd been especially savage. All of the whites lay scalped and mutilated in the dust, some of the settlers with their faces smashed and brains bashed in, while others lay sprawled on the ground next to piles of their own entrails. Holten spotted Ma Beaudeen's crumpled body lying in a pool of her own blood, her bloodied guts splattered on the dusty ground beside her. Throughout the clearing flies buzzed as they sucked the oozing blood from the stiffening corpses. The scout spied buzzards wheeling in the brassy sky above.

It seemed that only Holten had survived.

Then it struck him. Where were the whores?

Holten turned sharply, the pain in his head lancing down his entire frame, and glanced up at the grassy slope that led to the sacred burial ground.

He spotted the whores. He wished he hadn't.

The scout saw several naked Sioux warriors atop the moaning whores, the couples writhing under the last hot rays of the setting sun. The braves pumped their hardened cocks into the wiggling girls like bulls screwing cows in an alfalfa field.

Bridget screamed. Katie writhed. Lil squirmed.

Holten knew the end would come slowly for the struggling whores. The braves would take their time with the girls, screwing each of them several times until the warriors were completely satisfied. Then, if the girls were lucky, the Sioux would bring the whores to camp for others to sample. Finally, the scout knew, the white girls would be turned over to the vengeful Indian women, the savage squaws tearing the girls apart limb by limb.

Holten licked his parched lips.

Things looked bad. For him, too.

The scout had searched for Liver-Eating Jackson and Paco Riley. Instead, he'd found Red Hawk and his bloodthirsty renegades. Now, Holten was sure, Red Hawk

133

would take great pleasure in slowly torturing the scout to death.

Suddenly Red Hawk strode over to the scout.

The subchief beamed. "Now," he said smiling, "we take Tall Bear to our camp. We will see how strong the white man's scout really is."

Holten didn't like the tone of his voice.

Holten lay spread-eagled on the ground.

After a quick trip through the shadowy hills to Red Hawk's camp, the stunned whores and the wounded scout had been immediately stripped of every stitch of clothing and prepared for torture. The renegade village had turned out en masse to welcome home their conquering heroes, and to watch the slow death of the struggling white prisoners.

After he'd been stripped, the scout was slammed to the ground in the middle of the camp and tied spread-eagle to stakes, his arms and legs as far apart as they could go. The shrieking whores had been shuttled off to the teepees of drooling warriors for what the scout knew would be a very unpleasant evening.

Then the drums began to pound.

TUM, tum, tum, tum. TUM, tum, tum, tum.

The drumbeats echoed inside the scout's throbbing head, his still tender skull aching even more. Holten lay naked in the dust waiting for the slow excruciating pain he knew was sure to come. He'd seen it before in other Sioux camps.

TUM, tum, tum, tum. TUM, tum, tum, tum.

As Holten lay on his back in the middle of the camp, night fell over the prairie. The scout looked up and scanned the Indian encampment with his tired eyes, watching the eerie shadows cast by the many cooking fires, glancing at the distorted reflections that danced across the

134

tanned buffalo hides of the teepees.

TUM, tum, tum, tum. TUM, tum, tum, tum.

Holten thought how strange it was that his life on the prairie was going to end in almost the same place it had begun. He remembered watching the flickering Indian cooking fires the first evening he'd been brought to a Sioux camp after being captured out on the prairie. Twenty years had passed, but he had ended up in the same place.

Suddenly the drums stopped.

Silence fell over the renegade camp.

Holten turned his head and saw the circle of Indians tighten around him. Then the scout watched the circle of braves part for a moment to let Red Hawk and several other high ranking warriors enter. The haughty chiefs stepped over to where Holten lay looking up at them, knives and other weapons clutched in their hands. Right then the scout made up his mind not to give in to his tormentors, not to display any outward signs of pain during the torture. He'd show the gawking red bastards.

Then the torture started.

With an evil grin cracking his lean brown face, Red Hawk knelt beside Holten, took a long thin needle, and stuck it under the scout's skin between the shoulder and the elbow of his right arm. Holten stiffened. Then another subchief reached down, touched the long cold blade of a fearsome hunting knife to Holten's arm, and slowly sliced a small piece of skin from the scout's flesh. Holten grit his teeth.

The gathered renegades cheered.

Red Hawk repeated his jab with the needle, but this time in a different place on the arm. Again the other subchief sliced off a pea-sized bit of skin from Holten's arm. Again Holten stiffened and again the village cheered. Again and again the two Sioux warriors repeated the crude operation, piercing and slicing the scout's skin for over an hour until almost one hundred tiny bits of skin had been carved from Holten's right arm.

Then they worked on the left arm for an hour.

All during the slow excruciating torture session, Holten grit his teeth and kept his mouth shut. He didn't cry out at all, but kept his steely blue eyes focused on several twinkling stars in the inky sky overhead, his mind fixed on pleasant things like his lovemaking sessions with Rebecca Ridgeway.

Red Hawk pierced his skin.

Holten thought about Rebecca's golden thighs.

The other subchief sliced some skin.

Holten fixed his thoughts on Rebecca's firm round breasts.

For over two hours, Red Hawk and the other subchief picked and sliced the scout's skin between the shoulder and elbow of both arms until the ugly red welts looked as though a giant swarm of hornets had settled on his skin and stung him relentlessly.

It felt that way, too.

Finally Red Hawk grunted, tossed away his needle in disgust, and rose quickly from beside the scout. The Oglala subchief and his partner pushed through the circle of wide-eyed Sioux renegades and strode briskly toward a tall teepee. At the same time, the gawking Indians dispersed until the next round of the torture. Holten saw the parting Sioux talking excitedly among themselves as though they couldn't wait.

The scout sure as hell could.

A few giggling young Sioux women lingered near Holten pointing to his exposed penis and talking about its length. Suddenly the scout roared at them, the young squaws jumping and shrieking with fear as they scampered away.

Holten's upper arms stung as though he'd stuck his arms into a raging fire. The scout licked his parched lips and waited, smiling at the knowledge that he'd upset Red Hawk by failing to show any outward signs of his discomfort. But the scout knew the torture had only begun. By all Holten's previous knowledge of such events, he wouldn't last the night.

Suddenly he heard footsteps. Then he saw her.

A beautiful Indian woman padded over to where the scout lay bleeding in the dust, her finely sculptured face framed by long, silky black hair that glistened in the sparse firelight. As she knelt beside his head, her long hair falling over her shoulders, Holten gazed into her sparkling brown eyes and quickly scanned her lean shapely body. He noticed something familiar about her.

"Drink, Tall Bear," whispered the young woman in Lakota.

Holten hesitated. "Who are you?"

"I am called Yellow Shell," she replied softly.

"Yellow Shell?"

"From the camp of Crow Dog," she said. "I am the sister of White Bird."

Holten froze. His dead girl friend's sister.

Holten's blue eyes locked with hers, a sudden moment of understanding passing between them. His butchered girl friend's sister had come to him in his time of need.

"Drink, Tall Bear," Yellow Shell repeated. "Quickly before they come back."

Without speaking, the scout lifted his throbbing head and accepted the cool thirst-slaking water from the young squaw, his parched lips stinging as the liquid ran over them.

"White Bird spoke often of you," she said as she held the gourd of water near Holten's lips. "I will try to help you as much as possible."

137

The scout lay back after drinking. "You cannot help me, Yellow Shell," he said. "I am finished. Do not involve yourself or you, too, will receive Red Hawk's torture."

"I will be nearby, Tall Bear," said Yellow Shell simply, and rose quickly beside the scout. "May your pain be small."

The lithe Indian woman disappeared as suddenly as she had appeared. The scout craned his neck to find her.

"Yellow Shell?" he called.

Too late. She was gone.

Holten lay back again, grateful for the water and surprised to find White Bird's sister in Red Hawk's camp. As his mind drifted to the soft lovely Indian girl he once loved, the pain from his wounds almost disappeared. Too bad, thought the scout, he wouldn't be able to get to know Yellow Shell.

Excited voices rose in the camp. Braves gathered.

Here we go again, thought Holten.

Within minutes the tight circle of renegades surrounded the spread-eagled scout once again, Red Hawk and three other subchiefs kneeling beside his naked frame. This time they held handmade wooden pliers in their hands.

Holten knew what came next.

Quickly, Red Hawk reached down to the scout, grasped his forehead so as to hold him immobile, and with the wooden pliers, plucked a few hairs from Holten's right eyebrow.

The scout stiffened. The crowd cheered.

For the next half hour, Red Hawk and his cronies pulled the tiny hairs from Holten's eyebrows one by one until the scout's forehead glistened with little wounds above his eyes. The pain, like tiny pinpricks, became almost unbearable. But the scout just grit his teeth and didn't scream.

Then they worked on his eyelids.

138

For another agonizing half hour, the subchiefs pulled the tiny lashes from Holten's eyelids one by one, the scout's vision blurring as the renegade leaders plucked him clean. Again the pain became almost unbearable, but again Holten remained silent throughout the ordeal.

Finally, they started on his moustache.

Again came the agonizing pain as the Sioux renegade leaders bent over the spread-eagled scout and plucked the tiny hairs from his drooping moustache. And again the scout, now numb with pain, didn't cry out.

The crowd fell silent. Now they watched Red Hawk.

Holten blinked back the pain, a warm feeling spreading through his chest. The scout knew because he'd overcome Red Hawk's gruelling tests so far, the renegade chief was in danger of losing face in front of his people.

Then Holten smelled fire. He knew what came next.

He saw Red Hawk with a burning piece of punklike sunflower stalk, similar to the punk small boys use on the Fourth of July to light their firecrackers. With an evil grin cracking his lean hard face, the renegade subchief lay the slow-burning punk against Holten's right wrist. Another subchief did the same thing with the scout's left wrist. Then the smiling chiefs and the other excited Indians looked on with wide-eyed anticipation as the flame crackled its way across Holten's sensitive skin.

As the searing pain built on his wrists, the scout closed his tired eyes and grit his teeth so hard he thought they would crush into fine powder. For ten agonizing minutes the slow-burning sunflower punk singed its way across Holten's skin. Beads of sweat burst out on the scout's forehead, and he almost passed out twice. But he remained silent through the entire ordeal.

When the fires went out, the crowd gasped.

Red Hawk rose slowly beside the scout, his flashing eyes and scowling face fixed on Holten's ravaged body. The other subchiefs rose also.

Suddenly, a middle-aged stocky squaw burst through the circle of renegades, a glistening knife in her hand. The plump dark-faced woman strode purposefully to where Holten lay glistening with sweat on the ground and knelt beside his groin. As Holten watched with sudden horror, the laughing squaw reached out, fondled the scout's balls, and shouted in Lakota.

"A new tobacco pouch for my man!"

The crowd roared with laughter. Holten felt faint.

Suddenly, the woman reached toward the scout, grabbed Holten's testicles and cock even harder, and brought the knife forward slowly as though to slice the genitals neatly from the scout's body.

"No!" yelled Red Hawk.

The woman froze. She glanced up at the tall subchief.

"It is my turn!" she shouted. "My right!"

"No!" repeated Red Hawk. "Tall Bear did not cry out during the torture. It is bad medicine to disfigure him before he dies."

The woman hesitated as her trembling hands held the knife just inches from Holten's genitals. The scout winced as the squaw tightened her grip on his balls. Finally, with flashing eyes, the woman drew back the knife quickly and started to cut.

Red Hawk lashed out with a foot, kicked the woman's wrist, and sent the knife flying. The squaw shrieked with pain.

Holten took a deep breath.

"We will not cut the white man," snapped Red Hawk. The tall subchief, his eyes gleaming suddenly, glanced down at the scout. "We will take him to the Canyon of Death," said Red Hawk with a smile. "He has earned the right to die like a warrior."

Holten stiffened.

He'd heard about the famous Canyon of Death. No

140

warrior had ever escaped from the narrow ravine where the Oglala toss their most feared battle enemies. But given the option of being thrown into the famous canyon or being castrated in public, the scout knew there was no real choice.

At least this way he had a chance.

CHAPTER ELEVEN

The famed Canyon of Death lay nestled among the hills about a mile outside of Red Hawk's renegade camp. The naked scout, his wounds throbbing, hauled himself onto the back of a swift pony and followed Red Hawk and his braves away from the village. The small party of Red Hawk, Holten, and about a dozen high ranking warriors arrived at the Canyon with blazing torches sometime in the middle of the night. The warriors tethered their ponies and dragged the scout to the edge of the canyon.

Red Hawk laughed mightily. "Look, Tall Bear," he said, an evil smile cracking his lean hard face. "This is your final resting place."

The Sioux subchief motioned to the braves holding the flaming torches to dip them over the Canyon's edge. As the warriors held the flickering tongues of flame low to the ground, the scout peered into the famous Canyon of Death.

What he saw quickened his pulse.

The narrow canyon was only five or six feet wide, but about thirty feet deep, its slick hard rock sides devoid of any fissures or other hand holds. The canyon ran to a length of fifty or sixty feet, all the side walls as slick as the others. The tree-covered bottom of the narrow canyon was littered with bleached bones, decomposing bodies, and human rib cages that looked like the remains of a Christmas turkey after it had been picked clean.

Suddenly a deafening roar rose from the canyon.

Holten stiffened in the grasp of the braves.

"Some friends await you," said Red Hawk with a smile.

The scout peered intently through the eerie torchlight into the shadowy recesses of the deep slick canyon. Holten could barely make out some slow moving forms walking into the glare of the sparse light. Then he saw them.

The scout's heart began to pound.

From a deep cave at the base of the far wall emerged a couple of sinewy cougars, their flashing yellow eyes reflecting the flickering torchlight, their long white fangs bared as they growled their displeasure at having been disturbed in the middle of the night.

"The cougars keep the canyon clean," said Red Hawk matter-of-factly. "They can eat a whole man in just a short while."

The scout tensed his muscles. His wounds throbbed.

Red Hawk turned and glared at Holten. "Now you get what you deserve!" he said. "You used to be one of us, Tall Bear, but you are a white man. And all whites must die!"

The Oglala subchief nodded at the two muscled warriors who had the scout in a traplike hold. The braves started to drag Holten closer to the edge.

The scout had other ideas.

Summoning all his remaining strength, forgetting the sharp pain from the arrow wounds in his leg and arm, ignoring his throbbing head wound, Holten twisted suddenly and pulled his right arm free.

The warrior on that side stumbled.

The scout took advantage of his surprise move to bring his right knee up into the groin of the other warrior, the knee striking home and causing the lean warrior to gasp suddenly with pain. At the same time Holten slammed his right fist to the brave's jaw, snapping the Indian's head backward and sending him sprawling to the ground.

Then all hell broke loose.

Two warriors lunged for the scout, grabbing his flailing fists and pinning his arms to his sides. The scout struggled, but couldn't break free. Then Holten looked up quickly and saw a stocky muscled warrior walk toward him, a heavy war club grasped in his big hand and an evil scowl spread across his broad glistening face.

The scout kicked out with all his might.

Holten's feet caught the stocky Indian in the chest, the stunned warrior's flashing eyes widening suddenly with surprise. The muscled brave stumbled backward, teetered on the edge of the narrow canyon for a moment, then with the war club still clutched in his hand, fell to the lion-infested graveyard below, his horrible scream echoing in the night air.

The cougars in the canyon came to life.

"Get him!" snapped Red Hawk at his braves. "He is more trouble than he is worth!"

It took five strong warriors to subdue the struggling scout and push him inch by difficult inch to the canyon's edge.

"Good-bye, Tall Bear," said Red Hawk with a smile.

The braves pushed. Holten went flying into the air.

The scout felt himself falling for what seemed like minutes but was only a few seconds. He braced himself for a hard landing, figuring he'd land on the packed ground and be immediately attacked by the cougars.

It didn't happen that way.

Red Hawk's warriors had pushed the scout so hard, he sailed quite a distance from the edge of the steep cliff and landed onto the top branches of a sturdy box elder tree that stood about ten feet off the canyon floor.

The branches had broken his fall.

Holten winced as pointed sticks and branches jabbed into ribs and legs. Quickly he shook off the pain, grasped the limbs for dear life, and got his bearings. The scout glanced cautiously to where the warriors stood gazing down into the canyon.

Holten froze. He played dead for a few moments.

Soon, with the cougars' awful snarling ringing in his ears, the scout glanced carefully up at the top of the canyon and noticed that Red Hawk and his warriors had gone. The scout knew the Oglala subchief could hardly wait to return to camp and celebrate his great coup.

The cougars' growling caught Holten's attention.

The scout scanned the darkened canyon. Only the sparse moonlight illuminated the ravine now, the bone-cluttered ground bathed in a silvery light as Holten regained his senses after the fall. The scout watched five or six ravenous big cats tear and slash the body of the fallen, stocky warrior, the cougars lashing out at each other as they fought for scraps.

Holten didn't have much time.

Then he saw it.

The scout peered with his narrowed blue eyes at the long leather-covered war club that lay in the shadows about six feet from where the big cats ravaged the fallen Sioux warrior. The brave had carried the club into the canyon when he fell; now the scout's mind raced as he formed a plan to use it.

Suddenly the cougars spotted him.

One of the big males ambled over to the box elder tree, sniffed the air for a moment, then glanced up at Holten. The cougar's flashing yellow eyes narrowed and its fangs bared. Suddenly saliva dripped from its gleaming white teeth. An ear-splitting roar filled the Canyon of Death as the big cat threw back its head and growled at the scout.

Within seconds a few of the other cougars pulled their heads away from the dead warrior and glanced up at the box elder tree. Holten, his heart beating wildly, looked down at the blood-smeared feline faces that snarled up at him. The scout knew cougars well; he also knew what would come next. He braced himself for the attack.

145

The big male who had spotted him first leaped suddenly, its powerful legs propelling its lean sinewy frame upward at the cringing scout. As the cougar reached at him with snapping jaws, Holten grasped the strongest branch of the tree, bent his knees, and kicked savagely. His bare feet smashed into the big cat's sensitive snout. The cougar snarled sharply and fell to the canyon floor.

Holten had won the first round.

Soon all the other cats milled around the base of the tree, their flashing eyes fixed on the wounded scout. Holten knew time was running out. He could hold off one cougar, but not five or six.

Then he heard hoofbeats. Holten froze.

The scout glanced carefully above him at the rim of the canyon. He hunkered down in the branches as best he could and watched as several hard-faced warriors dragged three bodies to the edge of the steep cliff.

Holten felt a stab of anxiety.

Even in the sparse moonlight he recognized the corpses.

Bridget, Katie, and Lil. The three whores.

With a mighty heave, the three jabbering Sioux braves tossed the bloodied whores one by one into the Canyon of Death, the slim bodies sailing through the shadowy night air until they landed with sickening thuds on top of the bones on the ground. The cougars jumped slightly, sniffed the air, then growled with renewed vigor at the scent of fresh meat. Holten watched the big cats leap away from the tree and start in on the soft bodies of the whores.

Sudden anger coursed through Holten's veins. Even the throbbing pain of all his assorted wounds couldn't dull the hate he felt at that moment for Liver-Eating Jackson and the deserters. The dirty scalp-hunting killers had started the entire outbreak by looting and burning across the territory. Now, because of the hell they raised, innocent people like Ma Beaudeen and her girls had

146

died needlessly.

Then the scout thought of Rebecca. He grit his teeth.

Maybe the army would do what he would have done if he'd survived Red Hawk's hatred for white men—hunt down the murdering bastards, free Rebecca if she was still alive, and get some revenge.

"Holten!"

The scout froze. A soft voice called from above.

"Tall Bear!" called the voice. "Where are you? Are you still alive?"

Yellow Shell, White Bird's sister!

"I'm here!" shouted Holten in a cracking voice. He cleared his parched throat and tried again. "Over here, Yellow Shell!"

Above the snarling of the feeding cougars, Holten heard the rustle of buckskin clothing and the padding of moccasins. Then he saw Yellow Shell peer cautiously over the rim of the steep cliff.

"Over here!" he shouted.

"I've come to help you," said the slender Indian girl. "I have a rope."

The scout had never been more glad to see anyone in his entire life. "Toss it down," he shouted. "I'll catch it."

Within seconds a braided rawhide rope flew into the air, the last four or five feet landing on the canyon floor near the fallen war club.

"I have a pony," said Yellow Shell. "I'll tie the other end to its neck. Then you can pull yourself out of the canyon."

"I'm ready," said the scout.

As Yellow Shell disappeared to fasten the other end of the coarse braided rope to her pony, the scout swallowed hard. He was ready, but were the cougars ready to let him leave? He had to take a chance. Red Hawk's warriors could come back at any moment to check the canyon and its grisly contents. The scout had to make his move now.

"I'm ready up here," said Yellow Shell.

Holten waved his hand. "Here I come," he said.

He jumped from the box elder tree.

The scout landed with a thump on top of several bleached skeletons and next to the leather-covered war club, his weakened legs giving out as he struck the canyon floor. Holten rolled once and rose next to the rope.

A cougar looked up suddenly from his feast.

Without wasting any more time, the scout grabbed the heavy-headed war club, shot to his feet, and began to climb the rope toward the waiting Indian girl above.

The big cat charged.

Holten pulled on the braided rawhide with all his strength, his weakened arms straining to haul his tortured body out of the deadly ravine. The scout's assorted wounds throbbed as he climbed quickly to a height of ten feet above the bone-cluttered canyon bottom.

The cougar sprang at the climbing scout.

Holten saw the cat out of the corner of his eye, raised the heavy club with his right hand, and slashed downward at the snarling streak of fur and fangs. The heavy stone club smashed into the forequarters of the leaping cat. The big cougar growled sharply with pain and fell backward.

The stunned cougar slammed to the ground.

As Holten continued up the thin braided rope, he watched the enraged cat bare its fangs and crouch its long lethal body for another leap. The scout gripped the war club and waited for the attack he knew would come before he climbed much further up the canyon wall.

Suddenly the cougar leaped against the supposedly flat wall of the narrow Canyon of Death, grabbed onto several tiny footholds carved by nature into the rock, and began to climb toward Holten.

The scout's heart pounded against his ribs.

Now Holten knew how the big cats left the Canyon to

forage for food when the pickings tossed to them by the Sioux became kind of slim. A network of small slits honeycombed the sides of the ravine.

The scout saw the cat approach from his left.

As the snarling cougar reached out with a big paw full of fearsome claws, Holten slashed downward with the leather-covered war club as hard as he could while still swinging from the rawhide rope. The heavy stone weapon thudded into the forehead of the climbing cat and cracked its skull like a hammer cracking a walnut.

The limp cougar fell dead to the Canyon's floor.

The scout dropped the war club and continued his ascent out of the ravine. As he reached the edge of the cliff, Yellow Shell grabbed his tired arms and hauled him the rest of the way. Holten collapsed on the ground next to Yellow Shell's skittish pony.

"Here Tall Bear," said the young Indian woman thrusting a deerskin water bag at the panting scout.

Holten accepted the water and drank deeply, his tortured body absorbing the cool liquid like a dry sponge. The scout finished drinking and sighed. He glanced up at Yellow Shell, his burning eyes locking with hers.

"I owe you my life," said the scout in Lakota.

Yellow Shell looked at the ground. "You owe me nothing."

Holten struggled to his feet, his leg wound throbbing and the raw skin wounds on his upper arms biting him like bee stings. He grasped Yellow Shell's pretty face in his rough hands and kissed her gently on the forehead.

Yellow Shell's flashing brown eyes quickly roamed the scout's tall naked body. Suddenly Holten became fully aware of his nakedness.

"I brought this, too," she said tearing her gaze away from the scout's penis and holding up an Indian loin-cloth.

The scout smiled, then took the skimpy piece of Sioux clothing and slipped it around his groin.

"We must go now," said Yellow Shell softly. "Your horse and weapons are in the camp. I know where they are."

Holten smiled again. "Thank you," he said simply.

Quickly they gathered the rawhide rope, mounted the pony, and galloped off toward the whooping and the celebrating in the renegade camp a mile away.

Now he'd find Jackson after all.

Holten knelt in the tall buffalo grass beside Yellow Shell. Carefully clinging to the deep shadows, he peered through the inky midnight darkness at the yelping and dancing in Red Hawk's renegade camp in front of him. Wildly gyrating warriors, their painted bodies glistening in the sparse firelight, danced and twisted in a wide circle as war drums pounded out an incessant beat beside them.

TUM, tum, tum, tum. TUM, tum, tum, tum.

"Where are my belongings?" whispered the scout.

"Over there," replied Yellow Shell, nodding toward a tall painted teepee with a lone sentry slouching in front of it.

"Whose teepee is that?"

"It belongs to the medicine man."

"And my horse?"

"It is tied to a pole behind the teepee."

TUM, tum, tum, tum. TUM, tum, tum, tum.

Holten glanced one more time at the dancing braves, his heart beginning to pound with anticipation of the chores that lay ahead of him.

"Give me your knife," he said.

Yellow Shell reached to her belt, extracted a long hunting knife she used to skin buffalo and antelope, and handed it to the scout. Holten looked into the young

150

Indian woman's sparkling brown eyes.

"Thank you again, Yellow Shell," he said in Lakota. "I fear bad things will come to you for this."

She shook her head quickly. "Do not think of me, Tall Bear. I did what I thought was right. You were a good friend of White Bird."

TUM, tum, tum, tum. TUM, tum, tum, tum.

Holten reached out and grasped Yellow Shell's soft hand. He squeezed it gently, then slipped into the darkness toward the tall teepee and his belongings.

Padding barefoot through the green grass like an Indian hunter stalking a herd of grazing antelope, the scout edged his way around the renegade camp and ended up behind the tall medicine man's teepee. He watched the Indian camp so intently, he almost bumped into the tethered gelding. His big horse whinnied softly.

"Shh, boy," said the scout. He stroked the gelding's nose gently. "Wait a minute and we'll get the hell out of this place."

He hoped.

The scout continued toward the teepee until he reached the base of the tall conical lodge. His heart pounded against his ribs as fast as the beating drums in the middle of the renegade camp.

He stopped and listened.

Holten gripped the long hunting knife in his right hand and sneaked around the side of the medicine man's lodge. His tired eyes caught a glimpse of the central campfire and the wild celebration that took place there. He kept on moving toward the lone sentry.

TUM, tum, tum, tum. TUM, tum, tum, tum.

The scout peered around the teepee and saw the skinny disinterested renegade guard watching the dancing near the fire. He studied the warrior. Holten noticed the sentry cradled a Spencer repeating rifle in his arms, had a war

151

club hanging at his side, and a knife strapped to his belt.

TUM, tum, tum, tum. TUM, tum, tum, tum.

The scout tensed his muscles and prepared to leap at the sentry like the cougar that had charged him in the Canyon of Death. Holten crouched, gripped the glistening knife, and took a step forward.

Then the drums stopped.

Holten froze.

The scout remained motionless, the only sound he heard was the pounding of his heart against his ribs. Beads of sweat popped out on his forehead. His many wounds started to throb.

Then he heard Red Hawk's voice.

Holten listened as the tall subchief spoke to the gathered warriors and squaws in the middle of the camp. The renegade warrior told the Indians that the next dance would be a social dance, both warriors and squaws participating. The assembled Indians cheered and laughed, some of them calling out the names of lovers.

The scout stood still, his muscles tense and ready. He glanced quickly at the sentry and noticed the skinny warrior had started to laugh at the catcalls and yelping in the camp.

Then the drums began again.

TUM, tum, tum, tum. TUM, tum, tum, tum.

Now was Holten's chance to spring into action.

As quickly as a wildcat striking an unsuspecting jackrabbit, the scout lunged at the smiling sentry. With a strong forearm wrapped around the startled brave's throat, Holten slashed downward with the hunting knife and plunged the long glistening blade into the warrior's heart. The sentry died instantly, his blood spurting onto the dusty ground at his feet. The rifle fell from his hands.

Holten dragged the skinny body around to the back of the medicine man's lodge. Then the scout stopped and

152

listened to see if his sudden attack had been detected.

TUM, tum, tum, tum. TUM, tum, tum, tum.

Laughter and strident catcalls rose from the wild dancing throng in the middle of the renegade camp.

Satisfied that nobody had noticed him, Holten took a deep breath and returned carefully to the front of the tall teepee. He quickly kicked the dirt over the sentry's spilled blood. Then picking up the sentry's Spencer repeating rifle, the scout glanced around once and slipped into the medicine man's lodge. Holten pushed back the teepee flap and stepped into the dimly lit lodge.

The scout froze in his tracks.

A wizened old squaw, probably in her seventies, turned sharply at the sudden intrusion, her washed-out brown eyes widening suddenly as she recognized the scout. She opened her mouth to scream.

The old squaw never said a word.

Quickly Holten lashed out with the butt of the sentry's rifle and tapped the old woman gently on the head. The squaw's face slackened suddenly, her scream cut off by the knock on her head. Her eyes rolled toward the heavens just before she pitched over onto the thick buffalo robes on the teepee's floor.

Spotting his clothes and weapons immediately, the scout stepped quickly to the back of the teepee and started to dress. His senses remained alert for trouble and his ears strained to pick up any ominous sounds. Holten knew that if the renegades captured him again, they'd forget about any torture ceremonies. Death would be short and sweet.

The scout's upper arms ached as he pulled on his buckskin clothing, the hundreds of tiny cuts stinging like little pinpricks as his shirt passed over them. His arrow wounds still throbbed and his bruised head pounded when he bent over to grab his belongings. Holten touched his

153

eyebrows and eyelids once, the raw hairless skin burning with his gentle probe. His upper lip ached, too, where his long drooping moustache had once been.

As Holten finished dressing and fastened his .44 and his Bowie knife to his belt, he took a deep breath of relief. He knew he was lucky to leave Red Hawk's camp alive. The painful cuts and bruises would heal in time, but because of Liver-Eating Jackson and the deserters, he'd almost lost his life.

Then he heard it. Voices from outside the lodge.

"Two Elk?" called a brave just outside the teepee flap.

Holten tensed his muscles. He remained motionless.

"Two Elk?" repeated the brave. "Where are you? Little Dove is looking for you. She wants your body tonight."

The brave laughed, as did another nearby.

The scout had no choice. He muffled his voice and spoke.

"I'm in here," said Holten in Lakota. "I'm checking the white man's things. I like this rifle."

"Red Hawk will have your balls if you touch it," warned one of the braves.

Holten laughed. "That would spoil things with Little Dove."

The braves laughed.

"Tell Little Dove I will come soon," said the scout. "I finish here in a little while."

"She's horny as hell," said one of the braves, "but I'll tell her."

"Tell her I'm getting it big and hard for her," said Holten.

The braves roared with laughter. Then they left.

Holten sighed with relief.

The scout checked his pistol, adjusted the Bowie knife on his belt, and grabbed his Winchester .44-40. Peering carefully out of the medicine man's teepee, Holten slipped from the lodge and padded quietly up to the gelding.

154

"Now we're ready big fella," he whispered.

The scout swung his long tortured frame onto the strong back of his horse, clucked to the gelding, and trotted out onto the dark Dakota plains. Galloping into the night, Holten left the whooping and dancing behind and began to think about Liver-Eating Jackson.

And Rebecca Ridgeway.

CHAPTER TWELVE

The scout winced with pain.

Holten passed a moistened cloth over the wounds on his upper arms, the cool mountain water stinging the raw flesh as it cleansed the many cuts made by Red Hawk and his fellow chiefs. As the first warm rays of the rising sun slanted across the prairie, the scout paused for a couple of hours in a small clearing hidden from the main trail by tall, lush pine trees. He needed to get his bearings and to cleanse his wounds.

Holten felt like he'd just escaped from a nightmare.

Trying hard to forget the ordeal in the renegade camp, Holten concentrated on Liver-Eating Jackson and the deserters. Pulling on his clothes again, wincing slightly at the sudden contact with the raw flesh on his upper arms, the scout tried to reconstruct the facts about the killers as he remembered them.

The deserters had burned and looted the major ranches in the Dakota Territory, had provoked the treaty-keeping Oglala Sioux into a renegade uprising, and had kidnapped the widow Rebecca Ridgeway. The last thought sent a wave of renewed anger through Holten's body.

The scout strode to the gelding and hauled himself into the saddle. At Fort Rawlins, Maj. Nathan Phillips had told Holten to leave the punishment of the deserters to the army. But the major hadn't counted on kidnapping. The scout clucked to his big horse and trotted out of the clearing toward the wide grassy plains near Rebecca Ridgeway's burned-out ranch. Holten had done his best trying to lead settlers out of the ruckus. Now he renewed his mission of mercy.

The scout hoped Rebecca was still alive.

Holten urged the gelding into a full gallop across the brightening prairie, the big horse's well rested legs churning up the rich soil as it propelled the scout closer to Jackson and the deserters. Holten knew Red Hawk would discover that the scout had done the impossible and had escaped from the Canyon of Death. In fact, the scout figured the renegade chief had already sent his warriors out to track the escaped prisoner.

And kill him.

The scout rode hard for about an hour, then reined in the gelding. He dismounted and rested on a grassy ridge overlooking the trail he'd traveled. Holten peered through the early morning sunshine across the parched prairie and studied the trail that led from Red Hawk's camp.

Then he saw them.

Holten squinted and watched the small cloud of dust back on the narrow trail develop suddenly into four mounted warriors pushing hard in his direction.

The scout's pulse quickened.

Holten had to find Rebecca Ridgeway, but he knew Red Hawk's braves wouldn't leave him alone until they caught him and killed him. The scout had to take some kind of action.

He decided to set a trap.

Moving quickly, Holten mounted the gelding and galloped down into the small valley below. The scout reached a flat grassy clearing and reined in his snorting horse. He leaped from the gelding and began to prepare his trap.

Holten quickly built a huge roaring fire, unsaddled his horse, and took his bedroll to a spot next to the crackling flames. Stuffing grass and branches under the woolen blanket, the scout then took his wide-brimmed hat and

157

placed it on top of the bedroll near the fire. He stepped back to examine his work. If he didn't know better, Holten would have guessed that a tired plainsman lay sleeping away his troubles.

Then the scout tethered the gelding to a nearby tree and grabbed his Winchester from its sheath. Glancing quickly at the surrounding brush, Holten picked a good spot to wait for the tracking renegades and sprinted toward a clump of scraggly plum bushes.

The scout entered the clawing underbrush and hunkered down to wait for the warriors he knew would come soon. With the Winchester cradled in his arms and his sharpened senses working keenly, Holten remained as motionless as a coyote waiting for a prairie dog to poke its head out of its burrow hole.

He didn't have to wait long.

Holten glanced cautiously to his right and saw a sudden flash of movement. An inexperienced frontiersman might have missed it, but the scout had sneaked up on many enemies during his time with the Sioux; he recognized a stalking warrior when he saw one. He knew the jiggling branch and the sudden flight of a sparrow meant only one thing.

Then he spotted another. And another.

The fourth brave, Holten knew, remained with the ponies somewhere over the next ridge. It was a classic stalk, the three warriors fanning out around the clearing and the unsuspecting plainsman below.

As the braves sneaked closer to Holten's campsite, the scout shouldered his Winchester and readied his trigger finger. He'd wait for the right moment, then nail all the renegades in a matter of seconds.

Before they nailed him.

Finally, as tiny rivulets of perspiration ran down his leathery face, Holten sighted his rifle at a bold renegade who left the cover of the bushes and padded toward the sleeping frontiersman on the ground. The long-bladed hunting knife the scowling, muscular brave held in his hand glistened in the bright morning sunshine.

The scout readied his rifle.

Suddenly the warrior sprinted the final few yards toward Holten's blanket, his broad dark face set with determination, a slight smile on his lips at the ease with which he would make his kill. At the same time, the other two warriors burst from the bushes, long war clubs clutched in their hands. The gelding whinnied sharply at the sudden motion.

Holten squeezed the trigger.

Just as the first renegade let loose with a strident war cry and slashed his blade down into the grass-filled blanket, the Winchester roared. The hot slug slammed into the broad muscled chest of the brave with the knife, sending the warrior backwards into the air and onto the dusty ground, a widening circle of blood spreading across his brown-skinned chest.

The other Indians froze. Holten levered and fired.

Before the two remaining renegades had a chance to react, screaming bullets from the Winchester tore into their chests, the hot lead smashing their hearts to pulp and ripping all the way through their sinewy bodies. The Indians jumped backward from the impact and fell dead in the clearing.

It was over in a matter of seconds.

The gunshots echoed for a few long moments.

Holten kept low in the bushes and turned quickly toward the far ridge. He knew what would happen next. With his heart pounding in anticipation, the scout shouldered his Winchester one more time and waited.

The renegade with the ponies appeared suddenly on the hill. The puzzled warrior peered at the grassy clearing and

159

the bodies in the dust. It was the last thing he ever saw.

Holten's rifle spat fire.

Up on the ridge, the remaining warrior jerked from his pony like someone had hauled him off with a rope. The dead brave slammed to the rocky ridge, the scout's bullet lodged in his chest.

The scout waited and listened. He wanted to be sure.

Satisfied no more Sioux renegades lurked in the shadows, Holten rose slowly from his hiding place and ambled down toward the small clearing. The scout gathered his belongings and saddled the skittish gelding. With a final glance at the crumpled bodies in the dust, Holten clucked to his big horse and headed toward Rebecca's burned out ranch.

He had some tracking to do.

The lone soldier pushed his horse hard.

Holten sat atop the gelding in a stand of thirsty cottonwoods and watched the galloping deserter race across the dusty plains toward the hills beyond. Then the scout spurred his mount and followed the unsuspecting soldier toward, he hoped, Liver-Eating Jackson, Paco Riley, and Rebecca Ridgeway.

He'd been waiting in the trees for an hour.

After leaving the bloodied bodies of Red Hawk's renegades, the scout had galloped for a couple of hours until he reached the wide green valley where the three ranches had been torched by the marauding deserters. Remembering what the dying soldier at the small town of Buffalo Creek had said about the deserters using advance scouts to find possible settlers to rob and kill, Holten then set out to check the main trails. He hoped to find a deserter scout heading back with some hot news item.

Then he spotted the galloping soldier.

As the merciless midday sun beat down upon his weary

160

body, the scout kept a respectable distance and trailed the galloping soldier up into the purple hills. After an hour of hard riding, the deserter reined in his mount to a trot. Finally, the soldier led the scout up a narrow wooded trail to a large log cabin nestled among some tall stately pine trees. The scout halted in a copse of pines, dismounted, and tethered the gelding to a tall tree.

Unsheathing his Winchester, the scout then strode briskly toward the clearing below and the large log cabin. Grasping his powerful rifle firmly as he tramped through pine needles and under towering trees, Holten thought about Rebecca Ridgeway. The only reason he could think of why the deserters would want to keep her alive was for the big ransom she'd bring from her family back East. For that reason, the scout figured she was alive and relatively well. And if she was alive, Holten would bet anything she was being kept in the log cabin just ahead.

Holten stopped suddenly behind a row of blooming rose bushes that overlooked the cabin. He peered through the thorny branches and studied the activity below. Almost immediately he saw a flurry of action near the cabin.

As the scout watched from behind the rose bushes, the cabin door flew open and a steady stream of deserters poured out into the clearing. Holten saw the last of the soldiers leave the cabin, and watched two scowling frontiersmen follow them.

Liver-Eating Jackson and Paco Riley.

Holten's insides constricted. He could almost taste his fury.

Then while the scout watched from above, the six remaining deserters began to transform themselves into Sioux warriors. Holten watched in amazement as the soldiers slipped into Indian buckskin, smeared on yellow war paint, and fixed long flowing Indian scalps to their

161

heads. Even Liver-Eating Jackson turned himself into an Indian. Then, after picking up sturdy Sioux bows and heavy-headed war clubs, the newly-outfitted Sioux war party walked over to a small corral and mounted skittish Indian ponies.

As the deserters pulled themselves onto the bare backs of their snorting ponies, Holten strained his ears to pick up the conversation. The scout heard the harsh voice of Liver-Eating Jackson float up to the rose bushes.

"We'll hit them settlers," he said to Paco Riley, the only gang member not dressed in Indian garb, "then be back here to pick up the girl."

Holten's heart fluttered. Rebecca.

"How long you fixin' to be gone?" boomed big Paco Riley.

"About an hour. Unless we find us some women, too."

A chorus of laughter filled the tiny clearing.

"I'll take good care of missy," roared deep-voiced Paco.

"I bet you will!" shouted a deserter.

"Don't crush the girl to death!" yelled another.

Again, a chorus of evil laughter filled the clearing.

Holten felt a wave of anger mixed with anxiety spread through his chest. They might be holding Rebecca for ransom, he thought, but that wouldn't stop them from raping her. The scout's grip tightened on his Winchester at the thought.

A sudden flash of movement caught Holten's eye.

He glanced quickly at the planked door of the large log cabin and watched Rebecca Ridgeway, her new orange and white chiffon dress in tatters and her face smeared with dirt, bolt away from her captors.

"There goes your lady friend, Riley," shouted a soldier.

"Work for your fuck this time!" said another laughing.

Then as the scout watched with mounting anger, Liver-Eating Jackson kicked his pony in the ribs and galloped

162

after the stumbling blonde widow. Without breaking stride, the snake-eyed frontiersman raced past Rebecca and plucked the blonde off the ground. Jackson brought the kicking widow back to where giant Paco Riley stood chuckling and dropped her unceremoniously on the ground near the front door.

"Now stay put!" snarled Liver-Eating Jackson.

Paco Riley yanked the wide-eyed Rebecca to her feet. "I'll watch the little slut!" he boomed.

"Let me go!" yelled the young widow.

The deserters roared with laughter once again.

"Have fun!" said Liver-Eating Jackson.

Then with a swift kick to his pony's flanks, Jackson galloped out of the clearing and led the screaming deserters-turned-Indians through the tall pines and toward the main settler trails in the valley beyond.

Holten stiffened. He knew what he had to do.

As the scout watched, massive Paco Riley shoved the now sobbing widow through the doorway of the large log cabin and slammed the door. The way was clear for Holten to make his move.

The scout stood carefully and began his slow descent down the gentle slope that led to the cabin below. With his Winchester .44-40 gripped in his hands and his muscles tensed for action, Holten padded cautiously across the pine needle covered ground toward the deserters' forest hideout.

As he neared the cabin, Holten's mind drifted to Paco Riley and the big man's evil reputation. The massive 300-pound killer stood as tall and wide as a small grizzly bear, his thick powerful arms strong enough to break the back of a man unlucky to get caught in their traplike grip. The mammoth frontiersman was also a master knife fighter. His blinding speed with a blade had fooled many surprised opponents who, after seeing the giant mound

163

of flesh, took it for granted that Paco was slow and cumbersome. The startled opponents often paid for the mistake with their lives. Paco Riley was, indeed, similar to a grizzly in many ways—mean, tough, and unpredictable.

The scout reached the small corral and padded quickly past a half dozen disinterested army horses. Then gripping his rifle tightly, he slipped up to the rough outside wall of the log cabin. Holten pressed his back against the rough-hewn logs and listened.

What he heard turned his stomach.

Paco Riley's deep baritone voice boomed through a nearby open window. Rebecca's thin, frightened voice cut through the air, too.

"Take it in your mouth now," snapped Riley.

"I can't!" screeched Rebecca.

Then came the sickening slap of flesh against flesh. Holten heard Rebecca cry out in pain.

"Do it or I'll cut you to pieces, you slut!"

Then silence.

Quickly the scout stepped over to the small window in the middle of the outside wall. With his Winchester ready for action, Holten peered into the large log cabin at the desperate scene within.

His face slackened. His heart skipped a beat.

The scout saw big Paco Riley standing in the middle of the one building, his pants down to his knees as he moaned with sexual pleasure. On her knees in front of him, the big killer's huge elongated penis in her pretty mouth, was Rebecca Ridgeway, her supple lips sliding up and down the killer's big cock.

Holten boiled with anger.

Then the scout realized he'd caught the mammoth killer with his guard down, as well as his pants. Knowing a rifle shot into the cabin might kill Rebecca if she moved the wrong way, Holten unsheathed his ten-inch-long Bowie

164

knife and strode briskly to the cabin's front door.

Holten tensed himself like a bull ready to charge.

Suddenly the scout lowered his shoulder and smashed into the planked door. The flimsy slab flew from its hinges in a sudden shower of splinters. Holten burst into the cabin, regained his balance, and whirled to face the startled frontiersman.

Rebecca Ridgeway screamed. Paco went for his knife.

"Holten!" shouted the widow in a frayed voice.

"Stay out of the way!" yelled the scout.

Quickly, Paco Riley hauled up his pants and stood ready to fight the poised scout. The 300-pound killer smiled, a sudden gleam in his evil eyes.

"Yup, missy," he said in a deep voice. "Get out of the way. We'll take up where we left off after I get rid of this Injun lover!"

Holten laughed. "Long time no see," said the scout.

"When I get through with you," boomed Paco Riley, "you'll wish you had never laid eyes on me."

"Holten!" screamed the sobbing blonde widow.

"Stay put!" said Holten. "Everything will be all right."

Paco Riley roared with laughter. "We'll see," he said.

Then with a sudden slash of his glistening hunting knife, the 300-pound murderer rushed the scout. Holten jerked backward. The killer's blade whooshed just inches from the scout's weathered face.

"Losing your touch, Paco?"

The massive frontiersman faced the scout again, his long knife held flat and ready in his giant ham-sized hands, his thick grizzly bear arms outstretched and ready to strike again.

The scout and the giant killer circled warily inside the large log cabin. Each watched the other's flashing eyes. Each waited for the other to commit a fatal error.

Suddenly Paco Riley charged again. This time his long

razor-sharp blade struck Holten's buckskin sleeve and tore through the material as though it was made of tissue paper. At the same time, Holten lashed out with his Bowie knife. The fearsome blade caught Paco's leather belt and sliced neatly through it. The big killer's pants fell to his ankles.

Turning sharply, his pants twisted around his feet, Paco Riley suddenly lost his balance. The mammoth killer's broad gleaming face slackened and his big eyes widened with sudden surprise as he started to fall to the cabin floor.

The scout saw his opportunity.

With a lightning thrust of his Bowie knife, Holten jabbed the shining blade into Paco Riley's bloated belly. The big knife buried itself to the hilt in mounds of blubber.

Paco grunted. But that's all.

The scout withdrew the long blade and stabbed again, the big knife plunging once again into Paco Riley's overstuffed belly. The big frontiersman fell to the floor with a resounding crash. Paco roared with pain.

"You bastard!" he growled.

Riley lay struggling on the cabin floor like a roped steer, his pants around his ankles and blood spurting from his wounds. Holten crouched and held his Bowie knife. He waited for the right moment.

It came almost immediately.

Paco Riley made a desperate lunge at the scout's legs. With the quickness of a startled animal, Holten side-stepped the big killer's forearms and stood ready to attack once again. The scout saw that Riley's futile grab at his legs left his big broad chest unprotected; Paco now lay sprawled on the floor like a big bull waiting for the coup de grâce.

Holten struck with the speed of a matador.

The scout jabbed quickly with his ten-inch blade and plunged the knife into Paco Riley's heart. Holten drove the fearsome blade through flesh and muscle all the way to the hilt, the razor-sharp cutting edge slicing neatly through the big frontiersman's heart and killing him almost instantly.

Paco Riley's eyes widened. Then he died on the floor. The scout stood panting.

CHAPTER THIRTEEN

Rebecca Ridgeway ran into Holten's arms.

"Oh Holten!" she said sobbing.

The scout dropped his knife and enveloped the frightened blonde in his arms. "It's all right now," said Holten. She trembled in his strong embrace.

"It was so terrible!"

"It's over with."

Rebecca wiped away her tears with her hand. Then she looked down at Paco Riley's bloody body and shivered.

The widow made a distasteful face. "Let's get out of this cabin," said Rebecca in a quavering voice.

Holten escorted the sobbing blonde widow out of the large log cabin into the warm afternoon sunshine. He led her toward the tall pine trees where the gelding stood pawing the ground. Emotionally exhausted, they sank onto a blanket of brown pine needles.

Rebecca sighed. "That's much better," she said.

"You've been through a lot."

Rebecca nodded her pretty head slowly. "They burned my ranch and everything in it."

"I know," replied Holten. "And lots of others, too."

She sniffled. "Why?"

"Gold," he replied simply.

Puzzled at his answer, Rebecca looked at Holten. Then she gasped loudly.

"Oh!" she said, her delicate hand going to her mouth.

"What's the matter?" asked the concerned scout.

"Your eyebrows! And your lashes, too!"

Holten chuckled through his pain. All his wounds still throbbed. Especially the stinglike flesh wounds on his upper arms.

"What happened?" asked Rebecca, her long fingers gently touching his facial wounds. Holten flinched.

"It's a long story," said the scout.

Then as they sat in the shade of the tall dark pine tree, Holten told Rebecca everything that had happened to him from the time he last saw her in the Fort Rawlins general store to the knife fight with Paco Riley. All during his story Rebecca kept her hands over her mouth, her big blue eyes widening when the scout related the gory details of the torture session in Red Hawk's camp. When Holten finished they just sat in silence for a long moment.

"That's terrible," said Rebecca finally.

The scout nodded. "But I made it," he said. "And I got you back from those dirty bastards. That's what counts."

The blonde widow smiled. "You don't know how much I've missed you, Holten," she purred suddenly, reaching up to the scout's leathery face with her long tapered fingers. "I thought for a moment I might never see you again."

Holten thought quickly about his experiences in Red Hawk's camp and the Canyon of Death, a sudden wave of anxiety spreading through his chest as vivid memories of burning flesh and snarling cougars flashed in his head.

"There was a moment when I didn't give much for my chances, either," he said.

Their eyes locked suddenly. Holten felt a twinge in his loins.

"Please?" asked Rebecca softly. She slid her long fingers down the scout's shirt front and slipped them inside his pants where they gently massaged his suddenly enlarged cock.

Holten flinched again.

He took the luscious blonde's pretty face in his rough

hands and kissed her gently on the lips.

"You kept me alive," he told her.

Rebecca's eyebrows arched. "Me?"

"All during the torture in the Sioux camp," he explained, "I forced the pain out of my mind by thinking about you."

Her blue eyes twinkled with mischief. "What part of me?" she asked playfully.

The scout's big hands started to roam her shapely figure, starting with the firm round breasts. "Maybe it would be better if I showed you," answered Holten with a smile.

The scout's penis throbbed.

"Please!" said Rebecca in a hoarse whisper, her sparkling blue eyes pleading with Holten.

A wide grin cracked the scout's weathered face. "You know you don't have to ask," he said.

Then with the urgency of two teenage lovers having sex for the first time, they tore off their clothes and lay naked beneath the towering pine trees. Rebecca Ridgeway glanced at Holten's huge iron-hard cock.

"Oh my God!" she gasped, the scout noticing the admiration in her voice.

"It's yours," he said with a smile.

They attacked each other like sexual predators.

Holten reached out and gently stroked Rebecca's big soft breasts, his lean fingers kneading each of them, flicking the taut, hard nipples several times, causing the blonde widow to close her big blue eyes and toss her head backward with pleasure. A deep animal groan escaped from Rebecca's supple lips and her skin rippled with pleasure at the scout's firm yet gentle touch.

"Oooooo," moaned the writhing blonde as Holten's big rough hands slid down her flat stomach toward the waxy triangular patch of pubic hair at her crotch.

The scout's fingers dallied in the warm jungle of her

170

kinky hair and probed deeper into the wet and wonderful bush, his finger tips stroking the silky folds of sensitive flesh just inside the opening of Rebecca Ridgeway's aroused vagina. Holten slid his long forefinger in and out of the panting blonde woman's slippery channel, his finger probing deeper with each thrust, sending Rebecca into spasms of pure sexual ecstasy.

"Oh Holten!" she breathed. "Nobody can do it like you!"

Quickly the scout removed his dripping finger from her vagina and slid his rough hands around Rebecca's slim waist and down to her firm round buttocks, his big hands cupping them like a couple of ripe melons, and squeezed gently.

Rebecca's buttocks tightened at his touch.

Suddenly Holten shot his forefinger between her buttocks, the long finger darting toward her vagina from behind, striking the dripping target and the silky folds of flesh within.

"Oh my God!" said Rebecca in a hoarse whisper.

Just as suddenly, Rebecca went to the attack, her long delicate fingers grasping Holten's pulsating shaft and stroking it slowly at first, then more rapidly until her small hand was just a blur of motion as it raced up and down his incredibly long and iron-hard cock.

"Christ!" breathed the scout.

Quickly the two panting lovers fell to the thick carpet of grass and brown pine needles, Rebecca's hands fondling the scout's balls and stroking his penis as they slumped to the ground. Holten's arms enveloped the worked-up widow, his long fingers stroking her buttocks as she worked on his cock. The soft warmth of her flesh against his was almost overwhelming.

Without warning Rebecca pulled the scout's long penis against her dripping vagina and began to rub its sensitive tip in the warm wet folds of flesh at the head of the slippery

171

channel that led deep within her, the scout moaning at the sudden contact.

"Jesus!" he gasped.

"Do it!" pleaded Rebecca.

Suddenly Holten came down on the writhing blonde bombshell with all his weight, his hardened shaft slicing through her waxy pubic hair and ramming deep inside her wet and wonderful channel.

Rebecca arched her back to meet him.

The scout thrust his penis to the hilt inside of her, causing the young shapely widow to gasp suddenly, her big blue eyes rolling with pure ecstasy as Holten rammed his cock into her with a fervor he'd never felt before. All the frustration of the hellish nightmare at Red Hawk's camp and the Canyon of Death came forth in a savage animallike sexual display by the scout, his penis thrusting in and out, in and out until Rebecca nearly begged for mercy.

"Now!" breathed the young widow. "Please!"

"I'm coming!" said Holten panting.

In a sudden explosion of sexual release, the scout thrust into her one final time as he came in a hot milky flood that filled the writhing blonde to the brim.

"Oooooo!" moaned Rebecca as she arched to meet him.

They pressed together for a long moment, Holten draining himself of all his pent-up passion and Rebecca urging him on while meeting him and satisfying her own savage sexual desire.

They slumped to the ground exhausted.

Then they lay still for several beautiful minutes, Holten's long lean frame stretched along Rebecca's soft supple body, the scout's heart beating as fast as the noisy woodpecker in a nearby tree. He'd nearly forgotten the pain from his assorted wounds.

Finally the sinewy widow slid out from beneath the scout's long sweat-soaked body and glanced into his steely eyes, her sparkling blue eyes searching the scout's leathery face.

"I think I love you, Holten," she said softly.

The scout smiled. He kissed her on the lips, a long, lingering passionate kiss that sent shivers through his spine.

Then Holten heard it. He froze.

"What?" asked a startled Rebecca Ridgeway.

"I don't rightly know," said the scout. "Shhh."

The scout heard it again. But it was too late.

He shot to his feet.

"Very touching," said Liver-Eating Jackson.

Holten whirled to face the voice that came out of the pine trees behind him. Rebecca gasped, her slender arms going quickly to her billowy breasts.

"Sorry to spoil your fun, scout," snapped Jackson.

Holten stood motionless, and naked, beneath a tall pine tree, his brain working feverishly and his muscles tensed for action. The scout studied the snake-eyed frontiersman who sat sneering at him from atop a snorting Sioux pony ten feet away, a bearded deserter beside him on another stolen Indian mount. Both killers had ugly Spencer repeating rifles aimed at the scout's head. Holten looked for a way out.

He knew he didn't have a chance.

Liver-Eating Jackson cackled. "Well, missy," he said with a big smile. "Looks like your lover boy got himself some serious trouble, don't it."

"Leave us alone!" pleaded Rebecca in a strained voice.

Jackson's snakelike eyes roamed the widow's naked body, lingering for a moment on the glistening bush of pubic hair where her legs came together, the kinky patch of hair still dripping with Holten's juices.

Rebecca squirmed under his evil gaze.

"Don't touch the woman," said Holten. "She ain't done nothin' to harm you or your gang of killers."

Jackson squeezed the trigger of his Spencer, the big gun roaring in the small confines of the tree-shaded clearing, a hot slug kicking up dust just inches from Holten's feet.

Jackson's voice hardened. "You ain't in no position to give orders, mister," he snapped.

The shot echoed through the hills.

"At least let her get dressed."

"I kinda like her the way she is," said Jackson. He cackled again, his evil laugh roaring through the pines. Then Liver-Eating Jackson dismounted and strode forward toward the pair of naked lovers, his big repeater still fixed on Holten's head as he walked.

The scout's nerves tingled. His steely blue eyes darted from the wiry snake-eyed frontiersman on the ground to the hard-faced bearded deserter still atop the Sioux pony. Holten knew he had to make a move soon. Jackson planned to kill him, and the longer the scout waited the more chance the yellow-eyed bastard had to get set and carry out his plans.

"We was all set to head down into the valley," said Jackson as he ambled up to Rebecca Ridgeway. "Then I spied your tracks leadin' up toward the cabin. Since we ain't had no visitors the last two weeks, I decided to track ya and see what in hell you was up to."

Liver-Eating Jackson stopped at a spot in the pine needle-covered clearing where the blonde widow sat covering her exposed breasts. He glanced over at the scout with slitted eyes.

"And then we found Paco in the cabin," he grated.

Holten shrugged. "Just a slight misunderstanding."

"Seems it was a slight misunderstanding a couple of years ago when ya put this lead into my shoulder, too," said Jackson, flexing his shoulder as he spoke. "Bothers the hell out of me."

"You had it comin'," replied the scout.

Jackson's face darkened. "Now *you* got it comin'!"

he snapped.

The scout froze. He tensed himself for action.

Then while Holten stood and watched in horror, Liver-Eating Jackson placed his rifle on the ground, then reached down and grabbed Rebecca Ridgeway's big soft breasts with both hands and yanked her to her feet. The lean blonde widow shrieked with sudden pain.

Jackson cackled. "Nice tits!" he said. "Real nice."

"You bastard!" snapped Holten.

The scout took a sudden step toward Liver-Eating Jackson and Rebecca, his steely blue eyes flashing with hatred. The scout never made a second step. The deserter atop the stolen Indian pony squeezed the trigger of his big Spencer repeater, a searing slug slamming into the pine needles just a foot from Holten's bare feet. The horses whinnied. The scout froze.

Once again Jackson cackled. "You look kinda helpless, Holten," he said with a harsh laugh. "Standin' there bare ass naked with your weapons layin' next to your big-titted widow friend."

The scout grit his teeth. It looked bad.

Suddenly Holten watched as Jackson bent down and plucked his Spencer rifle off the pine needle ground cover with one arm, his other still wrapped around Rebecca's slim waist. The evil-eyed frontiersman raised the deadly repeater and sighted it at Holten's head.

"I got me an old score to settle," said Liver-Eating Jackson. "Never thought it would be so easy."

Holten swallowed hard. He felt helpless.

Then he saw it.

Out of the corner of his eye, the scout noticed the sudden swaying of a rosebush branch. It didn't move much, but enough to catch Holten's experienced eye. Then Holten saw the frightened flight of a couple of sparrows from a nearby pine tree. The busy woodpecker stopped its noisy pecking in the tall pine tree overhead. Holten read the

175

signs and knew what they all meant.

Indians lurked in the shadows.

Like Jackson, Red Hawk's warriors must have picked up his trail and tracked him to the cabin. And they were brought to the exact location by Jackson's and the bearded deserter's rifle shots. Trouble was, thought the scout, the painted braves who stalked silently in the bushes wanted his scalp not Jackson's. But one crisis at a time he told himself. Maybe he could use the dozen or so warriors to his advantage.

After all, he was running out of time.

Holten smiled. "Looks like ya got me, Jackson," he said, his steely eyes darting to the surrounding bushes as he spoke.

Jackson cocked his rifle. Rebecca gasped.

"Kinda looks that way, don't it scout," he said with an evil smile. "I waited two long years for this. Now I'm gonna do it."

"No!" shouted Rebecca Ridgeway.

With a sudden flash of movement the sinewy blonde reached out at the killer's pants and grasped Liver-Eating Jackson's crotch. She squeezed his balls as hard as her little hand could squeeze.

Jackson's snakelike eyes widened. He roared with pain.

Holten took advantage of the sudden flurry of action and started forward after the moaning snake-eyed killer, his lean muscled frame ready for action.

Then it happened.

The scout stopped in his tracks as he heard the whistle of an arrow through the sweltering afternoon air, followed immediately by the dull thud as the deadly shaft struck home in the chest of the bearded deserter atop his pony.

The soldier screamed and fell to the ground.

Then all hell broke loose as screaming Sioux renegades burst from the surrounding underbrush and charged the scout in the clearing, long fearsome war clubs grasped in

176

their hands and determined looks of revenge etched on their broad dark faces.

Rebecca screamed. Liver-Eating Jackson began to shoot.

Holten whirled to face several charging braves, his naked body crouched and ready to grapple with the whooping renegades who had only one thing on their minds.

Get Holten's scalp for Red Hawk.

Just as another arrow zipped past his head, the lean scout ducked quickly to avoid the deadly whoosh of a leather-covered war club that missed his skull by inches. Holten then grabbed the warrior with the club by his forearm, turned the startled Indian around sharply, and brought the brave's arm down across his knee with a resounding crack. The warrior yelped with pain as he slumped to the ground with a broken arm.

A shot echoed in the clearing. Holten turned sharply.

The scout watched Liver-Eating Jackson, his evil face still etched with pain from Rebecca's sudden attack on his groin, fire his Spencer rifle again, this time pointblank into the dark painted face of a charging Sioux warrior. The Indian's head exploded in a bloody red mist.

"Holten!" yelled Rebecca in a strained voice.

The scout spotted the naked blonde widow at Jackson's feet, her pretty face a sudden mask of fear as Indians leaped into the clearing all around her.

Holten started forward. He never made it.

Suddenly two wiry braves rammed into the scout's tall naked body, the impact sending all three men to the pine needle covered ground. Holten quickly regained his footing, the wounds on his upper arms starting to bleed once again as he did so. The scout lashed out with his foot and kicked one of the warriors in the face, the Indian's war club flying from his hands. The stunned brave slumped back onto the pine needles.

177

Holten grabbed the fallen war club, pivoted quickly, and with a solid swipe of the fearsome weapon struck the other wiry brave on the side of the head. The warrior grunted as the blow cracked his skull, his flashing eyes suddenly wide with astonishment. The brave slumped to the ground like a sack of potatoes.

The scout heard a horse whinny sharply.

Holten whirled and glanced across the small pine-tree-shaded clearing. His pulse quickened at what he saw. The scout watched Liver-Eating Jackson shoot rapid-fire at the nearby warriors from atop his prancing Indian pony, the naked squirming Rebecca Ridgeway lying on her belly across the horse's wide back.

"Rebecca!" shouted the scout.

Jackson levered and fired many times, his Spencer repeater smoking as Indians dropped like quail in the clearing. Holten stood stunned beside the fallen warriors, his mind working rapidly. Suddenly he saw his chance to escape.

The scout bolted toward the woods.

Holten pumped his long legs and sprinted away from the shots in the clearing. As the scout crashed through clawing rosebushes and grabbing pine branches, he knew he'd have to escape from both the renegades and Liver-Eating Jackson if he was to have any chance of rescuing Rebecca later on. He raced through the pine trees.

About a hundred yards from the clearing, the scout stopped and looked back at the scene he'd left behind. Holten's chest heaved and his breath came in uneven gasps. His many wounds throbbed as he peered through the shadows and tried to figure out what had happened behind him.

Holten's heart leapt to his throat.

As the scout watched helplessly, Liver-Eating Jackson galloped away from the pine tree clearing, the wide-eyed widow, Rebecca Ridgeway, sprawled across the broad back of the killer's pony. Rebecca's naked white body gleamed in the late afternoon sun as the evil frontiersman raced into the surrounding tree-covered hills.

Suddenly an arrow whistled through the air.

Then another and another.

The scout glanced at the sudden flurry of activity in the clearing. He felt a stab of panic shoot through his chest. Half a dozen screaming Sioux warriors had spotted him and raced through the woods in his direction.

Holten turned and began to run again.

CHAPTER FOURTEEN

"He couldn't have gone too far," said a hard-faced renegade warrior in Lakota.

"We already searched the woods."

"Search them again."

"Ahhh," complained another brave. "I think this white scout is bad medicine."

"Red Hawk wants his scalp. Find him!"

"All right," replied a brave. "But save his belongings until we get back. I want a chance at that horse."

"The gelding goes to Red Hawk."

"Then save that knife. I at least have a chance for that!"

"Find Tall Bear or none of us will be able to go home!"

The scout's heart pounded against his ribs.

Holten crouched inside a hollowed-out log and watched the lean painted warriors in front of him fan out into the woods. The scout had been lucky to find the big log just as the screaming renegades had closed in on him. Now he remained motionless, breathing as quietly as possible, while the hard-faced warriors tried to find him.

The scout knew he had to move again. The secret of avoiding a search and destroy war party, he'd learned long ago, was to keep moving from one hiding place to another. Keep one step ahead of your pursuers was the rule.

As the scout waited for the warriors to leave the immediate area, he took stock of his situation. He rubbed his aching leg muscles, checked the bleeding wounds on his upper arms, and shivered slightly with the cold. Things could be better, he thought. He lay naked in the forest without weapons or a horse while half a dozen savage Sioux renegades tried to track him down and scalp him. Liver-Eating Jackson had raced into the surrounding purple hills with Rebecca Ridgeway. The deserters still plundered the prairie.

And a gold shipment was due any day.

Holten peered through the gathering dusk and decided it was time to move. He rose slowly from his hiding place and padded into the woods toward the clearing. The last place he figured the renegades would suspect him to hide would be the place he started from.

Holten glided through the woods as quietly as a stalking cougar, his long graceful strides bringing him quickly to the small pine-shaded clearing.

He stopped and listened. Nothing.

The scout glanced around, his steely eyes scanning the body-cluttered clearing and the Indian ponies tethered nearby. Holten heard a couple of the horses snort and paw the ground. Then he heard a familiar whinny, as distinctive as the voice of an old friend.

The gelding.

The scout padded to the tall pine tree where he had made love to the luscious widow and spotted his buckskin clothes scattered on the ground. His Winchester and other weapons lay propped against a nearby tree. He started forward to claim his belongings.

Then he heard them. The renegades headed for the clearing.

Quickly Holten whirled and studied the surrounding terrain. He spotted a rocky hollow off to one side of the clearing. With long powerful strides, the scout reached a small pile of rocks that covered a mild depression in the soft pine-needle-covered ground and began to uncover it. Within seconds Holten lay hidden among the rocks and bushes, his lean tortured frame cramped and bleeding.

But hidden.

From inside his new hiding place, the scout watched the lean scowling warriors march into the clearing. From the evil looks on their faces, he figured they weren't in too good of a mood.

"Where could he have gone?" asked a brave in Lakota.

"Into the air," replied another.

"Tell that to Red Hawk!"

"Where are his belongings?"

"He gives us the slip and all you think of are his belongings?"

"I like that knife!"

"You better think of something to tell Red Hawk!"

"To hell with Red Hawk," said the scowling brave as he walked over to the gelding. "We risked our lives, now we can claim our prizes."

"I want the knife!"

"I claimed it first!"

Holten saw the glint of steel as the two warriors unsheathed their long glistening knives. Their leader stepped between them.

"Stop this fighting!" he snapped. "There is enough for all of us. We will decide who gets what just as we always do it."

The two combatants scowled at each other.

"Now let's make camp," said the leader. "We have all night to decide."

Holten's stomach froze. All night?

"Kill some rabbits. Better still, get us some antelope. Tonight we deserve to eat well."

Holten watched the Indians go about the tasks of pitching camp. Several of the warriors headed on foot into the forest in search of fresh meat. The others gathered their ponies close to the camp, built a small campfire, and brought the scout's belongings alongside.

Holten knew it was going to be a long night.

Darkness fell quickly over the pine-covered hills, and

with it came a bone chilling cold that seeped through the rocks of Holten's hiding place and caused him to shiver. The scout lay as still as a field mouse next to an unsuspecting cat, his cold, cramped body staying as motionless as possible. In front of him around the campfire, Holten saw the six renegades gorge themselves on fresh antelope and rabbit meat, then haggle over the ownership of his guns and horse.

The scout stayed still and watched. And waited.

The time passed agonizingly slow for the scout. After the first few hours, his left foot went to sleep and his upper arms began to throb as never before. The jagged rocks that covered him like a blanket dug into his flesh and pinched his skin. As the hours dragged into early morning, the Indians continued to haggle about his belongings, smoking and eating until Holten finally managed to spot a few pink streaks of the new dawn in the horizon beyond.

Toward morning the scout flinched slightly as he felt the smooth skin of a long thin snake across his legs, the beady-eyed reptile passing over Holten's motionless body on its way to breakfast in the grass. Other creatures scampered around the scout's cramped body. A couple of furry mice paused once to sniff at the scout's bloody upper arms before dashing off into a hole in the soft earth.

Finally the morning broke clear and cool.

And finally the Indians slept.

As the first bright rays of early morning sun slanted into the small clearing, the scout began to take action. One by one, and as quietly as possible, Holten removed the blanket of rocks from his naked body. Within ten minutes he had removed all of the stones and lay motionless on the cold ground. Then he started to move.

His body protested. His legs remained asleep.

Quickly, but without much noise, the scout massaged his long cramped legs until the blood flowed freely once again and brought them back to life. Then Holten stood carefully just twenty feet away from the slumbering renegades.

The scout scanned the clearing. His piercing blue eyes spotted his Winchester beside a sleeping warrior who lay just a few quick strides away. He noticed the gelding remained tethered to the tall pine tree on the far side of the clearing. Holten spotted his buckskin clothing in a pile near the fire and noticed his .44 pistol and Bowie knife beside another sleeping Sioux warrior near the ponies.

Holten began to make his move.

Padding as quietly as a large predator sneaking up on its unsuspecting prey, the scout glided over to the clearing where the Indians slept soundly. Holten reached down carefully and grabbed his Winchester .44-40.

A wave of confidence spread through his chest.

Grasping the rifle's cool wooden stock, the scout stepped lightly through the clearing toward his other weapons. His legs remained cramped and caused him to walk unsteadily past the snoring braves. Holten reached the pistol and knife and bent over to pick them up.

Then the Indian ponies began to whinny.

Two of the warriors stirred. Holten froze.

"What is it?" mumbled a sleepy brave in Lakota.

"The ponies," answered another.

The braves sat bolt upright on their blankets and turned sharply to look at the horses. Their flashing brown eyes widened with shock as they locked with Holten's.

The scout had no choice.

With blinding speed, Holten levered a cartridge into the chamber of the big Winchester and fired at the braves. The hot slug slammed into one of the stunned warrior's chest sending him tumbling backward into the dying fire. Holten levered again. And again the rifle spat fire, another hot bullet ripping into the second warrior's chest just as he was about to draw his .45 pistol. The brave shrieked with pain and jumped into the air with the impact of the slug.

Then all hell broke loose.

The other four warriors snapped awake in an instant, all of them going for their weapons with lightning fast reflexes. Holten picked his targets.

The scout levered and fired, then levered and fired again. Two of the startled renegades jumped backward as bullets from the .44-40 slammed into them, killing them almost instantly.

But a third warrior attacked the scout.

The lean dark-skinned brave leaped at Holten, a glistening blade in his hand and an ugly scowl on his broad gleaming face. Holten reacted with the sudden reflexes of a scared wildcat. In a flash of motion, the scout jabbed the barrel of the Winchester into the charging warrior's face, the hard metal slamming into the brave's forehead and stopping him in his tracks.

The stunned warrior froze for a moment.

Holten then reversed his grip on the rifle and clubbed the tottering renegade on the back of the head with a resounding crack. The Indian's eyes rolled toward the deep blue morning sky as he pitched forward and fell dead onto the pine needles.

A flash of movement caught the scout's eye.

The lone remaining warrior bolted toward the pine forest, his long lean legs pumping as fast as they could go. The scout shouldered his Winchester and squeezed the trigger.

He heard a metallic click. The rifle was empty.

Swearing under his breath, Holten dropped the Winchester and looked at the ground. He reached down and plucked his Bowie knife from the pine needles and took off after the fleeing renegade. The scout didn't want any survivors heading back to tell Red Hawk that he was still alive. The tall Sioux subchief would figure that out in due time.

Holten sprinted after the warrior.

Still naked and stiff from his all-night ordeal under the blanket of jagged rocks, the scout tried as hard as he could to loosen-up his long leg muscles as he raced past tall pines and through clawing underbrush. Finally, with his lungs heaving and his heart pounding, Holten began to gain on the lean warrior ahead of him. The scared brave glanced once over his shoulder to check the position of the scout, his broad gleaming face a mask of sudden fear when he spotted Holten just a few yards behind him.

The scout lunged like a cougar making a strike.

Holten smashed into the stumbling warrior and slammed him to the ground. The two panting combatants scrambled to their feet and whirled to face each other, glistening knives in their hands and determined looks on their faces. Holten watched the lean warrior's flashing brown eyes and waited to make his move.

As the early morning sun broke through the tops of the towering pine trees and struck the scout's naked body, the two knife fighters circled warily. Each of them knew one mistake could be fatal.

Finally the warrior struck.

The scout noticed the sinewy brave's flashing eyes widen a split second before he charged. Holten was ready. The scout jerked suddenly to his right, avoided the deadly blade thrust by the lunging brave, and, at the same time, slashed his long fearsome Bowie knife down toward the stumbling warrior's back.

The glistening blade struck home.

The warrior screamed.

Holten's blade slammed into the lean brave's bare back all the way to the hilt, the razor-sharp knife slicing through the Indian's lungs and reaching his liver. Blood spurted onto the brown pine needles. The warrior arched his back, dropped his knife, and fell dead to the ground.

The scout stood panting in the sunshine, the summer sun warming his chilled and tortured body for a long moment as he caught his breath.

It had been a hell of a night.

Finally Holten turned and walked steadily back to the small clearing. He quickly hauled on his buckskin clothing, checked and loaded his weapons, and then claimed his gelding. With a final look at the small rock pile where he'd spent the long night, the scout smiled and hauled himself onto the wide strong back of his big horse.

He had some tracking to do. The deserters had Rebecca.

The big jack rabbit stood frozen in the grass.

Holten reined in the gelding, slipped off his big horse, and drew his bow from its saddle sheath. Taking a long iron-tipped arrow from a quiver next to the Winchester, the scout notched the deadly shaft and aimed at the twitching forequarters of the unsuspecting rabbit in the field off the trail to Holten's left. The scout figured he would stop to eat before continuing after Jackson and his boys.

The long bow twanged. The arrow skittered through the air.

The long wooden arrow sliced neatly through the long-eared jack rabbit's heart killing it instantly. The scout ambled over to the fallen animal and gathered his breakfast. Holten's growling stomach was a constant reminder of how long it had been since his last meal.

The scout tethered the gelding in a copse of cotton-woods, built a small cooking fire, and began to prepare his first meal in many hours. While he waited, Holten moistened a cloth with some water from his canteen and cleansed the burning flesh wounds on his upper arms and face. He winced at the sudden pressure of the wet cloth, and thought he'd never see the end of Red Hawk and his braves. They seemed to be hounding him all over the Dakota plains.

The sizzling fire told him his breakfast was ready. The

scout reached for the slender wooden spit and the crackling rabbit meat. He could almost taste the sweet fresh meat with his eyes.

"Hold it right there, mister!"

Holten froze. The gruff voice came from behind.

"Don't move a muscle or I'll blow your head off!" came another voice off to the side, near the gelding.

"I ain't movin'," he said, his eyes flicking to the bushes to his right. The scout swore at himself for letting down his guard. The combination of Red Hawk's torture, the renegades' attack, and his own hunger had weakened his concentration. Men had died on the prairie by making the same mistakes. The scout tensed his muscles and waited.

Holten heard the press of boots on pine needles and suddenly saw two bearded frontiersmen, their big Henry repeaters pointed at the scout, sidle into his campsite. One of the men stood as tall as the scout, but carried about fifty more pounds. His partner, a scrawny little character, scowled at Holten through a bushy black beard. The scout noticed both had been shot recently. Fresh blood oozed from a couple of bandages that each wore around recent bullet wounds in their arms.

The big man glanced at Holten's bow. "That yours?" he asked in a gruff voice.

Holten nodded slowly.

"That settles it," said the big man. "Get a rope Ike."

The scrawny frontiersman nodded and strode briskly from the scout's campsite.

"What's this all about?" asked Holten.

"We're goin' to hang ya!"

The scout's pulse quickened. He knew they meant it.

The scrawny frontiersman returned to the campsite with a coil of rope clutched in his hand. With a quick flip he tossed the coil over a big branch of one of the cottonwoods and began to make a hangman's noose.

"Mind if I ask what for?" said the scout, his brain

working rapidly. He had to stall for time.

The big man laughed. "As if you didn't know!"

"I don't know what in hell you're talkin' about."

"You killed my brother! I seen ya do it!"

"Me?"

"You and your partners all dressed up like Injuns. You didn't fool us none, eh Ike?"

"Rope's ready," said the scrawny plainsman.

"Now wait a minute—" said Holten.

The big man cocked the Henry rifle. "You didn't wait no minute before you killed my brother. Now get up nice and slow and march over to that rope. You're gonna get what ya deserve!"

The deserters had struck again, thought Holten.

"I know who killed your brother," he said in a last ditch attempt to reason with the big scowling frontiersman. "I can even help you track 'em down."

Holten watched the man's face harden.

The big man squeezed the trigger of his Henry repeater, the big gun roaring in the confined space of the cottonwoods like an army cannon. The slug zipped just inches past Holten's head.

"I said get to your feet!"

So much for last ditch attempts at reasoning.

The scout had to act.

"Whatever you say," replied Holten.

With the lighting reflexes of a cougar, the scout flung the sizzling rabbit he still clutched in his hand up into the big frontiersman's bearded face, the crackling meat striking the startled plainsman's eyes and blinding him momentarily. The big man shrieked with pain and dropped his rifle.

Holten turned to face the other man.

The scrawny plainsman had already reached for the Henry he'd left standing against a tree trunk. The scout had no choice. Holten drew his long Bowie knife and with a quick flick of his wrist threw the glistening blade at the lunging frontiersman. The fearsome ten-inch blade buried itself in the wiry man's chest, slicing his heart as it tore through flesh and bone. The bearded frontiersman cried out sharply, then fell dead to the ground.

A flash of movement.

The scout ducked quickly as the big frontiersman, still half blinded by the hot jack rabbit that struck his eyes, swung his Henry rifle at Holten's head. The scout reached out and grabbed the other rifle that leaned against a nearby cottonwood. Holten grasped the cold metal barrel and swung the heavy wooden stock upwards toward the stumbling half-blinded big man. The rifle struck the big frontiersman square on the side of his big hairy head with a sickening crack.

The plainsman went down like a felled tree.

The scout stood panting and surveyed the damage.

As he glanced at the two crumpled bodies sprawled in the small wooded clearing, Holten realized he couldn't even have a quiet meal any more. Jackson and the deserters had made life almost unbearable out on the plains.

They had to be stopped.

As he gathered his gear, Holten retrieved his cooked rabbit from the dust and began to eat. Finally the scout swung his long lean frame onto the back of the gelding and headed for the prairie once again.

He had a long day of tracking ahead of him.

CHAPTER FIFTEEN

Holten followed Jackson's well-defined trail.

Starting from the large log cabin, the scout kept his eyes glued to the dusty, alkaline trail and followed the overburdened Indian pony that carried Liver-Eating Jackson and the naked widow, Rebecca Ridgeway. Holten felt uneasy. In the back of his mind, he knew that the gold shipment mentioned by General Corrington was due at any time. He figured the deserters, led by Jackson, would more than likely try to grab the loot before it reached Fort Rawlins.

The scout tracked all day.

The trail led Holten across a wide expanse of parched Dakota prairie, past pitiful stands of thirsty cottonwoods, and over dusty sand hills dotted with green and white Spanish dagger plants and scraggly sagebrush. Holten kept his burning eyes on the scorched trail, the afternoon breeze occasionally blowing swirls of alkaline dust up into his nostrils and clogging his windpipe.

He knew Jackson had to be just up ahead.

By nightfall the scout had tracked over some fifty miles of dusty, parched prairie and still hadn't caught up with the deserters. He decided to bed down for the night. After noticing the direction Jackson took away from the log cabin, Holten's intimate knowledge of the Dakota Territory told him that Liver-Eating Jackson and his gang of killers would probably rendezvous somewhere near the western section of the vast territory—far enough away from all army posts to avoid any sudden rescue by more troops, and close enough to Sioux country to discourage any competition from other white bandits.

The scout would arrive there in the morning.

Awake before the crack of dawn, Holten clucked to the gelding and started off at a trot toward the still shadowy hills that surrounded him. Further back in those same hills, he knew, was Red Hawk's renegade camp—and the Canyon of Death. The sudden thought sent a wave of anxiety through his chest. He spurred his horse and broke into a gallop.

As he urged the big gelding up a narrow incline toward a jagged rocky ridge, Holten thought about Rebecca Ridgeway. He knew the deserters wanted as much ransom as she'd bring; he just hoped to hell they didn't damage the merchandise too much before he arrived to help her.

The scout reined in his big snorting mount at the top of the hill and scanned a small wooded valley below. Beyond stood the shadowy Black Hills—and the Sioux renegades.

Then he heard it.

A low moan carried to the scout on the morning wind.

Holten strained his ears to listen for the direction of the terrible sound. He sat frozen atop the restless gelding. Somewhere down in the valley lay a wounded man. Or woman.

Rebecca?

The scout clucked gently to the gelding and began a slow descent into the valley. As he bounced atop his big mount, Holten's hand dropped to his Winchester just in case. His big Bowie knife and .44 pistol hung ready at his belt. He figured it was about time he made contact with Jackson and his boys. And Rebecca.

Then he saw her. She was tied to a tree like a dog.

Holten stopped in his tracks. The gelding snorted in protest. The scout's muscles tensed and his nerves tingled. He peered through the early morning haze at Rebecca Ridgeway, dressed only in an oversized army deserter's shirt, tied by the wrists to a rutted cottonwood tree in the middle of the grassy valley.

Holten knew a trap when he saw one.

But the scout also knew he didn't have any choice. He had to save Rebecca. And do it now.

Holten dismounted, tethered the gelding, and unsheathed his Winchester .44-40. His steely blue eyes scanned the surrounding woods for signs of trouble, his sharpened animallike senses on edge as he headed toward the moaning widow. As he padded like an Indian stalking an antelope on the plains, the scout felt as though a hundred eyes watched his every move. But he kept on walking.

When he reached a spot about fifty feet from the gasping blonde, the scout saw what they'd done to her. His stomach turned. Holten noticed the ugly bruises on her once beautiful face, the swollen welts around her now glazed eyes, and the black and blue marks around her thighs where the deserters must have taken turns mounting her.

Holten froze. His grip tightened on the rifle.

"Holten!" gasped Rebecca. "Go back! It's a trap!"

Before the scout could react, he heard the sudden drumbeat as half a dozen horses burst from the surrounding woods. A rifle cracked, then another and another. Several bullets kicked up the dirt beside his feet.

The scout was, indeed, trapped.

Holten stood motionless and waited for the smiling riders to reach him. The scout noticed a big potbellied sergeant and several other laughing army deserters.

Then he saw Liver-Eating Jackson.

The snake-eyed frontiersman reined in his snorting pony just a few feet from where the scout stood ramrod straight in the tall buffalo grass, a shower of rich dark soil spraying over Holten's boots as the horse braked.

"Well, well!" snapped Jackson. "We meet again!"

"Unfortunately," replied Holten dryly.

In a flash, one of the deserters dismounted, wrenched the Winchester from the scout's hands, and took his other weapons. Holten stood defiantly in front of the wiry narrow-faced killer.

"Go ahead and get it over with, Jackson," he said. "Shoot me."

Jackson cackled. "If I had my druthers," he said with an evil smile, "I'd shoot ya on the spot."

"Well?"

"I ain't callin' the shots, Injun lover."

Suddenly Holten saw a flash of movement from over near the woods. He turned his head sharply and saw a rider approach them in the clearing. Holten squinted at the uniformed figure and tried to recognize the face.

It hit him like an Indian war hatchet. Major Phillips!

"Here comes the boss now," said Jackson. "Maybe he'll let me pull the trigger."

The boss? Now all the pieces came together.

Phillips reined in his army horse. "Mornin' scout," he said tipping his wide-brimmed officer's hat. "Glad you could join our little group."

Holten listened to the major's clipped voice and looked at his glistening brass buttons. It was an inside job all along. Phillips *had* met with Jackson and Riley back near the fort, probably to plan their brutal attacks on the innocent white settlers.

"I ain't joined nothin' yet," said the scout.

Major Phillips chuckled. "Don't bet on it."

"Stay away from the deserters, you told me," said Holten. "Let the army take care of them. You just round up all the settlers and bring 'em in."

"You should have done like you were told, scout."

"And let you butcher half the territory?"

Phillips shrugged. "Now you're going to have to play our game with us."

"Your game?"

Nathan Phillips extracted a long green cigar and lit it slowly. "Gold," he said through a cloud of smoke. "Army gold."

"Indian gold," corrected the scout.

Phillips shrugged again. "What's the difference?" he said. "It'll be our gold in just a few short hours."

Suddenly Rebecca moaned loudly from where she lay tied to the cottonwood tree.

"That another one of your games?" asked Holten nodding in the blonde widow's direction.

"Hell of a fuck!" said Liver-Eating Jackson.

"You sure know how to pick 'em, scout!" snapped another of the deserters.

The entire gang roared with laughter.

Holten started forward. Guns flashed.

"I wouldn't if I was you," said Jackson. "He may be the boss around here, but one wrong move and I might just forget about that."

The scout stared into Jackson's snakelike eyes.

"That's enough," said Major Phillips. "We have some plans to discuss with the scout."

"Plans?" asked Holten.

Phillips nodded. "Jackson wanted to shoot you as soon as you poked your Indian-lovin' face over that ridge. But I convinced him that you would be valuable to us in taking the gold shipment off the army's hands."

Holten's face hardened. "Go to hell!"

"I may go later," said Major Phillips coolly, "but right now you don't have much choice, scout." Phillips nodded in Rebecca Ridgeway's direction. "You help us or she dies. Simple, no?"

The scout stiffened. He glanced at the moaning widow.

"Let me shoot him," said Jackson. "He ain't worth it."

"I think he'll help us," said Phillips. "Right Holten?"

The scout didn't know what the traitorous major had in

mind for him, but whatever it was it sure as hell beat dying right now. And whatever happened, without him alive Rebecca stood about as much chance as a prairie dog in a rattlesnake nest.

Holten nodded. "What do you want me to do?"

Phillips smiled. "Good," he said, and started to dismount. "Visit with your girl friend for a moment, then we'll talk about what we have in mind for you."

The hard-eyed officer strode up to Holten and glared at the scout, his eyes flashing with sullen hate.

"Of course you won't get a share of the gold. You'll just come away with your life."

The mounted deserters roared with laughter.

"Sergeant Ames!" snapped Phillips. "Take Mr. Holten to see the—lady."

"Yessir!" said big Luther Ames with a reflex action carried over from his army days.

Then while Maj. Nathan Phillips and Liver-Eating Jackson led the former soldiers over to a small clearing, Holten followed big dumb-looking Luther Ames to the moaning widow. The sergeant cut the rope from Rebecca's slender wrists.

"Just five minutes," snapped Ames. The sergeant turned and walked back toward the other soldiers.

"Rebecca?" said Holten softly.

"Oh, Holten," she gasped weakly.

The scout raised Rebecca's head and placed it on his lap. Holten scanned the blonde widow's bruised and battered body and felt the anger boil up inside of him.

"Look what they did to you," he said through clenched teeth. "I'll get 'em for this!"

Rebecca's blue eyes flashed suddenly. "No," she said in a frayed voice. "Do what they say—or they'll kill you."

Holten nodded. "Do you feel better?" he asked.

She nodded and smiled. "Remember what you told me?"

"About what?"

"About your torture in the Indian camp and how you passed the time by thinking about me."

The scout nodded. The sudden memory pained him.

"Well," said Rebecca. "While they—while they did all those things to me, I just thought about you." She smiled up at Holten, her old flashing smile once again melting his insides as it used to do.

"What part of me?" he asked playfully.

Rebecca's long fingers slid up Holten's leg until they reached his groin. The blonde widow's small hand grasped the scout's penis through his buckskin pants and squeezed gently.

Their eyes met. Holten knew she would be all right.

"Holten!"

The scout turned sharply. He saw Luther Ames.

"Holten," repeated the big dumb-looking sergeant, "the major wants you over here right now. Move your ass!"

Holten started to rise. Rebecca grabbed his rough hand.

"Don't do anything foolish," she pleaded. "Please?"

The scout hesitated, then smiled. "I won't," he said.

"Promise?"

Holten nodded. "Promise."

The bruised widow smiled back at him, then lay her puffed and swollen face on the cool grass. He wouldn't do anything foolish, he thought, but he'd get the ones responsible for treating a lady like a common pack animal.

Holten marched over to Maj. Nathan Phillips.

"The gold wagon drivers know you, Holten."

"Who are they?"

"Marshall and Sims from Fort Sampson. They trust you. They'd stop the gold wagon to listen to you."

"What do you want me to say?"

197

"Nothing," said Major Phillips. "Jackson here will do all the talking."

"And those Indian costumes?"

Jackson cackled. "We got us some new army duds," said the snake-eyed killer. "Courtesy of the major, here."

"With you ridin' at the point," added Major Phillips in a cool clipped voice, "the deserters and Jackson will trot right up to the wagon dressed in gleaming new uniforms fresh from the quartermaster's tent at Fort Rawlins."

"And I just tell them guards," said Jackson, "that we're an escort to take 'em all the way to the fort."

"And if they don't believe you?"

"With you riding alongside Jackson," said Phillips, "the guards will believe almost anything he says."

The major puffed on his cigar, then glanced at Holten. "Your word means something on the prairie, scout."

Liver-Eating Jackson cackled again. "After the robbery, it won't mean shit!"

All the deserters roared with laughter.

"So all along you planned to take the gold," said the scout. "Why kill a lot of innocent settlers?"

Phillips shrugged. "What's a few farmers? We're talking about one hundred thousand dollars in gold coins, Holten!"

"Gold that's supposed to go to the Indians on the reservations," added Holten. "You think Black Spotted Horse and the others are goin' to sit still and see every treaty they sign with the army get broken?"

"Who gives a shit what they think!" snapped Jackson.

Phillips exhaled some smoke. "By the time they react to all this," he said, "I'll be down in Mexico with a señorita on each arm."

The soldiers burst into laughter again.

The scout nodded at Rebecca. "And her?" said Holten more seriously. "Why'd you even bother with a widow

198

who's got nothin' to do with all this?''

"She's our insurance," said Phillips tossing his green cigar to the ground. "If you don't do your job, or the whole thing falls apart, then we hold her for ransom."

"You could have treated her like a lady!" said the scout in a harsh voice.

"She was one hell of a fuck!" snapped Liver-Eating Jackson.

The anger boiled over inside the scout. Holten lunged for the snake-eyed killer, but a heavy army boot and several arms restrained him. The scout sat back and glared at Jackson, his pulse racing and his muscles twitching.

Holten took a deep breath.

"What if I don't go along with all this?" he asked.

Phillips shrugged. "We kill the woman."

Holten sat on the ground and regained his composure. He'd have to wait for his chance, then stick it to all of them. He just hoped to hell he got that chance.

The scout nodded. "All right," he said somberly. "I'll do whatever you want."

Maj. Nathan Phillips grinned from ear to ear.

"Good, Holten," he said. "I knew you'd see it our way."

"What about my weapons?" asked the scout. "The guards will sure as hell get suspicious if they see me without my guns."

Jackson shook his head. "No way, scout."

"Jackson's right," added Phillips. "Just sit on your horse and shut up. You won't need your guns."

"And the widow?"

"We'll keep a good man here to watch her."

"Just like Paco Riley watched her?"

Jackson chuckled. Phillips smiled.

Holten felt a lump in the pit of his stomach.

For one week he'd been running across the murdering deserters all over the Dakota plains. Now he'd have to help

199

them rob and kill again—or they'd sure as hell butcher Rebecca. For all the scout knew, they might do that anyway.

But he didn't have much choice.

"Let's get those new uniforms on," shouted Major Phillips. "Then let's ride for gold!"

The deserters let out a whoop and started to dress.

The scout didn't feel much like celebrating.

CHAPTER SIXTEEN

Holten hunkered in the tall grass.

Next to the scout on the rocky ridge crouched Liver-Eating Jackson, big Sgt. Luther Ames, and Maj. Nathan Phillips. As pregnant black storm clouds scudded across the Dakota sky and blocked out the sun, they all studied the slow-moving wagon in the narrow valley below.

"They got a gatling gun," said Jackson.

"We got surprise on our side," remarked Phillips.

"Surprise can't stop no bullets."

"There won't be any bullets," said Phillips with a sideways glance at the scout. "That is, if Holten does his job."

Jackson cackled. "He'll do the job," said the snake-eyed frontiersman. "He wants to see his little miss pussy!"

Dim-witted Luther Ames guffawed. Holten just stared.

While the dumb-looking deserter roared with laughter, the scout watched the slow procession below. He noticed four mounted guards on both sides of the heavy gold wagon, and a big gatling gun trailing behind on its carriage. He saw the two dusty drivers, Marshall and Sims, flick the reins and shout at the lazy team of six gleaming horses. The guards, he noticed, cradled Springfield carbines in their arms and scanned the surrounding countryside like buck antelope protecting their herd at a watering hole.

"Candy from a baby!" said Liver-Eating Jackson.

Luther Ames' eyes danced. "Let's take 'em!"

"Ready Holten?" asked the major.

"Ready as I'll ever be to help you bastards."

The unlikely quartet rose slowly and eased away from the edge of the valley. A few large drops of rain splattered in the dust at their feet. They strode briskly toward the three remaining deserters and their sluggish army mounts. Another deserter stayed behind to watch Rebecca. Holten thought the soldiers looked quite spiffy in their stolen uniforms; spiffy enough to fool the men in the valley. Maybe the scout could warn the drivers.

But how?

"Remember," said Maj. Nathan Phillips as he hauled his erect frame onto his horse. "I'll be waiting up near the trees. Let Jackson do the talking."

"Let's get us some gold!" yelled Ames.

"No tricks, Holten," reminded Phillips.

The scout glared at the major. "Let's get this over with."

"And Jackson," added Phillips. "Once you get the guards to relax, you know what to do."

Holten saw a gleam in Jackson's yellow eyes. "Yeah," said the snake-eyed frontiersman patting his war hatchet.

"Good luck," said the major finally.

"Let's go!"

"Gold!"

With a sudden drumbeat of pounding hooves, the band of uniformed killers raced down the slope in a cloud of dust and galloped into the narrow tree-lined valley below. Holten wasn't looking forward to the trip.

"You go first, Holten," shouted Jackson as they rode. "And remember, I'm right behind ya!"

Without his weapons, the scout felt naked.

As they rode into the narrow valley, Holten saw the gold wagon pull up short. He watched the armed guards trot around to the front of the horses in the usual army manner. The scout noticed the wizened faces of the two old drivers wrinkle with concentration as they tried to read the

202

faces of the approaching uniformed riders. Then Holten saw the lean wrinkled face of Pop Marshall spread into a grin as the old man recognized the scout.

Damn fool, thought Holten.

Jackson raised his hand in the accepted army fashion and the deserters slowed to a trot. As they approached to within fifty feet of the unsuspecting party of soldiers, the scout saw Pop Marshall speak to one of the guards and point toward Holten. The armed guard then lowered his Springfield carbine.

The fools fell for the trap.

"Get ready," said Jackson over his shoulder.

Jackson and Holten stopped the small party of deserters beside the drivers of the wagon. The armed guards scanned the faces of the deserters, then lowered their carbines and seemed to relax.

The surprise was complete, thought the scout.

"Eli Holten!" shouted Pop Marshall.

The scout glanced sideways at Jackson. "Hi Pop," said Holten softly.

"Never thought I'd see you ridin' out to greet us!"

"Scout Holten is accompanying us through Indian country," replied Liver-Eating Jackson in an official manner. He squirmed with obvious discomfort at his freshly starched uniform.

"We saw some signs of hostiles," said a hard-faced armed guard off to Holten's left. "Saw some burned out ranches, too."

"Renegades, most likely," said Jackson.

"We heard 'bout some army deserters up these parts," said old Pop Marshall in a wheezing voice.

"Nothin' to worry about," said Jackson. "But just the same, we've been sent to give ya some more protection all the way to Fort Rawlins."

"Mighty obliged," said the armed guard. "All this gold

makes me kinda nervous."

"I can imagine," said Jackson with a grin. "Well, suppose we better get movin' before them renegades or deserters decide to show up."

Then it happened.

"Luther Ames!"

Holten froze.

The other old driver, Jawbone Sims, pointed at the sergeant. "It's Luther Ames!" shouted Sims again. "That sonofabitch deserted three months ago! I saw him drunker 'an a skunk just two weeks ago! He done killed the stationmaster's boy over a spilled drink, of all things!"

Holten watched Ames lick his lips and squirm in his saddle.

The old driver started to rise. "You bastard!" he said.

"Wait a minute," shouted Jackson. "Sergeant Ames is a good soldier who's been with us for years!"

"Like hell!" yelled Jawbone Sims, climbing down from the wagon at the same time.

The scout saw Ames' hand drop to his gun.

The scout smelled trouble.

It came immediately. Luther Ames drew his pistol.

The dim-witted sergeant's army .45 roared in the narrow valley, the hot slug slamming into the slender old frame of Jawbone Sims, sending the wizened wagonmaster flying onto the dusty ground. The shot echoed among the pine trees.

Then silence filled the valley.

The hard-faced army guard looked up slowly, an expression of sudden realization etched on his stubbled face. "Deserters!" he breathed.

Liver-Eating Jackson went for his pistols.

The other deserters slapped their leather holsters.

The armed guards started to bring their Springfield carbines into play at the same time. Holten flinched atop the suddenly skittish gelding.

All hell broke loose.

Within seconds the quiet valley erupted with gunshots, Jackson drew his two .45's and blasted away, his accurate bullets finding their mark in the chest of the hard-faced guard, the stunned soldier spinning off his horse to the ground. Behind the scout the other deserters opened fire, their bullets whistling past Holten's head and slamming into the other equally startled armed guards, sending them flying from their prancing army horses. The stench of gunpowder filled the air.

It was over in seconds. Holten surveyed the grisly scene.

The scout saw the four armed guards lying in spreading pools of their own blood, several ugly wounds oozing fresh crimson onto the valley floor. Pop Marshall lay sprawled on the driver's seat of the gold wagon, his head half torn off, a gaping wound oozing brain matter and blood onto the ground. Scared army mounts raced into the hills. Only the skittish team of horses remained unscathed by the sudden blast of six-gun fury unleashed by Liver-Eating Jackson and the deserters.

Holten heard hoofbeats. He whirled and saw Phillips.

The major reined in his snorting horse. "Good job!" he shouted. "A hell of a job!"

"We're rich!" shouted big Luther Ames.

"Let's check the gold!" yelled Jackson.

Like kids rushing to the tree on Christmas morning, Liver-Eating Jackson and the three wide-eyed deserters leaped off their mounts and sprinted to the back of the army gold wagon.

"Very efficient, wouldn't you say Holten?" asked Phillips.

"Bastards!" replied the scout.

Phillips laughed shortly. "The weak fall by the way-side."

Holten turned and glared at the major.

"It's all here!" shouted a delirious Luther Ames.

"He's right," confirmed Jackson. "Here's the box!"

As Holten watched in disgust, the four army deserters hauled the gold-filled strongbox out of the wagon and tossed it on the ground. Liver-Eating Jackson aimed his .45 at the big lock and squeezed the trigger. The heavy lock disintegrated with the impact of the hot slug.

Luther Ames tossed back the cover. They all gasped.

Holten peered down at the big strongbox jammed full of gold coins. The glittering cargo glistened brightly even under the now threatening skies.

"Goddam!"

"Will ya look at that!"

"Jesus!"

Then the scout heard something else. He listened hard.

While the excited deserters jumped around the glittering strongbox like children at a party, Holten's trained ears picked up other sounds from the surrounding bushes and trees. Suddenly the scout's animallike senses began to work keenly and his muscles began to tense. His instincts, sharpened from years out on the lonesome prairie, began to speak to him.

Holten heard birds, crickets, and prairie dogs.

Except they were fake.

Sioux warriors lurked somewhere in the shadows that surrounded the gleeful band of deserters, their bows notched with arrows and their guns aimed at the white men's backs. The scout listened intently.

A metal click.

A pistol being cocked snapped Holten back to the scene around him. The scout turned and looked into the deadly bore of Maj. Nathan Phillips' Colt .45.

"Thanks for your help, scout," said Phillips smiling.

"The payoff?" asked Holten.

The major nodded. "What did you expect?"

"I expect you'll do the same to them, too," replied the scout nodding at the laughing deserters near the wagon.

"You're so right."

Crickets. Prairie dogs. Birds.

Then it happened. Bows twanged and arrows skittered. The renegades attacked.

"Jesus Christ!"

"Indians!"

"Where's my gun?"

Panic struck the band of deserters. Holten watched the confidence drain suddenly from Maj. Nathan Phillips' lean, hard military face. The major's widening eyes darted to the screaming renegades who poured out of the hills. The scout lashed out and knocked the .45 from the major's hand.

Then Holten turned toward Liver-Eating Jackson's horse, grabbed his own weapons from the frontiersman's saddle, and pulled back on the reins of the frightened gelding. The scout looked at the gold wagon and watched the struggling soldiers heave the gold-laden strongbox into the back of the heavy wagon.

The scout knew what he had to do.

While arrows skittered over his head and bullets whistled through the air, Holten leaped from the gelding and led the big horse to the rear of the wagon. Quickly the scout unhitched the cumbersome gatling gun and tethered the gelding to the back of the heavy wagon. Then with his Winchester in his hand, he jumped onto the driver's seat, shoved Pop Marshall's battered body onto the ground, and grabbed the reins of the team of six skittish horses.

Then Holten saw him. Red Hawk.

The tall scowling renegade chief rode his sleek war pony in a circle around the suddenly embattled deserters, leading his screaming warriors into the valley while taking pot shots at the white men with a rapid-fire Spencer repeater.

Holten figured Red Hawk wanted him so much that this time he didn't entrust any more braves with the task. He came himself. That meant the entire force of renegades had to be in the valley with him. Too bad, thought Holten, the Sioux subchief wouldn't catch him with the others. The scout got set to leave.

Suddenly a wiry brave appeared from nowhere atop his galloping pony, a fearsome war hatchet in his hand and a wild look of hatred on his dark painted face. The warrior raised the hatchet and tossed it at Holten's head. The scout jerked backward with the reflexes of a scared wildcat, the deadly tomahawk thudding harmlessly into the wooden frame of the gold wagon.

The scout raised his Winchester and fired several rapid shots at the passing renegade, the hot slugs tearing into the lean brave's side and almost cutting him in two. The screaming warrior fell heavily to the ground and landed in a cloud of alkaline dust.

A scream of pain rose from Holten's right.

The scout whirled and saw one of the deserters fall to the ground, a couple of Sioux arrows deeply embedded in his chest. A couple of twitching army horses lay dead in the dust near the wheels of the wagon full of gold.

Then Holten saw it. An arrow aimed at his head.

The scout arced his Winchester .44-40 upward in a flash and fired just as the gleaming painted warrior released his arrow. The bullet tore into the startled brave's head and ripped the top of his skull off before he even knew what hit him. The renegade's arrow zipped past Holten's face and thudded into the wagon.

Holten felt the gold wagon tilt suddenly. He whirled and saw two hard-faced Sioux renegades coming straight at him from inside the wagon. The fierce looking warriors had jumped onto the back of the heavy army wagon and leaped at Holten with glistening blades in their hands.

Holten braced himself for the attack.

"Your scalp is mine, Tall Bear!" said the first brave in Lakota.

"Come and get it!" replied the scout.

The lean warrior leaped at Holten, his flashing blade tearing the sleeve of the scout's buckskin jacket. Holten jumped backward, almost falling from the driver's seat, and kicked savagely with his heavy boots.

The boots struck the brave's groin.

The warrior gasped. His eyes widened with pain.

At the same time, Holten unsheathed his ten-inch Bowie knife and slashed downward at the stunned warrior's back, the long fearsome blade plunging to the hilt in the screaming renegade's body.

A flash of movement. The second warrior charged.

With a mighty heave, Holten shoved the limp dead body of the first brave up into the lunging second warrior. The Indian fell with a grunt to the floor of the gold wagon, the bloody body of his dead companion covering him like a blanket.

The scout didn't waste a moment.

With a flash of glinting steel, Holten reached out and slashed his Bowie knife at the exposed neck of the wide-eyed warrior. The razor-sharp blade sliced neatly through the renegade's jugular and almost decapitated him with one swipe. Blood splashed onto the wagon. The brave gurgled once, then slumped dead onto the wagon floor in a pool of widening crimson.

Holten stopped and breathed deeply. His heart pounded.

From outside the wagon came the fierce screams and loud shots of a pitched battle. Horses whinnied and renegades shouted. The deserters fired desperately at the circling warriors. Holten knew he had to make his move now or never.

The scout flicked the reins. The wagon jumped ahead.

Holten yelled to the skittish team of gleaming horses, urging the tired army mounts toward the hills that surrounded the narrow valley. As he pushed the wagon forward, the scout glanced at the beleaguered deserters who shot from a ragged skirmish circle at the whooping warriors. He saw Major Phillips on his feet now, directing the soldiers and firing his .45 army pistol at the circling braves.

"Hey!" yelled Luther Ames. "The gold wagon!"

"Holten come back!" roared Jackson.

"Stop him!"

Holten slapped the reins against the ample butts of the horses and sped away from the shooting behind him. The scout ducked quickly as several shots splintered the wagon near his head. Within seconds he steered the bouncing wagon full of gold up the gentle slope leading to the hills.

And to Rebecca Ridgeway.

The scout stopped suddenly at the top of the hill and peered down at the wild fighting below. He'd taken both the soldiers and the renegades by complete surprise with his mad dash from the valley. The Indians concentrated on the mounted soldiers; the soldiers were trapped by the circling braves.

The scout heard a sharp volley of shots.

Holten glanced at the gatling gun and saw big Luther Ames cranking the machine gun's handle and spewing hot lead at the screaming Sioux warriors. Renegades dropped like clay pigeons at a skeet shoot.

Suddenly Red Hawk's hands flew over his head as bullets tore through his lean body. The tall renegade chief screamed and fell dead to the ground. It wouldn't be long now, thought the scout.

Holten flicked the reins. The wagon spurted ahead.

At the rate the big sergeant felled the braves in the valley, the scout knew the deserters would be on his trail in about five or ten minutes. He flicked the reins again and raced toward the dark brooding forest ahead.

He had the gold. But they had Rebecca.

CHAPTER SEVENTEEN

Holten's mind raced as fast as the wagon.

The scout slapped the leather reins against the ample butts of the snorting army horses and pointed the six galloping mounts toward the clearing where a lone deserter held Rebecca Ridgeway prisoner. Holten had two things on his mind now.

Save Rebecca. Keep the gold.

As the big horses churned up the dark rich Dakota topsoil, the scout glanced skyward at the black clouds that threatened to explode into a raging storm at any minute.

He had to work fast.

Holten knew that with Red Hawk dead, the renegades would soon retreat into the surrounding hills. The sudden withdrawal of the Sioux warriors would send Major Phillips and Liver-Eating Jackson after the scout and his valuable cargo.

Holten shouted at the horses and raced ahead.

Within fifteen minutes the scout pulled back the reins and braked the panting team of tired mounts on a wooded knoll that overlooked the clearing where Rebecca waited. The horses snorted and Holten listened. The scout scanned the woods with his piercing blue eyes, his senses alert for any movement that might indicate additional signs of trouble. Holten spotted the lone deserter leaning against a rutted cottonwood trunk.

And he saw Rebecca slumped beside him.

Quickly the scout formulated a plan of action. He didn't have much time, but surprise was on his side. Holten leaped from the heavy wagon, unhitched the gelding, and grabbed his Winchester. Then with a resounding smack on the butt of the lead horse, Holten sent the rattling wagon hurtling into the small clearing and toward the suddenly startled guard.

The scout watched surprise spread on the man's face.

Holten hauled his still aching frame atop the prancing gelding and dug his heels into the big horse's gleaming flanks. The well-rested mount surged forward in the tracks of the rumbling, old gold-laden wagon.

Holten watched the lone deserter twist his lean stubbled face in thought and try to figure out what in hell was happening. The delay was all the scout needed to complete his ruse. As the six wide-eyed army horses galloped into the clearing and raced past the puzzled guard, Holten hid the gelding behind the hurtling gold wagon as long as he could.

Then the soldier spotted him. He arced his gun upward.

Holten grabbed his Winchester with both hands and aimed down the long barrel at the firing deserter. The Winchester spat fire several times, hot lead spewing into the quiet afternoon air toward the stunned soldier. Before the guard could even squeeze the trigger of his Springfield carbine, the bullets from the scout's repeater ripped through his slender body and slammed him to the ground, the widening circles of crimson staining the front of his dirty white shirt.

Rebecca Ridgeway screamed. The scout braked his horse.

"Holten!"

"It's all right," said the scout in a soothing voice.

The blonde widow, her bruised face now a mask of sudden relief, leaped at Holten with her slender arms outstretched. The scout held the trembling young woman for a long moment.

"I knew you'd come," she said in a frayed voice.

Holten smiled. "Wish I was as sure as you."

"And the others?"

"Right on my trail," said Holten. "We don't have much time to lose."

"What are you going to do?" asked Rebecca wiping away a tear with her delicate hand.

The scout released the now fully composed young widow and strode briskly to where the snorting team of wagon horses stood pawing at the loose dark soil in the clearing. As he walked, Holten felt a couple of large raindrops splat against his buckskin clothing. He spoke over his shoulder.

"Prepare a welcome for our gold-lovin' friends."

Rebecca wrinkled her brow. "I don't understand."

"Hopefully the deserters won't either."

"You can't fight them all," said the widow.

Holten grabbed the reins of the six horses and led the wagon back to where the gelding stood impatiently.

"I'm gonna have help," said the scout.

"Me?"

Holten chuckled. "You've been through enough," he said. "I plan to use some big cats and a lot of surprise. It's our only chance.

The scout hefted the slender widow onto the broad back of the gelding and handed her the reins. Then Holten climbed into the driver's seat of the gold wagon and tried to calm down the skittish horses.

"We've got a little time," he said, "but not much. We gotta ride like hell."

Rebecca nodded. Holten flicked the reins.

As the heavens opened and rain slanted down into their determined faces, the scout and the blonde widow raced out of the small clearing toward the misty hills beyond.

And toward the Canyon of Death.

Holten smacked the reins onto the wide butts of the galloping horses and steered the struggling mounts through the fresh mud in the deeply rutted trail. Rebecca Ridgeway trotted alongside atop the steady gelding and held on to the big horse for dear life. The sudden downpour drenched the scout to the skin, and lowered the visibility to almost nothing.

The scout knew he had to resort to cunning and surprise if he was to overcome Major Phillips' and Liver-Eating Jackson's love for glittering gold. He also knew the killers would do anything to recover their lost treasure—even kill the widow Ridgeway if necessary. As he bounced atop the driver's seat in the creaking gold wagon, Holten planned his next moves.

Maybe the rain would even help him.

Thunder rumbled through the heavens.

Holten sat under the cover of the canvas rear portion of the gold wagon and stripped off his rain-soaked clothes. The rain pounded a steady drumbeat against the canvas. Rebecca Ridgeway sat beside him and looked with horror at the bloodstained floor. The scout had tossed the dead renegades onto the muddy ground just before they entered the wagon to rest for a few moments, but the crimson stains remained.

"Ugh!" said Rebecca glancing at the gleaming blood.

"The deserters caused lots of blood to flow," said Holten.

"I know, but why?"

"Gold," remarked the scout wringing out his buckskin shirt, "and greed. Major Phillips used his position as an army officer to plan a major robbery."

"They killed lots of innocent people, too," added Rebecca.

Holten shrugged. "It's always the innocent who get hurt the most when marauders start burnin' and lootin' on the plains."

Rebecca sighed. "At least you're safe, Holten."

"For the time being," said the scout.

Holten hauled off his buckskin trousers and started to wring the rain water from each of the pant legs. The downpour increased and the patter of raindrops against the canvas cover was almost deafening. The scout sat buck naked on top of the cold metal strongbox that contained one hundred thousand dollars in gold coins, his tortured frame just starting to return to normal.

Holten knew the rain would slow the deserters in their pursuit of the scout and the gold. But even so, he didn't want to spend any more time than necessary in this rest stop. The tired army horses needed to rest more than anybody. And now, after a ten-minute break, the scout figured the rested horses could take a few more miles of punishment through the muddy hills. Holten prepared to dress.

Then he felt her hand on his penis. She squeezed gently.

The scout looked up.

"I almost forgot what it felt like," said Rebecca with a smile.

Holten glanced quickly at the lean young widow's sinewy body. Rebecca had stripped off her rain-soaked army shirt and sat gleaming naked across from the scout, her firm round breasts barely visible in the dim light of the wagon and her patch of pubic hair glistening as she sat smiling at him. Her soft blue eyes danced with mischief.

The scout's penis throbbed in her gentle grasp.

Rebecca squeezed his cock. "You ready?"

"Rebecca, I—" started Holten, trying to protest. He was certain the deserters galloped only a few miles behind them on the trail.

She leaped beside him in a flash.

Before the scout could speak again, the lithe blonde widow took his incredibly long and hard cock in her mouth, her soft supple lips stroking the pulsating shaft slowly, exquisitely.

"But the deserters?" gasped Holten.

"To hell with them," said Rebecca pausing for a moment.

As the scout tossed back his head with pleasure, the gentle widow's mouth massaged his throbbing penis, her lips sliding from its hard base to the sensitive pink tip where she flicked the tip of her tongue sending Holten into spasms of pure delight.

"Damn!" said Holten.

Rebecca worked feverishly on him now, her mouth caressing his shaft and bringing him on, trying desperately to milk the pent-up passion from deep within the scout's tortured frame. Holten writhed atop the strongbox, his long lean body twisting with each sensuous flick of Rebecca's tongue against his fully aroused penis.

He grabbed her shoulders and moaned.

The lithe widow brought the scout close to the delicious moment of sexual explosion, then eased off again, her delicate tongue sliding slowly to the hard base of his enormous cock to start all over again. Holten felt himself coming.

All the terrible thoughts of Red Hawk's torture, the deserters' atrocities, and the savage deaths of Ma Beaudeen and her girls evaporated from the scout's cluttered mind as he closed his eyes and let Rebecca drain him completely, her supple lips clasped to his jerking frame as he came into her, her eager mouth urging him on until he was completely drained and satisfied.

The scout slumped on the strongbox. Rebecca sighed.

For a long moment they sat still and listened to the pounding of the summer rain on the canvas of the wagon, their minds a hundred miles away from the problems they faced and the danger that chased them on the trail behind.

A bolt of lightning flashed. Thunder rumbled.

Rebecca jumped. Holten sat up quickly.

"Time to go," he said.

"So soon?"

Holten grabbed his clothes. "Trouble is on the way."

Rebecca reached out and grasped the scout's now flaccid penis. Holten froze suddenly and looked past her bruised face into her sparkling blue eyes.

"I want you, Holten," she said softly.

After all she'd been through, thought the scout, that was a hell of a thing to say. Holten just hoped he could get her out of this final jam.

"Let's go," he said simply.

The scout hauled on his still wet buckskin clothes, the contact with his raw upper arms sending hot shafts of pain through his entire body, and hopped up to the driver's seat.

"Stay in the wagon," he told Rebecca. "The gelding will trot along behind. No sense gettin' any wetter than you have to."

"Where are we going?"

Holten grabbed the reins. "To a place just right for Liver-Eating Jackson and the others."

"Where?" asked a puzzled widow.

The scout urged the tired army horses back onto the main trail and flicked the reins gently. He knew what he'd have to do, and the place to do it. Outnumbered as he was, Holten knew the best way to even up the oods. He spoke to Rebecca over his shoulder.

"An old Indian burial ground," he said. "The Canyon of Death."

Holten smiled and shouted at the team of glistening rain-soaked mounts. Maybe his experiences in the Canyon would prove beneficial after all. He started to whip the horses into a full gallop.

Another bolt of lightning. A crash of thunder.

Rebecca screamed. "Look!" she cried.

Holten reined in the horses and glanced suddenly at the trail behind them. The scout peered through the pouring summer rain at a small ravine that had started to fill with fresh rain water. More lightning illuminated the woods—and three mounted figures.

His heart leaped to his throat.

Holten spotted Liver-Eating Jackson, Maj. Nathan Phillips, and the big dim-witted Sergeant Luther Ames on the far side of the ravine, their skittish mounts pawing at the water in an attempt to reach the clearing where the scout and Rebecca waited. The scout saw an evil grin spread across Jackson's narrow face. Holten also watched Luther Ames haul a Springfield carbine from its saddle sheath and bring it to his shoulder.

Time had run out.

The scout flicked the reins against the butts of the snorting horses. The wagon shot forward toward the Canyon of Death. Holten knew the three killers would have trouble crossing the rain-filled ravine. He knew the raging water would give him more time to prepare his defense.

But not much time. He shouted at the tired mounts.

A rifle cracked behind him.

As Holten turned the heavy gold-laden wagon around and urged the galloping team of horses up a slight incline, a bullet splintered the wooden frame just above his head.

The rifle cracked again. And again.

"Get down!" he shouted at Rebecca.

Two more slugs splintered the water-logged wooden frame and ripped through the canvas cover. Holten whipped the horses and headed for the grassy ridge ahead of them. A few more feet and they'd be behind the cover of the small hill.

Two other rifles barked behind them.

The scout reached the top of the slope and reined in the glistening army team. The wagon rolled to a stop behind a couple of large boulders. With the slanting rain slapping him in the face and drenching his buckskin clothes,

Holten reached for his Winchester. A bolt of lightning lit up the darkened sky.

"What are we waiting for?" asked a startled Rebecca.

Holten shouldered his rifle. "We need more time," he shouted above the din of the pounding rain.

The scout saw Phillips, Jackson, and Ames atop their skittish mounts on the far side of the narrow water-filled ravine. They all held repeating rifles at their shoulders. Holten hoped to gain some more getaway time by sending the murderous trio diving for cover.

He squeezed the trigger. The Winchester spat fire.

Holten's first bullet whistled past Liver-Eating Jackson's narrow face. The scout continued to lever and fire, lever and fire, lever and fire. He sent a sudden hail of hot lead zipping through the summer rain toward the surprised killers.

The threesome rushed for cover.

A wide grin cracked the scout's leather face as he watched Jackson, Phillips, and Ames lower their rifles and turn the heads of their snorting mounts toward the trees behind them. Holten fired a final time, then returned his Winchester to the driver's seat beside him.

"Hang on!" he yelled at Rebecca.

As a bolt of lightning flashed in the sky above and a long roll of thunder boomed all around him, the scout slapped the reins. He sent the team of six glistening horses galloping through the downpour toward the hills.

And toward the Canyon of Death.

CHAPTER EIGHTEEN

Holten shouted above the din of the horses' hooves and the pounding rain.

"We'll be there in about ten minutes."

"Then what?" shouted Rebecca from inside the wagon.

Holten smiled. "I'm gonna fix a warm welcome for our gold-lovin' friends."

"Can I help?"

"Just stay out of the way," yelled the scout. "After all we've been through so far, I'd hate to lose you at the last minute."

"What are you going to do?"

"Rig some traps."

"But you said the Canyon is full of cougars!"

The scout smiled again. "I know."

Holten flicked the reins and urged the tired army mounts toward the narrow ravine just ahead. The scout figured he had about five minutes to do what he had in mind. By that time, the three killers would be hot on his trail.

At least he hoped so. His traps would be ready.

The scout reined in the snorting rain-soaked horses just before the wagon reached the top of the cliff above the Canyon of Death. Ignoring the driving summer rain that pelted his weathered face, Holten leaped from the wagon and grabbed his Winchester.

"Come on!" he told Rebecca. "You'll have to wait in the underbrush for a few minutes."

The scout helped the bruised widow down from the

waterlogged wagon onto the slimy Dakota soil. Rebecca skidded slightly as she touched the ground.

"Head for cover," said Holten over the din of the pounding rain. "I got some things to do here. Then you can get back into the wagon."

Rebecca nodded quickly, rivulets of rain racing down her still swollen face, and ran for the relatively dry cover of a copse of tiny cottonwoods off to one side. The scout watched the sinewy blonde scamper away, then turned his attention to the dripping wagon.

And the gold.

Quickly Holten hauled the heavy strongbox from the back of the canvas-covered wagon. If the three killers' love of gold was stronger than their sense of danger, as he figured, then what he had planned for them should work. The scout dropped the bulky gold-filled box on the ground where it landed with a splat in the mud.

Holten strode quickly to the gelding and removed the long coil of rope from the saddle. He glanced once at the trail where they'd just been. He knew time was running out. The scout walked briskly back to the strongbox, cut a ten foot length of rope with his Bowie knife, then fastened one end of the rope to it. Then he quickly tied the other end to the saddle horn and mounted his big horse.

As a flash of lightning illuminated the shadowy cliff area, the scout dragged the heavy gold-filled box through the mud to the edge of the steep drop-off. Dismounting quickly, Holten glanced at the surrounding trees and bushes.

He spotted just what he needed.

Pulling with all his might, the scout lugged the heavy strongbox a few more feet until he reached a sturdy box elder tree that hung slightly over the edge of the cliff. Then he looped the rope over a thick branch, guided the gelding backwards a few yards until the box rose into the air and swung freely, and fastened the rope to the tree trunk. The gold box hung like a big piece of ripe fruit waiting to be picked.

The killers couldn't miss it.

Suddenly a deafening roar pierced the air. Holten froze.

From deep inside the rain-slicked ravine came the mixed chorus of growls and snarls as the family of hungry cougars suddenly noticed the scout high up on the cliff. Holten peered through the sheets of warm rain at the milling cats on the canyon floor. Vivid flashes of the memory of pearly white fangs tearing apart the three whores, piece by bloody piece, filled the scout's brain.

He shivered involuntarily. Then he heard a yell.

"Holten!"

The scout turned toward Rebecca. "What is it?"

"Look!" shouted the blonde widow. She pointed at the trail leading up to the Canyon of Death.

Holten peered back at the muddy trail, his steely blue eyes slitted against the driving rain. Then he saw them, bent against the sheets of rain and reading signs as best they could in the blinding deluge.

Jackson, Phillips, and Ames. Only half a mile away.

"Get back in the wagon," shouted the scout.

Rebecca nodded and sloshed back to the wagon from her dripping cover near some plum bushes. Holten watched the shapely widow haul herself up into the canvas-covered rear portion of the wagon, then went back to work.

Now time was really running out.

Quickly the scout took the remaining coil of rope and strode briskly through the mud in front of the steep drop-off. Holten studied the cliff for a moment, then tied one end of the rope to a tree. Then he stretched the long line across the ground for about thirty feet in front of the edge. He fastened the other end to a large boulder. The rope stood about two feet off the ground and was stretched as tight as a fiddle string. Any horse hitting the taut line would tumble head over heels into the canyon—so would its rider.

The trap was perfect for unsuspecting gold robbers.

The scout then foraged in the surrounding brush for armfuls of water-logged sticks and branches and quickly covered the rope as best he could.

Now he was ready. And not a second too soon, either.

Holten looked up and saw the three soaked riders trotting just a few hundred yards from the Canyon of Death. The scout turned and sprinted through the still driving rain to a bush-covered spot near the cliff. With his heart pounding and his muscles tense, he waited for the killers to race into his trap.

Holten gripped his Winchester just in case.

Liver-Eating Jackson and Luther Ames came into full view first, their evil faces illuminated suddenly by a flash of lightning. Maj. Nathan Phillips trotted just behind them. Holten waited for them to spot the gold. Then he'd end the problem of deserters on the Dakota plains with a bang.

But the killers stopped short. Holten stiffened.

The scout listened to their conversation as best he could.

Luther Ames reined in his horse. "Where are we?"

"Sioux country," answered Jackson atop his snorting horse.

"Where's the goddam gold?"

"There's the wagon," said Jackson.

"Let's go get it!" yelled Ames.

Major Phillips held out his hand. "Wait a minute," he ordered. "Let's be careful. Holten's no fool."

"Hell," said Ames, "that scout and his little blonde slut are more 'an likely miles from here by now."

"Don't be so sure," cautioned Phillips.

A sudden bolt of lightning streaked the sky and illuminated the Canyon area.

"Look!" shouted a suddenly excited Luther Ames.

Jackson smiled. "The gold," he said.

"Be careful," warned Phillips. "Go check it out."

"Yahooooo!" yelled Ames, as he spurred his tired horse.

With a sudden splash of water and mud, Liver-Eating Jackson and Luther Ames galloped through the blinding rain toward the cliff and the swinging box of gold.

And toward Holten's trap.

A wide grin spread across Holten's leathery face. He hunkered down in the bushes and grasped his Winchester. The action would start at any moment.

The scout wiped the rain from his face with the back of his big hand and watched Jackson and Ames gallop toward the cliff. The visibility was so poor, Holten could barely make out the racing mounts as they zipped past him.

Hopefully, the killers couldn't see the trap, either.

Ames spurred his snorting army mount and surged ahead of the more cautious frontiersman riding with him. Holten noticed Liver-Eating Jackson's head turn slightly and scan the surrounding terrain. Both riders continued their frantic pace.

Just a few seconds more.

The scout shouldered his Winchester and waited. He glanced at the trail and saw Major Phillips waiting in the pouring rain for Jackson and Ames to grab the gold. Holten thought about shooting the son of a bitch right away, but he didn't want to spoil the fun of his trap. He returned his gaze to the cliff.

Then it happened—just as he'd planned it.

First Luther Ames' tired mount galloped into the taut rope, its front legs buckling suddenly as it struck the trap at full speed. The wild-eyed horse whinnied sharply and flipped head over heels, its big glistening body sprawling in the mud as it slid inexorably toward the cliff.

And the Canyon of Death.

Luther Ames flew from the back of his horse as though he'd been shot from a cannon, a look of shocked horror etched on his broad dumb-looking face. The big former sergeant sailed through the air and smashed to the ground at the edge of the cliff. The forward momentum of his big potbellied body propelled him across the slick, muddy ground into the narrow ravine. He fell to the Canyon floor right behind his stumbling horse.

"Aiiiieeeeee!" he shouted, as he fell into the gorge.

Liver-Eating Jackson's mount struck the taut line just a fraction of a second after Luther Ames went flying. And with the same result.

Holten watched the snake-eyed killer's stunned horse tumble head over heels and fly into the narrow ravine just behind the screaming sergeant. Jackson shot from the back of his mount as though he'd been yanked by a rope, his narrow evil face contorted into a mask of sudden fear. The scout saw Liver-Eating Jackson slam to the ground, skid for a few feet in the mud like a stone sliding across a frozen pond, and disappear over the edge of the cliff.

But the snake-eyed killer didn't fall.

As Holten watched with horror, the wiry narrow-faced frontiersman grabbed a scraggly bush at the top of the steep drop-off and held on for dear life. Liver-Eating Jackson reached up with both hands and started to haul his lean wiry frame out of the snapping jaws of death in the canyon.

The scout heard the big cats suddenly.

From deep in the canyon came the sharp whinnying of the fallen horses as the family of hungry cougars pounced on them and began to tear the flesh from their broken bodies.

Then came another bloodcurdling sound.

Holten heard the terrible screams of Sergeant Luther Ames rise into the rainy afternoon air as the cougars started to maul his big potbellied body.

"No, no!" yelled Ames. "Oh my God!"

Then it ended. The scout heard only the patter of rain.

A flash of movement on the trail caught his eye.

Holten turned sharply. He saw Maj. Nathan Phillips spin his horse around and begin to gallop away from the sudden screams near the Canyon of Death. The scout aimed down the barrel of his Winchester and squeezed the trigger.

The rifle cracked through the silence.

Down on the trail Holten saw Phillips jerk in his saddle as hot lead slammed into his right leg. The officer screamed with pain. The hard-faced major's horse reared suddenly and tossed the struggling soldier to the mud where he landed with a splash.

Now the real battle began. Holten was ready.

With the snarls of the feeding cougars ringing in his ears, the scout slipped through the warm driving rain toward the cliff. He wanted to finish off Liver-Eating Jackson before the struggling frontiersman regained his bearings. Two against one were tough odds for the scout even in the rain.

A shot whistled past Holten's ear. He fell to the mud.

The scout quickly scanned the terrain. He saw Major Phillips, bright red blood gushing from his leg wound and a Springfield carbine clutched in his hand, racing toward the cover of the wagon.

And toward Rebecca.

Holten's pulse quickened.

The scout leaped to his feet and sprinted across the open ground near the cliff. Another flash of movement caught his attention.

Liver-Eating Jackson crawled out of the ravine.

Quickly Holten dove for cover behind some box elder trees. He landed just as Jackson fired two shots from his army .45 revolver, the hot slugs splintering some bark just inches from the scout's head.

The scout arced his Winchester upward and squeezed off a quick shot. The bullet zipped through the air toward

227

Jackson and struck the killer's .45 with a metallic clang. The snake-eyed frontiersman screamed with shock as the gun flew from his hand and fell into the ravine. Jackson ducked quickly behind some rocks.

Rebecca! Holten remembered Major Phillips.

But it was too late!

The scout glanced up sharply and saw the wounded army officer limping toward the edge of the cliff, the wide-eyed and completely drenched young widow grasped firmly in one arm.

"Holten!" screamed Rebecca.

"Shut up!" yelled Phillips as he struggled through the mud toward the cliff and the gold.

Holten shouldered his Winchester, but paused before he aimed the rifle. It was too risky. A good shot would drop Phillips where he stood; a bad shot might kill Rebecca. The scout just waited helplessly and watched the wounded officer drag the frightened blonde closer to the Canyon of Death.

Suddenly Phillips stopped in his tracks.

"Holten!" he yelled. "Do you hear me Holten!"

The scout peered through the driving sheets of rain at the bleeding officer. Phillips shielded his body by holding Rebecca in front of him. The traitorous army officer stood with his back to the Canyon and his feet on the edge of the steep cliff. The scout had no choice.

"I hear ya," he shouted through the pounding rain.

"Throw down your gun and come on out!"

"Let the woman go first," answered Holten.

"Come out or I'll toss the woman into the ravine!"

Holten glanced at the ground for a moment as he thought things over. He could still hear the snarling cougars battle for bloody bits of the horses and Luther Ames in the canyon below. It looked like he sure as hell didn't have any choice.

Rebecca screamed suddenly. Holten looked up.

"Do it now!" shouted Phillips.

At the same time he yelled at Holten, the hard-faced army officer held Rebecca's sinewy frame over the edge of the cliff. The blonde widow's eyes saucered and her mouth hung open with fear.

"Holten, please!" yelled Rebecca.

The scout stood slowly, his Winchester at his side.

"Good, Holten," said Phillips. "Now throw down your gun."

Jackson's voice rose from the edge of the cliff. "I've got him covered, Phillips," he said.

Holten saw the evil-eyed killer kneeling in the mud just twenty feet away, his fearsome war hatchet in his hand poised to throw.

"Take his rifle, Jackson."

"Right," said the smiling frontiersman. "With pleasure."

Liver-Eating Jackson rose cautiously and strode over to where Holten stood near the box elder trees. Holten saw the glistening war hatchet in Jackson's hand.

"One false move," yelled Phillips, "and the woman gets it."

"Holten!" screeched the terrified widow.

Jackson walked up to the scout. "Gimme the rifle," he snapped, his snakelike eyes dancing with anticipation.

Reluctantly, Holten started to hand over his Winchester.

Then they heard it. A sudden snarl from the cliff.

Rebecca screamed.

The scout turned and glanced at Phillips. His heart leapt to his throat at what he saw. In a sudden flash of fur and fangs, a big male cougar jumped from the canyon and wrapped its long forelegs around Major Phillips' body. Holten figured the cat had been attracted by the flurry of action up on the cliff and had climbed up the tiny footholds to get at Phillips. As the scout watched, the cougar bared its fangs and sunk them deep into the wide-eyed army officer's exposed throat.

Blood spurted onto the muddy ground.

"Ahhhhh!" screamed the major.

"Oh my God!" shouted Rebecca.

Suddenly Rebecca pulled away from the clutches of the struggling officer and fell heavily in the slimy mud. The cougar tore its fangs from Phillips' neck, the sudden ripping action severing the major's jugular vein and killing him almost instantly.

Blood splattered onto Rebecca.

As Holten watched, the big cat started to drag Major Phillips' lifeless body over the edge of the steep cliff and down into the Canyon of Death.

Suddenly Holten flew into action.

The scout raised his Winchester and started to club Liver-Eating Jackson, who stood frozen next to him. The snake-eyed frontiersman came to life, reached up with his war hatchet, and deflected Holten's blow.

The Winchester flew from the scout's hands.

Jackson's narrow face cracked into a wide evil grin.

"Now I gotcha, you son of a bitch!" snapped Jackson.

The scout drew his Bowie knife. "Not yet," he said.

As the driving rain intensified, the two combatants crouched and circled warily, Holten gripping his long fearsome knife and Jackson holding his razor-sharp Indian war hatchet. Holten studied the circling frontiersman, rivulets of rain water streaming down his weathered face as he did so. The roars of the feeding cougars rose from the narrow Canyon of Death as they fought.

Holten had fought many such battles in his years with the Oglala Sioux. The war hatchet was a favorite weapon of the plains Indians. The Sioux warriors were pretty good with the slashing hatchet; but Holten was one of the best.

And the evil killer knew it.

Suddenly Jackson reached out and slashed at Holten's

arm, the deadly hatchet whooshing just inches from the scout's buckskin-clad limb. Holten jerked backwards and countered with a downward slash of his Bowie knife.

The knife caught Jackson's wrist. The killer screamed.

"You bastard!" he snapped as blood spurted from the superficial flesh wound.

"You had it comin'," said Holten with a wry grin.

"And you have this comin'!" said Jackson as he lunged suddenly at the scout.

The sudden blow caught Holten off guard. The scout's boots slipped in the slick footing as he tried to back away, and the evil frontiersman's slashing blade caught the falling scout's shoulder with a glancing blow.

A hot shaft of pain sliced through Holten's arm.

The scout staggered. Jackson charged.

Suddenly Holten was caught in a desperate fight for his life. Like an enraged bull buffalo, Liver-Eating Jackson pushed forward toward the stumbling scout, his glistening blade thrashing away and barely missing Holten's flailing arms and legs. The two fighters stumbled through the driving summer rain toward the lonely wagon just behind them.

Finally Holten recovered his balance and warded off a glancing blow from Jackson. Then the scout went on the offensive, his ten-inch long Bowie knife becoming just a glistening blur of motion as he slashed and hacked at Liver-Eating Jackson's lean frame.

"Holten!" shouted Rebecca. "Let me help you!"

"Get back!" warned the scout.

Jackson chuckled. "Better get back missy," he said with an evil smile on his face. "I want ya in good shape when I finish off this Injun lover."

The two combatants slashed and hacked for a few more minutes, their desperate struggle bringing them closer and closer to the edge of the cliff as they fought.

Suddenly Rebecca grabbed Holten's Winchester.

"Look out Holten!" shouted the widow as she aimed. Jackson's eyes widened with fear.

The rifle spat fire. Rebecca fell backwards.

Liver-Eating Jackson screamed as a hot slug from the .44-40 ripped through his left arm and spun him to the muddy ground. Holten turned sharply and glanced at Rebecca.

"Get to the wagon!" he told the stunned widow.

Rebecca nodded and ran like hell to the wagon.

Holten turned back to Jackson just in time. A flash of movement had caught the scout's eye. He ducked quickly. Liver-Eating Jackson had scrambled to his feet and slashed wildly at Holten's head, the glistening hatchet blade whooshing just a fraction of an inch from the scout's rain splattered face.

Holten fell backwards. Jackson bolted.

Hauling his long lean frame from the slimy mud, the scout watched the bleeding frontiersman race toward the edge of the cliff. Holten sprinted after Jackson.

Suddenly the snake-eyed frontiersman whirled to face the scout, an evil snarl on his face and his yellow eyes flashing with sullen hate.

"Come on, scout!" taunted Jackson.

Holten stopped in his tracks and braced himself for a fight, his muscles tense once again and his grip on the Bowie knife tightening. He watched Jackson's flashing eyes.

Without warning the wiry frontiersman lashed out with the glistening war hatchet. Holten jackknifed away, the deadly blade whooshing through the air just inches from his stomach. The two combatants began to circle once again.

Holten's mind raced as he formulated a plan for finishing off the stubborn killer. The scout looked out of the corner of his eye at the edge of the cliff just a few feet away. He knew he'd have to maneuver Jackson to the edge and then finish him off.

But how?

Suddenly Jackson lunged at the scout; he'd caught him deep in thought. The fearsome hatchet blade slashed at Holten's head. The scout raised his Bowie knife just in time to deflect the savage blow, but the force of Jackson's thrust sent Holten slamming to the mud near a couple of small trees.

"I gotcha now, scout!" said Jackson with a gleam in his evil snake eyes.

Holten lay flat on his back near the trees and waited for the lean narrow-faced frontiersman's final attack. Suddenly the idea struck the scout like a lightning bolt.

The gold. And Jackson's greed.

"What about your gold, Jackson?" asked Holten quickly.

The frontiersman froze. "What about it?"

"Go get it!" snapped Holten.

With a sudden flash of his Bowie knife, the scout sliced neatly through the rope that held the strongbox suspended over the cougar-filled Canyon of Death. The heavy box fell to the canyon floor like a giant rock.

Jackson's eyes widened as big as gold coins.

Holten flew into action.

Leaping from the muddy ground like an enraged cougar, his long knife leading the way, the scout plunged his Bowie knife deep into Liver-Eating Jackson's chest. The razor-sharp blade sliced the killer's heart in two.

Jackson's mouth hung open with shock.

The force of Holten's blow sent the snake-eyed killer stumbling backward toward the edge of the steep cliff. The scout withdrew his blade and watched Liver-Eating Jackson teeter on the edge. Then as his eyes rolled toward the rain-filled heavens, Jackson sailed into the Canyon of Death and landed amidst a renewed chorus of growls and roars from the cougars below.

Holten stood panting for a long moment.

When the fierce snarling abated, the scout walked slowly to the edge of the cliff and stood holding his bloodied knife. As the summer rain began to let up, Holten stared down at the family of cougars and their fresh meal of horses and men. The scout paused for a moment, then turned and strode briskly toward the wagon and Rebecca.

Suddenly the sun burst out from behind a cloud.

CHAPTER NINETEEN

The gold was safe. So was Rebecca.

General Frank Corrington spat an amber stream of tobacco juice into the brass spittoon on the floor of his Fort Rawlins office, stroked his iron-gray beard, and looked up at the scout.

"Maj. Nathan Phillips?" he said shaking his head. "I never woulda guessed he was in cahoots with them deserters."

"All the way," said the scout.

"He knew about the settler killings, too?"

"Planned 'em."

Corrington spat again. "No wonder them settlers out on the prairie are scared shitless," said the general. "They can't even trust the army officers who are supposed to protect 'em!"

"Phillips got what he deserved," said Holten.

"And the gold?"

"In the quartermaster's office."

"All of it?"

"Every last coin."

Corrington shifted the chaw of tobacco in his cheek and moved from behind his mahogany desk. "The people of the Dakota Territory owe ya a lot, Mr. Holten."

The scout shrugged. "Just doin' my job."

"Gettin' tortured by renegades goes beyond the call of normal duty."

Holten's eyebrows arched. "You know about that?"

"The widow Ridgeway," said the general with a smile.

"She seems to think you're kinda special, too."

"She's lucky to be alive."

"She was lucky you kept lookin' for her."

Corrington thrust a big cigar box in front of Holten. The scout selected a long fresh cheroot. Both the scout and the general stood smoking in silence for a couple of minutes. They listened to the familiar military sounds that drifted in from the fort's parade grounds.

"She's a hell of a woman, Holten," said the general.

The scout nodded. "I know," he said. Visions of firm round breasts and golden thighs danced in his brain.

"Be just the right woman for ya, scout."

Holten chuckled. "Nice thought, general," he said, "but reckon I'd look kinda silly struttin' down Philadelphia's main street in my buckskins!"

Both Corrington and the scout laughed.

"Well, Holten," said Corrington. "I thank ya once again. If it wasn't for you we never woulda cleaned up the deserters so soon. Or the renegades."

Holten took a drag of his cheroot. "See that the Sioux on the reservations get the money that's due 'em, will ya?"

"Of course, of course," said the general with a smile.

The scout stuck his cigar in his mouth. "Well," he said, extending his hand toward Corrington, "let me know when ya need me again."

Holten leaned down to the general's ear and whispered.

"But not for at least a couple of hours," said the scout. "Gotta say goodbye to the widow Ridgeway." Holten winked.

General Corrington smiled, then winked back.

Eli Holten, Chief Scout for the Army's 12th Cavalry, turned and strode purposefully to the general's office door. He pulled back the pine slab and squinted into the gathering dusk in the Fort Rawlins parade grounds. A couple of early stars twinkled in the distance.

"Goin' to be a beautiful night," said Holten.

Then he closed the door and started to walk toward Fort Rawlins' visitors' quarters—and Rebecca Ridgeway. Holten was glad the deserter problem had ended at last. He'd been lucky to grab the gold away from the feasting cougars in the Canyon of Death, haul it into the heavy wagon, and gallop through the mud with Rebecca back to the fort. Then without even changing his water-logged buckskin clothing, the scout had gone straight to General Corrington's office to give his report. Now he looked foward to a hot bath, fresh clothes, and a big meal with all the fixins.

Among other things.

The sudden thought of Rebecca's long lean body sent a twinge of desire through his loins. Holten felt the beginnings of an erection in his pants. He walked a little faster.

The scout crossed the parade grounds, grabbed the door knob of Rebecca's quarters, and burst into the room. He stopped in the entrance.

The room was empty.

"Rebecca?" he called as he shut the door.

Holten stopped and listened. He heard nothing.

Finally, with his wet buckskin clothes starting to irritate the many tiny pinprick wounds on his upper arms, the scout just shrugged and started to undress. He spotted a fresh change of army clothes he could use until his own duds were dry and ready to wear. Within seconds Holten stood buck naked in the middle of the room, his cold tortured body warming from the heat of the roaring flames in the nearby fireplace.

Then he heard her. He whirled around.

The scout's eyes widened.

"What took you so long?" asked Rebecca as she emerged from the bathroom—stark naked.

Holten's flashing blue eyes searched the lovely widow's shapely body, darting quickly from her big round breasts down her flat smooth stomach to the waxy patch of pubic

237

hair at her crotch. His eyes lingered for a moment at the glistening mat of kinky hair that hid the warm and wonderful treasures deep inside of her.

The scout's penis grew to its full length.

Rebecca's soft blue eyes watched it.

"I've come to say goodbye," said the scout simply.

"I'm ready," she said, her eyes still fixed on his cock.

Holten stepped forward and took her in his long powerful arms, her golden flesh feeling warm against his cold lean frame. The scout closed his eyes and felt Rebecca's trembling body press against his pulsating erection. Her breasts flattened against his matted chest as she did so.

"Oh Holten!" said Rebecca softly. "I don't want to go, but I have to. My family wants me back in Philadelphia."

"Shhh," said the scout. "Don't talk."

Suddenly they looked at each other, their flashing eyes saying everything that was necessary. Then they became savage sexual animals, first one reaching for the other, then the other returning the favor. Holten moaned with pleasure.

Rebecca grasped the scout's throbbing shaft in her delicate hand and began to stroke it, slowly at first, then more rapidly from its hard base to the sensitive pink tip until the scout moaned with ecstasy.

"Jesus!" he breathed.

At the same time, Holten's long fingers probed Rebecca's waxy bush, his fingers plunging inside of her slick wet channel. The lean blonde widow jumped at his touch.

"Oh Holten!" she gasped. "Do it!"

Holten removed his sticky fingers and began to roam Rebecca's soft body with his big rough hands, starting at her delicate shoulders and working down to her round plump buttocks. The scout shot a finger into the crevice of her buttocks, sending the blonde widow into a writhing spasm of pure sexual delight.

They fell to the bear rug near the fireplace.

Holten quickly mounted the writhing widow and maneuvered his long iron-hard shaft over her glistening vagina. Rebecca grasped Holten's penis and began to rub it in the soft silky folds of flesh at the entrance of her slippery channel, the sudden contact with the tip of the scout's penis causing her to groan with desire.

Suddenly he came down on her. Holten rammed in his cock.

"Oooooo," gasped Rebecca. Her big blue eyes rolled.

The two lovers thrashed and rolled atop the downy bear rug, Holten pumping his iron-hard penis inside the writhing widow, the gasping blonde arching her body to get every inch of him inside of her.

For almost half an hour they brought each other to the brink of sexual climax over and over, only to ease off and start again. Holten nearly exploded into Rebecca several times, but held back at the last moment and pumped her even harder. The lean soft blonde pressed against the tall muscular scout until it seemed as though they were glued together.

Finally he came in a hot milky flood of passion that filled Rebecca to the brim and made her arch her sinewy body one final time as she gasped with delight.

Then they collapsed on the bear rug.

The lovers lay panting for several long minutes.

Finally Holten rolled off of Rebecca, kissed her gently on the cheek, and began to dress. He pulled the dry army clothes over his battered body in silence. Occasionally he caught the golden-skinned widow studying him from her spot on the fluffy bear rug, her flashing blue eyes welling with tears.

When he finished, the scout picked up his own damp buckskin clothing and looked down at Rebecca. She still watched him, but now rivers of tears streamed down her pretty face.

"Goodbye, Rebecca," said Holten simply.

The blonde widow just nodded slightly.

The scout turned and walked toward the door.

"I'll never forget you, Holten," called Rebecca in a frayed voice. "I—I—"

"You'll be okay," said Holten.

Rebecca sniffled. "Goodbye," she said softly.

The scout pulled open the door and went out of the room. He closed the slab door softly behind him, squinted into the darkness, and headed for the stables to retrieve the gelding. As he walked, Holten glanced up at the vast canopy of stars that hung over the prairie.

It was going to be a beautiful night.